This LIFE OF Mine

VICTORIA LYNN

ADVANCED PRAISE FOR THIS LIFE OF MINE

"Some books stir the imagination, but *This Life of Mine* stirs the soul. A journey of hope from brokenness, strength in weakness, and power in unity. It's impossible to miss Victoria Lynn's passion in this heart-written story and if you open your own heart as you read, you'll leave behind the world of Elira as changed as its characters."
- **Nadine Brandes**, author of *Wishtress, Fawkes, Romanov*, and the *Out of Time Series*

"Make sure you're stocked up on tissues because Victoria Lynn has crafted yet another masterpiece. *This Life of Mine* is a poignant, contemplative tale of profound loss, struggle, healing, and faith. Its powerful message, compelling characters, and sweet romance will tug at your heartstrings and push you toward Jesus."
-**Megan McCullough**, author of *We Could Be Villains*

"This Life of Mine has earned a forever home on my bookshelf and in my heart. Featuring memorable characters and a powerful stance on the sanctity of life, it had me in tears with its story of redemption in the wake of regret. Victoria Lynn has done it again, weaving a tale that holds out hope to the ones who have been broken…and to the ones who have broken others."
-**Laurel Luehmann**, author of *This Will Not Last* and *Clarion Hope*

THIS LIFE OF MINE

g.w. press

Published by Glory Writers
www.glorywriters.com

Victoria Lynn is a credited author with The Glory Writers.

Printed in the United States of America

Library of Congress Cataloging-in-Publication Data

ISBN –
Paperback: 979-8-9857294-3-6aa
Hardcover: 979-8-9857294-4-3
eBook: 979-8-9857294-5-0

This is a work of fiction. Names, characters, incidents, and dialogues are products of the author's imagination and are not to be construed as real. Any resemblance to actual events or persons, living or dead, is entirely coincidental.

Scripture quotations from The Authorized (King James) Version. Rights in the Authorized Version in the United Kingdom are vested in the Crown. Reproduced by permission of the Crown's patentee, Cambridge University Press

Cover Design by: Victoria Lynn Designs in conjunction with The Glory Writers for Glory Writers Press
https://glorywriters.com/

First Printing

*To my six baby siblings in heaven. May your little lives
speak worth and value from the gates of heaven as you
worship our King together. I can't wait to meet you one day.*

*And to the millions of tiny lives who never saw a day outside
of the womb on this side of heaven. You are remembered.
You are treasured. And your life matters.*

*And to their mamas—those who know what they are missing
and those who do not. May you find healing and comfort in
the arms of Jesus, assured that you will see your babies
again one day soon.*

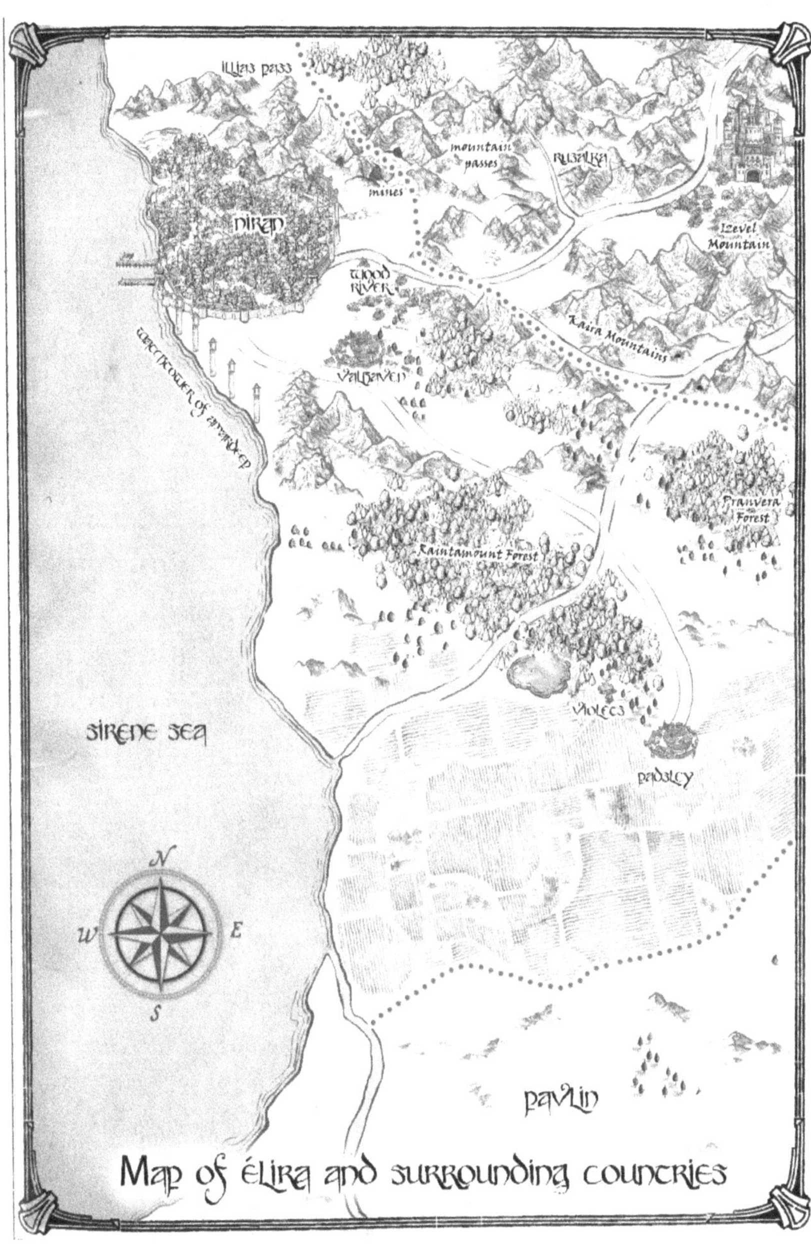

Map of Élira and surrounding countries

FORWARD

Dearest Reader,

This book was not an easy one to write. I felt led to do so, in spite of my misgivings and I hope that despite the difficulty of the subject matter, you find hope, life, and truth amidst these pages.

Abortion and human trafficking have been my two 'passion projects' since I was a child. At the age of 13, I felt called to stand up and fight against these two evils. I was scarcely old enough to truly understand the monstrosity of both of these subjects, but I was called nonetheless.

William Wilberforce has been a hero of the faith to me for many years and it is His mission and unswerving dedication that I hope to emulate as I fight for Christ and His kingdom in a world full of evil. One of his models for encouraging others to stand up was to educate and truthfully portray the immorality and wickedness of the slave trade, while honoring and humanizing its victims.

I did my best to write these stories as tactfully, gently, and realistically as possible, all while maintaining a level of decorum that will allow this book to be enjoyed by many ages. If you are a parent reading this book, this may be an amazing discussion starter to explain the trauma and pain of trafficking and abortion, the affects and the spiritual component behind them. I hope this story fills you with compassion and motivates you to stand and speak for those that cannot speak for themselves.

For His Kingdom, Victoria Lynn

TABLE OF CONTENTS

Life is never wasted.

It always has value.

Even when dark and deformed.

Because even dead things can live again.

The dead of winter can pass away.

The dark stain of sin washed white as snow.

But green explodes with new life.

And flowers bloom,

Resurrected with hope and washed by blood.

*Hearts blossom as winds of grace and mercy blow through,
cleansing the dust from the room.*

*Chains fall with a thud and are buried with the shame and
the grief.*

*New life has come, Hope eternal has sprung. From great
shame and guilt, a story of purity and redemption has begun.*

HYMN OF NEW LIFE

Prologue

THE AIR WAS STARTLINGLY COLD, chilling her to the bone and sending shards of pain through her chest with every inhale.

Panic hung on the wind, its broken song whistling through the treetops, the branches barren—as empty as she felt.

Her thin dress provided little protection against the mountain chill, the blood frozen to her legs.

Her breath came fast and heavy, her heart beating against her ribs with the weight of what felt like a blow to her side with every thud.

She was numb.

Her hair whipped at her face in the wind, stinging her skin with its frosty bite. She had ceased to shiver, but still her legs tumbled on, her feet frozen within her thin, deerskin shoes.

She stumbled against a tree, tripping as she pushed herself onward again, collapsing against the snow that cut and stung her bare arms.

She squeezed her eyes shut, her hands buried in the ice crystals, each one a different shape that swam in her blurry vision. A sob wrenched from her throat. Gripping the snow, she shoved herself upright, gathering her feet under her in stumbling movements and fighting the fogginess that clouded her head.

A lone wolf howled in the gathering dusk.

She needed to get away.

Forcing her feet forward, she stumbled on as the darkness quickly closed in, the last hazy rays of light disappearing into the swallowing thickness of the forest, the pine trees so tall they spun around her. She imagined that their tips touched the heavens, making her feel even smaller and more alone. Desperately alone.

Heaven was a long way off.

And she needed to survive the night.

One

SECRETS UNBURIED

MARCUS FELT THE late fall breeze sweeping through Ratintamount Forest from his place on his knees before the thyme plant. His fingers skillfully harvested leaves for medicinal purposes. Winter was nearly upon them and had already settled upon the mountaintops, clothing the stone with its white, frigid atmosphere like a woman crowned with silver hair. Raintamount stood nestled in a valley on the opposite side of the King's Highway from the Kaira Mountains, so winter settled a little later in Padsley than in the eastern regions of Elira. It made their land better suited to the farming and agriculture they were famous for.

Sighing, he winced and shifted uncomfortably on his right leg and groaned as some of the blood returned. The limb gave him trouble all of the time, but it often worsened in the cold months of winter. He bit his lip, fighting the pain and waiting it out until the very last minute so that he could harvest as much as possible. The pinched nerve finally sharpened, and with a gasp, he set the last twig in the basket and reached for his crutch, floundering to his feet as quickly as he could.

Dragging in a harsh breath as he leaned heavily on his crutch, he eliminated the weight from his right leg with his crutch to give it the time it needed to let the blood flow return. A branch cracked behind him, and Marcus's heart ricocheted into his throat as he turned sharply. His leg collapsed beneath him, sending him flat on his back in a pile of leaves. Some of the branches above him were naked, while others clattered with the oak leaves that would remain until the new buds in the spring pushed them from where they clung.

Steps clumped heavily through the underbrush. Marcus tried to draw a breath, but his lungs were frozen from the fall. Everard's face suddenly popped into view, and the massive man needed no words to communicate his apology and concern.

Marcus waved a hand to absolve him from guilt, but his lungs were bursting and his eyes started to water. Suddenly, his gut thawed, and he gasped in a gulp of air, aspirating and choking on a cough as he struggled to sit up. Everard looped an arm behind him, supporting his shoulders. Marcus twitched to the side as he sat up, and the tendons in his hip joint pulled uncomfortably.

Fendrel, the town's medicinal and Marcus's mentor, said that by the best he could tell, Marcus's hip had been disjointed during the attack he had sustained long ago as a boy. He had been thirteen when his life had been upended by the vicious assault from the Kingsmen that had left him lame for life. With a hip out of place, and too many broken bones to count, his life had been completely changed forever in the short span of fifteen minutes. Now, he gripped Everard's hand and nodded that he was all right, allowing the large man to pull him to his feet and support him with a strong grip while Marcus situated his crutch under his arm. Sometimes, all he needed was a cane, but on days like today, where he was venturing farther from town or was simply having a rough go of it, the crutch was necessary to support him fully and help him remain mobile.

Rubbing his abdomen where his lungs had stopped, he took a deep breath, steadying himself. He was used to having to rely on others. It was a part of his life now and had been for the last seven years.

Everard dusted Marcus's back off. He must be covered in the dead leaves of the past season, much like the hopes and dreams lying dead within him.

That was a rather gloomy thought. He was usually the bright one, the happy one, the one who could bring joy to those around him even if there was no other way he could help. But since Violet had married the man who was now their king, she had taken those subtle hopes that had been his mainstay for so many years and flown off with them like a dove startled from her nest in the brush. And she had taken his heart with her.

He shook his head. Violet had never truly been his. She was a dear friend—a sister, someone he had once hoped to spend the rest of his life with, but now was someone he was learning to live without.

He tried to reach for the basket of herbs at his feet and would have fallen again had Everard not pulled him upright and taken the basket in his own capable hand, supporting Marcus with his opposite forearm. Everard didn't say a word, but Marcus took the offer gratefully, despite the frustration that he needed it at all.

Drawing in another deep breath, he tried to relax, letting the aching bones from his fall settle back into their normal position. He had accepted a long time ago that this would be his lot in life. But it was still hard being a man who wanted to be able to at least fend for himself and could not. He was a burden. And even though he was a help to Fendrel—he knew he was—somehow there was still that feeling of being useless, and he wondered why. Ever since Violet had left, he had been fighting these thoughts every single day. It was wearing on him, and his body was starting to feel it.

"Have you heard the news?" Everard's deep, scratchy voice probably sounded that way from its lack of use. He helped Marcus over a particularly knotted tree root on the way back to the trail. A blustery wind blew through the wood, setting the boughs to creaking and the oak leaves to chattering in the cold. Marcus himself shivered. Winter would be here soon.

"What news? There seems to be much of it these days."

"With Elgon…the king's announcement of the nullification of the chancellor's treaty with Rusalka, there seems to be a rush for the border. Some of the merchants who came through yesterday were saying that it looks bad."

Marcus's heart sank. There was bound to be some turmoil as a result of Elgon's backing out of the treaty. Rusalka had been promised a lot of money; it had been the reason the people's tax in Elira became so burdensome. Someone needed to pay what the treaty promised, and it was little wonder the Mountain King would retaliate. Marcus drew a breath. He wasn't sure he was prepared for what that might look like.

They had all settled into some level of peace as a result of the whirlwind takeover of Elgon as the ruler of Elira and his subsequent marriage. But it was clear, though the peace was much welcome, things were still astir beneath it all. There was much to be wary of. Elgon had warned them before he and Violet had left for Niran. He still didn't know who among the Kingsmen were to be trusted. Enguerrand had swayed many over to his allegiance while in power, and there was little telling who would stay with the king if things worsened and the balance tilted.

Marcus tripped over a stone and was borne over it by Everard's muscular arm. He swallowed with a wry grin to himself. If only he always had the arm of someone like Everard to lean on.

You have mine. Marcus's heart ached. He had been ignoring that still, small voice of late, but he latched onto it with the desperation of a drowning man. He needed the voice of his Heavenly Father now more than ever.

"What is there to be concerned about?" Marcus prodded Everard. The man wouldn't say much unless pressed.

A massive sigh heaved up from the depths of Everard's soul, and Marcus felt the weight of it within his own. "There has been fighting. Many are attempting to flee Rusalka before the soldiers arrive and close down the border. There is talk of much bloodshed."

Marcus felt his stomach cramp and his muscles clench in pain. The idea of what that might look like filled his heart with trembling. "Lord protect them."

Everard grunted in agreement.

There was little wonder why anyone would try to flee Rusalka. They were renowned in the continent for their brutality, lawlessness, and as one of the few countries that permitted slavery. Elira had always kept its distance, and King Indulf, Elgon's father, had fought to keep their borders intact for many years. But after his death, during the regent's reign, Enguerrand had bowed to them, attempting in some overt and other covert ways to weasel his way into the affection of the Mountain King, Zuko. The treaty would have sealed a relationship between both kingdoms and joined the Rusalkan and Eliran armies, in addition to giving the people of Rusalka free passage and commerce within the lands of Elira.

Marcus shuddered. The idea of what that commerce would be filled him with horror. He had not witnessed slavery in his lifetime, and he hoped that fact would never change. They had been what felt as close as one could get to it when the Kingsmen, under the rule of Enguerrand, had worked hard to instill fear and enforce his rule with an iron fist amongst every town, village, and dale throughout Elira.

As they neared Padsley now, a slight buzz came from amongst the people within it. Marcus smiled slightly. Padsley was always a-bustle in some way. The only village on this side of Raintamount Forest, it was the only spot around for connection, trade, and community. He loved the feeling of quiet that the forest and surrounding hills provided, but he also felt at home amidst the gentle flurry of the village. It would always be his home. He probably knew the streets better than anyone, as he had run them like a maze as an orphaned urchin before Violet's family and Fendrel took him in after the accident. He still knew the byways, alleys, and streets like the back of his hand. It just took him longer to traverse them these days.

"You'll tell me if you hear any more news?"

Everard nodded and handed him back his basket with a heavy, but gentle, hand to the shoulder and an even more pointed look. Marcus started to shrivel beneath the perceptive and piercing gaze of his friend and, after a moment, ducked his eyes, settling the leather strap of the basket over his shoulder and adjusting his crutch. He then looked back up, his feelings, and hopefully his face, composed once more. "I'm fine."

Everard paused a moment, then nodded in acknowledgment of Marcus's assurance before sauntering off toward the blacksmith shop. Marcus smiled when Everard caught a wayward ball that had sailed over his head and bent double to toss it underhand back to the little boy who caught it, grinned, and ran off again. That was Everard. A friend to everyone— man, woman, beast, or child, with the exception of anyone who had an evil streak. Everard never had to raise a hand, but his scowl as dark as the midnight sky, his clenched fists and set shoulders enough to make any man quaver and think twice before attempting to hurt anyone the large man chose to protect.

Once back within the confines of Fendrel's abode and medicinal dispensary, Marcus set the basket down and approached the little huddle gathered around the exam table toward the back of the room.

Marcus made a silly face at the small little girl who sat on the table. The crocodile tears spilling from her massive blue eyes wet her face and caught in the shelf made by the cleft of her trembling lip. She clutched her arm to her side as Fendrel talked in soothing tones, using his fingers to gently examine the child's obviously broken arm.

Marcus's efforts at distracting her were rewarded with a sniff and an even greater widening of her eyes. They blinked slowly, then a dimple showed at the corner of her mouth.

He redoubled his efforts, twisting his features into the most outlandish of expressions that he possibly could, and in response, she let out a giggle, peaking shyly around Fendrel's shoulder.

Fendrel threw a grin over his shoulder at Marcus. "Would you be so kind as to assist me with the setting of the bone? But first, I'll need the willow bark tea, if you please."

Marcus nodded and wagged his tongue at the girl one more time before hobbling over to the kitchen stove where the kettle of willow bark tea rested on the trestle. It was often kept near the stove, as it was the most used medicinal they had at hand. Good for combating fevers and reducing the pain, it was a remedy they made every morning to have at the ready since it was so often needed. He poured a small pottery cup full of the warm and bitter liquid, paused, then gathered a generous scoop of honey on the wand and dipped it into the mug, stirring it thoroughly before hobbling back across the room.

The little girl still grimaced and squirmed away from the tea when her mother tried to hold it for her to drink, but

Marcus bribed her to finish it with the promise of a new doll to add to her collection. He talked to her reassuringly as he sat behind her on the table, gripping her shoulder in his hands and turning her face to look at him instead of Fendrel, who was taking a good hold on her wrist and forearm.

She cried when Fendrel set the bone, but it was a mild break and one that Marcus was glad to see she would recover from quickly. He shook his head and smiled as he petted her hair back from her face and told her a joke about falling flat on his back in the woods that morning. Her laugh revived his spirit. Children had an innate ability to recover quickly from anything. If only adult hearts mended so soon.

Halfway through the plastering process, Fendrel looked up with his eyebrows curved in chagrin, pushing his spectacles farther up his nose with the back of his hand. "I'm about out of plaster, and I forgot to get some from the mason's this morning when I was out. I'm sorry to ask it of you, but would you do me a favor? Run 'round and retrieve some?"

Marcus almost laughed sardonically with the use of the phrase "run 'round." But he would do his level best to hurry. "Of course. I'll be back in a tiff!" He swung his arms back and forth in an exaggerated movement that rewarded him a giggle from little Aria who was getting fidgety with the long waiting under Fendrel's hand.

Gathering his crutch again under his arm, he sallied forth with the lurch and shuffle that were his daily companions. He knew how to make quick work over the cobbles, even if he was still slower than most, and he also knew ways to shorten his walk. Small alleys and short-cuts had become his best friends over the years.

Nearing his destination, he swung a quick hop on his crutch that sent him a little farther along the cobbles than he could manage and nearly sent him sprawling. He was grateful for the wooden rail outside the blacksmith's shop to catch his step—and his breath. The long-faced horse that gave him a stare from the other end of the post made him feel as if he were interrupting some important meeting of the equestrian kind. Who knew a horse could look so disgruntled and un-horselike all at once? Marcus stuck his tongue out at the animal which reared his head back in disdain and turned his shoulder to Marcus with a few hoof clops along the cobblestones.

Glancing around himself to make sure his immaturity hadn't been seen, he moved the last ten feet to the stonemason's front step.

Eskel opened the door after a few of Marcus's knocks.

The man spoke before Marcus could even get a word out. "Fendrel forgot the plaster this morning. I'll fetch it." He turned without inviting Marcus in and disappeared into the house. Marcus grinned anyway. Eskel was abrupt, but he also kept a running tally in his head. He knew his entire stock, every contract and bill by memory, and never kept any books, much to his wife's chagrin.

Taking the moment to lean against the door frame, he drew in a deep breath, wincing at the radiating pain from his hip that shot down his leg when he tried to situate it in a better position for comfort. He rolled his neck back and rested his head against the lintel with a wince. The fall from earlier would not help with the pain, and he worried how sore he would feel in the morning.

Pain made him feel invisible. It felt like a heavy weight hanging around his neck and dragging him down, but he never wanted to make others feel bad. He hated pity, he hated the stares, and so he chose to hide it. But with hiding pain came shame and loneliness. He became the bearer of a burden that no one else can see.

"Such a sham, really. A peasant girl marrying the crowned prince." The female voice came from around the corner on the main street where a few skirted shadows shifted slowly into Marcus's view. He frowned. It did not take a scholar to know that they were talking about Violet. His dear friend and sister, Violet.

"How can you say that? She was clearly the woman he chose," said a more timid voice.

"But to *marry*? My dear. He would have been better off with a royal or a courtier. Much more befitting of his station, yet no, he chose to marry the first simpering peasant who cast eyes at him."

Marcus swallowed down the fire that rose in his throat and clenched his crutch, his fingernails digging into the wood.

"But her? I really do not know how she could have done it. The very idea of her marrying the man responsible for her father's death…" The words trailed off with a 'tsk' at their end like unfinished punctuation.

"Wasn't her father killed because he saved the urchin boy, Marcus, who works at Fendrel's now?"

Marcus's blood froze in his veins, and he felt as though his heart had fallen to his very toes. He couldn't breathe, couldn't move. His back cramped up, but he didn't care in the slightest.

"Yes, such a shame, really. I am grateful, I suppose, that King Elgon has put a stop to that nonsense. It really was preposterous, but if Richard had left well enough alone, the boy would be out of his misery and wouldn't be a burden to poor Fendrel. I'm sure it would have been much easier for him to die and not experience such a harsh life. That limp really is pitiful. My heart aches to see it every time he walks by."

His eyes were burning, and every single part of him felt like it was on fire. No air entered his lungs, and the memories from that day flooded his mind like a dam that had burst with the weight of the spring floods.

How had he never known? He was all but conscious after it happened. Barely able to move or defend himself at first, but then succumbing to unconsciousness as the kicks had broken one bone and then another, he had slipped away into oblivion. He had only woken weeks later in excruciating pain, the fever having left him so weak he could barely move.

Violet had been a shadow of herself, but she hadn't left his side through those dark days, as he was confined, unmoving, to a bed at Fendrel's.

How had she never told him? Was it truly his fault that her father had met his death? She had always been so vague. The Kingsmen had taken Richard away. But why? His brain fairly exploded, and every subsequent word of the gossiping pair was lost to him as his legs trembled beneath him and he sank to a seat on the flagstone. He stretched his bad leg out straight in front of him. Staring at the floor, he shook from the top of his head to the bottom of his feet.

Fendrel would tell him the truth.

"Here ye be, Marcus. I put in a bit extra. Just tell Fendrel that I won't be needing pay this week and that I'm still gra'ful that he was able to take care of Lila's foot; she be walking right proper now. She be… Eh, you aw'right there, lad?" Eskel shifted the fabric sack of plaster powder and tucked it under an elbow, crouching beside Marcus with an inquiring look at the boy.

Marcus swallowed, trying to drag his mind back from the fiery pit that consumed it as it had not consumed Shadrach, Mesach, and Abednego. If only he had been privileged with the ability to walk with Jesus through fire. He coughed into his elbow and took the man's hand as Eskel helped him to his feet. He still felt wobbly as he slung the sack from Eskel over his shoulder and gripped his crutch like a lifeline. "I'm fine. Thank you for the plaster."

"You sh'ore you're aw'right? You look a bit unsteady, and the last thing I'd want was to find out ye fell on yer way home."

"I'm just fine." Marcus felt a fingernail crack beneath his grip on the crutch, and he winced. "Thank you again," he squeaked out before turning and hobbling as quickly as he could down the alley and onto the street.

He needed to talk to Fendrel.

Now.

Finally bursting into the door, barely able to stand, he gasped for breath.

Fendrel looked up, his brow furrowed and his eyes wide. "What happened to you? Are you alright?"

Marcus drew himself up short when he caught sight of the little girl, her eyes wider than Fendrel's and her lips parted in shock at the sight of him. He must look crazed. He drew a breath and swallowed down the panic. His own problems could wait; others were more important.

Shaking his head, he set down the plaster and made it to his own room off of the kitchen and main exam area. Shutting the door harder than he intended to, he leaned against it and finally gasped in the air he needed to fill his lungs.

Could those women possibly be right? All these years, and no one had ever told him. The weight of the shame and guilt felt like it was going to swallow him whole. No wonder Violet had been distant of late. Ever since meeting Obed…or rather, Elgon, she had distanced herself from him, and now he knew why. Perhaps she had discovered that he was responsible for her father's death? Or had she simply known all this time?

He gulped, his mind suddenly remembering all of the moments when she had shushed, distracted, or hushed a crowd around them. Had she protected him from this knowledge all these years? All it had taken was her being gone for just a few weeks for the truth to come out. He sat on his cot and rubbed the muscles in his thigh, wincing with the intensity of the pain while his brain exploded with all of the thoughts that cluttered there. He remembered nothing of the moments when he had been injured. But Violet had told him later how she had followed her father's march to Niran and witnessed his death. He had assumed it had been a result of something else, but now it made sense. Had her father done something to upset the Kingsmen as a result of his attack?

Was Richard's death his fault?

Fendrel knocked, then pushed open the door when there was no response. "What on earth is the matter, dear boy? You seemed incredibly upset..." He froze as soon as he caught sight of Marcus's face. "What's going on?"

"Am I responsible for Violet's father's death?"

Marcus could tell by the blank look on his face that the man had been far from expecting that question.

"I—" The pause that followed filled Marcus's heart with dread.

"Am I?"

The continued silence sent a dagger into Marcus's heart. No wonder Violet could leave him so easily. If he was the one who had caused her father's death, what more was there for her here?

If only he had died that day instead. What of value did he have to offer that could have possibly justified taking the place of Richard in Violet's life?

His eyes burned. Fendrel seemed about to say something when the front door burst open, catching their attention.

The shadow looming in front of the doorway was charged with energy, rippling from every muscle with the static of a lightning storm.

"Fendrel, you and Marcus are needed if you can be spared. I just received word. Rusalka is closing the border crossing, and they are slaying anyone trying to escape. The refugees who made it over are in dire straits. We are needed." Everard's voice was low, husky with emotion.

Fendrel swallowed and straightened his shoulders, pain sweeping across his face and making his eyes droop. Then he turned to Marcus, his mouth open to speak.

"When do we leave?" Marcus smiled softly.

Two

WORTH THE COST

MARCUS'S VERY BONES seemed to rattle as the wagon wheel ran over a rut. He stiffened, attempting to adjust his position on top of a sack of oats in the back of the wagon. They had gathered all that might be needed for the refugees rumored to be pouring over the border near Pranvera Forest and into the neighboring town. It would be a full night's ride before they arrived, and Marcus hoped he could rest. Or better yet, sleep, though perhaps that was hoping for too much on this rickety byway.

They hadn't thought it prudent to wait to leave. Though Everard, who now drove the wagon, spared many a word, as was his habit, the others who joined their small caravan of aid spoke freely, and the looks of fear and anger on their faces were enough to set his own blood boiling. With the new king seeking to bring freedom and honor the Lord with his actions,

19

they had just escaped the harshest life any of them had ever known. But now, the Mountain King rising up in such anger and striking down his own people, those who so obviously sought only to flee their land of indecency and abuse—it was unthinkable. Were their lives not of as much value as the king himself?

Marcus knew that their lives were just as valuable to God as to each other. He was greatly encouraged by the group who had been willing to drop everything and come at a moment's notice to lend aid and perhaps even lodging for the refugees who would surely need more than physical aid and comfort after their escape.

They were homeless. Without anywhere to go. More than likely the Rusalkans sought refuge in Elira because it was the only country they felt could be trusted.

Marcus was glad to see that the people of Elira would not betray that trust. He was proud of those who had mustered forth with little notice to lend a helping hand to the least of these.

It afforded him a helpful distraction. Though, that distraction was not working well due to the inordinate amount of time he now had upon this cart to think before they arrived.

Fendrel had said little as they had gathered all of the herbs, bandages, clean clothes, blankets, vittles, and stores that they could get their hands on. The miller had offered several sacks of necessary food stuffs such as flours, oats, and ground meal that could be turned into simple camping fare. Eskel had come as well, driving the other wagon, which carried his wife and one of the farmers and his wife.

Marcus pulled his cloak tighter around his shoulders to ward off the chill. The closer they got to the mountains, the colder it grew as the elevation rose. The clouds shrouded the moon from them, and it was a shame. They could have moved much faster if they weren't relying on the lanterns fitted with mirrors that lit the ground in front of their wagons. They lurched along as if the horses hesitated over where to put their hooves.

With the hurry and flutter of actually departing finally over, there was little else to occupy Marcus's mind than the overwhelming guilt, sorrow, and shame that tore at his mind. It dragged his heart down into the depths like a millstone tied around the neck.

"It's not your fault." The whisper reached his ear in the darkness.

He turned back to look at Fendrel, doing nothing to hide the tears that gathered in his eyes. Fendrel wouldn't be able to see them in the black inkiness of night. They were too far out of reach from the yellow orbs that lit their path.

"Then it's true." The words came out like a sharp object being wrested from impaled flesh being wrested from flesh. Leaving more damage behind than if it had just been left alone.

"True, perhaps, in the sense that Richard moved to defend you, and in so doing, incurred the wrath of the Kingsmen."

"They said that I was to blame."

"Who?"

"Just…" Marcus shook his head and folded his arms tighter over his chest to keep the sorrow from exploding out of him at any moment. "Two women. I was gathering the plaster when I overheard." He clenched his teeth hard. "Am I a burden to you? If I am, please tell me." His breath shuddered on the intake after the words left his mouth.

A hand—kind, gentle, the one that had comforted him in his deepest pain and nursed him back to health, such as it was—gripped his shoulder and squeezed. "My dear boy. You? A burden?" Fendrel's voice was harsh with emotion and grave with the repressed feeling it still conveyed in the simplest of words. "If so, it has been the one I have borne the most gladly and with the greatest reward."

"You can't mean it." Marcus fought against the urge to collapse, but he held back the emotions that welled within him.

"I do, and most earnestly. When you were brought to me, nearest death, you do not know the burden that was placed on my heart to see you well again." Fendrel's voice was rough. "Marcus, I fairly stormed the gates of heaven on your behalf. You are like a son to me, a son I could never have had if God had not given you to me. So don't you dare for one moment feel yourself a burden. Your interest in my work and the skill you have shown thereof has far outweighed any inconvenience your condition has burdened anyone with. Your life has purpose, and it was worth any cost."

The tears fell now; gone was any strength to hold them back. The shame still reared its ugly head, the pain black and thick like a storm cloud about to unleash its terror. "But how can my life be worth…Richard's? I am to blame for that loss. How could Violet have possibly forgiven me? What must she think? The whole town knows it, though I did not. If Richard had just left me to die that day, would he still be here? Would his life be forfeit if not for what I have done? Me, an urchin and a farmer's orphan with nothing to give or offer."

"You were not to blame, Marcus. Richard counted the cost and found you, urchin and farmer's orphan though you were, worthy of the cost he would pay. Violet does not blame you. What use have you for the opinion of the taverner's wife and her friend?"

Marcus choked and looked up quickly, catching the anger in the faint glow on Fendrel's face. "I never told you who I overheard."

Fendrel smiled sardonically, though it disappeared almost as instantly as it had come. "You did not need to. Gossip is as gossip does and there are few, God be praised, who would speak so lowly, so publicly."

Marcus felt a cramp in his hip and a flare of anger at it. The constant reminder of what the sum of his life had been. Forfeit for that of a man greater than he and worthless in the realm of what he had to offer the God who had seen fit, for some reason, to save him.

He drew a breath. Better to get his mind off this subject. "They also spoke of Violet."

A grumble from the man's chest was his only response, and the hand that still rested on Marcus's shoulder tightened its grip.

"Was Elgon truly responsible for Richard's execution?"

"How could he have been? Though the next ruler in line to the throne, he was but a boy, scarcely older than you and Violet at the time. Only an idiot—pardon my unkindness— would presume to speak such stupidity."

"They also spoke of Elgon and Violet, as if their marriage was an indiscretion on the part of our new monarch."

Fendrel huffed, releasing Marcus's shoulder, flicking his cloak, and resettled into a more comfortable position. "Only a fool would dare sully the name of the king. They seemed pleasant enough at the wedding that they enjoyed alongside the rest of the town when the King decided to bless us with his presence and with the wedding of the century." Fendrel shook his head. "We ought to have little use for such talk, and it is not profitable to repeat. Put it from your mind, I pray you, and don't let's speak of it again. Gossip is bad enough when originally spoken, let alone when repeated idly. Violet and Elgon are above reproach, as are you. Try to get some sleep, Marcus. I know it's a tiring and painful ride, but we will need your skills, your light heart, and your gifted hands on the morrow when we reach our destination."

Marcus nodded, readjusting to a more reclined position, half on his good hip so that his sore one could be given somewhat of a rest. He closed his eyes. If only the words of gossip Fendrel so readily disposed of did not still slither with a shred of truth. A truth, however disproportionate in Fendrel's mind, that still fought for supremacy in Marcus's brain like a drowning man fighting for air.

Marcus had rarely felt this way over the course of his life, but somehow, God felt distant, and with a tiny thorn of rebellion and anger within him, he declined to reach out and instead pushed the beckoning desire to commune with his Maker aside.

Her heart froze as cold as the ice that clung to her clothes and skin as the dark, clear sky spun above her, no stars or moon to illuminate her way. She was so frigid she could not even shiver, but even with everything within her fighting for her to lay down and give up…there was a fire still left burning in her heart.

Her foot crashed through the upper, crusted layer of snow at her feet, and she sank up to her knee. A sobbing gasp escaped her raw and ragged lungs as she fought to free it, wrestling it out of the hole and grasping a pine branch with the little strength left in her numb fingers. The bark broke through the fragile skin, but she didn't care. With a groan, she hefted herself another step, and then another.

Voices shouted behind her at a distance in the wood, and she pressed on, heaving ragged breaths, one after the other, to fill her dying lungs. She had not thought it possible to drown on dry land, but the pressure that built within her chest felt as close to it as she ever dared to be again.

She fell to her knees at the top of the rise and looked down at the half-frozen lake below her. The border she sought was just around the lake and through that portion of the Pranvera Forest. Her mother had told her the way many a time throughout her growing up years. She had been eight when she had been sold, but she had always remembered that it was not her mother's doing.

With a tear falling from her eye and freezing to her cheek, she wrested herself from the grip of the snow and the exhaustion that sought to kill her.

Death beckoned to her, welcoming her into its comforting embrace, but she had looked death in the face enough to know that she would not succumb to its siren call. Not unless it was beyond her own choice.

Life would have to be pried from her cold, fast grip.

Her stumbling steps led down the mountain, and a wolf howl split the echoing night air. Her heart was already in her throat, and she had more things to fear than the she-wolf that had been following her for the last several miles of her journey.

Another human shout joined the wolf call, and her head throbbed as she picked up speed, crashing down the hill, more afraid of the voices that matched her own than the mother wolf crying for her cubs. Her feet seized with frozen cramps, and she wondered if her deerskin shoes still even clad her feet. It would not surprise her if she had lost them in the trek through the mountains. More shouts followed the first, and she tried to swallow against her dry throat. One man seemed to cry out in pain, another in anger, and she felt sick at the visualization in her mind of what could be occurring far behind her in the woods.

Her heart willed her on when she reached the bottom of the hill, but she knew that unless she drank something, she would not make it through the forest and into Elira before it was too late. Her chances were already slimmer than she would have hoped. She could make it without food, but eating the snow would only suck the life from her bones faster than it already fled.

Testing the ice with a trembling foot, she sank to her knees, crawling across the frozen face of the lake that was hidden beneath its winter coat. Her bare and bleeding hands trembled as she tested the ice before she put weight on it. If she could only make it far enough out to reach the unfrozen water, she could bathe away the blood that was frozen to her skin and drink enough to make it the rest of the way. On her stomach, she edged herself the last few feet and reached a hand into the shockingly frigid water that somehow warmed her skin with its burning touch in a way the wind had not. The blood that coated her legs and bled from her scratched hands blended with the inky black of the water and colored the white, icey coat.

Now with clean hands, she scooped up the water and brought it to her cracked and trembling lips, drinking as much from her hands as she could before using the hem of her dress to clean the blood from her legs. A sob sliced through her like a knife, and she shoved the rest of the inner pain farther into her belly. If she made it through this night, there would be time to dwell on her sorrow at a later date.

But first, life. While her heart, however unsteady, beat within her breast, there was hope. And she intended to run out every last second of that pounding to see herself free.

Nothing would stop her. She had lost everything, but while there was life, there was hope. And she would fight with that tiny flicker until nothing else remained.

Three

THE WALL BETWEEN WORLDS

MARCUS JOLTED AWAKE and squinted into the light of the rising sun as he pulled his hood off his head. He slowly rotated, sitting up and testing his limbs one by one. The wagon still rattled on, and he was definitely sore, but the pain could have been so much worse. He swallowed. *Thanks, Lord.*

He cringed at the slight twinge of guilt that stabbed at him. He had been ignoring the Lord and fighting Him on so many things of late, self-aware enough to know that. He knew he was being a fair-weathered follower at the moment and that he was wrong, but his heart was a little too angry to admit it to the Lord.

Fendrel was rolling bandages from the basket of unwrapped strips of cotton that had been boiled and bleached out in the sun. They had thrown the basket into the wagon in preparation

29

for needing more than what they had stored and prepared. Marcus yawned and reached across for a strip to start rolling himself. Many hands made light work.

"Do you see what you are doing?" Fendrel's words were sharp with his morning voice, and Marcus froze.

"What do you mean?"

Fendrel smiled sadly. "You wonder if you are useless, yet look at what your first instinct is, my boy. Your heart is one to help. And yet you ask me if *you* are the burden." He shook his head and smiled sadly.

Marcus swallowed. "I could never repay you for all that you have done for me."

Fendrel threw a bandage at him and Marcus reared back in surprise, unsure if he should smile or frown, but a grin tugged at the corners of his mouth over the playful gesture anyway.

Fendrel's smile held less sadness and more love that deepened and moistened his eyes. "You have already done so, many times over. Now stop listening to idiotic nonsense that replays in your head and help me with the rest of these."

Marcus reached for another bandage with a shake of the head. There was a little more life in his soul after a good night's sleep and his lessened pain. Though, the words of the town gossips still lingered in the back of his mind like creeping moss clinging to trees. The words hung in the shadows, and he knew that though he put them away for the moment, they might come back to haunt him.

"How far away are we?" Marcus rubbed his aching shoulders.

Fendrel glanced at Everard, who still sat at the front of the wagon, the reins threaded effortlessly and loosely through his massive fingers, his palms resting upward on his knees. "Should be there within the hour. We have to go through the town of Pranvera first, but it's not far from there."

The trees grew thinner before they left the woods. Drawing near Pranvera, Marcus could hear shouting. He pulled himself to a standing position with the back of the driver's seat and peered over Everard's shoulder, supporting his full weight with his arms and standing on the toes of his good leg to see over.

"What's going on?" There was a buzz in the air. The horses sensed it, their ears flicking back and forth and their steps now prancing more than plodding.

Everard swallowed, and his eyebrows lowered. The cleft in his forehead that had once been a fixture, but had disappeared after Elgon's ascension, was now back in its place, and it made Marcus's heart drop clear to his feet. He had hoped to never see that look again.

Instead of answering, Everard simply shook his head with a look of confusion and gripped the reins tighter, keeping his horses in check.

Pranvera's village consisted of widespread houses with grass and gardens, long since harvested and bare, laid out between them instead of being built right on top of each other as was custom in Padsley. There was a cluster of several larger buildings, an inn, tavern, and a few smaller custodial buildings, one of which looked to be a combined smithy and stable. People who were out and about seemed to be in a bit of a hurry, and there was a general rush in the direction of the wall beyond the town. It was over a hill and abutted the forest, so it was out of sight, but Marcus could sense the fear and panic that pervaded the area.

A lump grew in his throat, and his pulse quickened, making his chest feel fluttery and his stomach sick from the movement.

He hadn't known what to expect, but it certainly hadn't been this.

The first sight of a kingsman's uniform brought back a weight crashing upon his shoulders. He flinched, losing his balance at a bump in the road and gripping Everard's shoulder to keep from falling sideways. Fendrel's arm reached around his waist and supported him beneath the shoulder as they both stood.

They crested the hill. Shouts from people fighting, the clamor of weapons, the frantic calls to lost relatives, cries and moans from the refugees, and the commanding calls of the leaders and townspeople met their ears. Coupled with the sight of the melee below them, the uncontrolled energy made Marcus's throat close up; his eyes watered, and a sob tried to escape the weight that felt like it was growing in his stomach.

The foreboding of fear and pain washed over him like a scalding wave, a sensation that brought back far too many unkind and ugly memories.

Ones he had hoped never to relive.

He shoved the thoughts of dark days and painful nights behind him and prayed for strength. Not for himself, but for the people below who needed the healing hand of their Creator and not just his mortal touch. *Let me be your hands and feet, my Lord. Give us all that gift.*

Every one of them focused on the valley below, and Everard "hupped" to the horses, holding them in a controlled, but quicker, descent into the crowded valley and wooded field below.

The moaning, pain-filled cries, and the sight of the broken and desperate people as they joined the crowd below crushed Marcus with its overwhelming presence. Everard pulled the wagon to a stop, and within moments, Fendrel was over the side with his elderly, but spry, legs moving quickly to the most injured person within close distance.

Marcus followed more slowly as he struggled off the wagon. The others had pulled up behind them and were already well on their way to determining the most in need among them.

Shivering at the cold air around him as it poured over the mountain top and blew through the surrounding forest, he slung the leather bag of medicinal supplies over his head and shoulder, gathered his crutches, and used them to propel himself faster than he thought possible.

Marcus passed a groaning man who clutched a bloodied cloth to a gash on his head. He was already being tended by the farmer's wife who had accompanied them. A woman clutched a child to her breast and sobbed, her hands blistered and red, and Marcus's stomach flipped when he realized it was frostbite. Her face was pocked and marked with the frozen blisters as well. Stepping to their side, he spoke comfortingly to her, offering to take her child. He bent to his left knee, keeping his right leg laid out to the side so it didn't cramp the muscles in his joint as he took the baby from her. The child was white as a ghost, and it didn't take him long to realize with horror that he had no pulse. The poor thing was lifeless—probably had been for some time judging by the stiffness. Marcus stared at the perfect little face, eyes closed in peaceful rest. Sickness rose in the back of his throat, and he reached a hand to the mother. She was rocking back and forth, her cries unintelligible, but the brokenness and sorrow needed no interpretation. She already knew.

He covered the little one's face and gathered the mother's hands in his to tend to their frost-burned patches. Staring past his shoulder, tears streamed unchecked from her eyes as he coated her palms in a salve from his bag and bandaged them with care, praying for her all the while.

Her lesser wounds would need to be tended to later when they could find the people shelter, but for now, as desperately broken as he was over leaving her to herself, he stepped away to help another individual. He passed Fendrel, who was stitching a nasty gash on a man's arm that poured blood on the green grass fast turning yellow and freckled with frost. Marcus stopped, his hip cramping beneath the stress and quickness of his movements as he looked up.

Everard was helping more wounded over the stone wall, and a precise, military shout came from within the woods. More kingsmen rushed in defense over the wall, built out of rocks caked in moss and dirt that had been piled high to form a rampart. It had been erected in an attempt to keep any of those who had enacted such reckless violence from following the refugees over to this side of the wall.

There were so many. His chest heaved with each belabored breath. He didn't know where to turn. So many wounded. So many with eyes of broken glass. So many with hearts torn asunder and bleeding before his very eyes with internal wounds his hands could not fix. They stretched along the field covered in trampled frost and dotted with trees where they sat against or leaned upon the boughs to gather their strength and nurse their own wounds. Relief had not come to them as yet. For though they were on the right side of the wall now, the past on the other side still haunted them like ghosts among the living.

His heart jumped and beat anew. He must help. He needed to find *the one*. When in doubt of what to do, he only had to find one and tend to their needs. It all started with one. His eyes fixed on a man whose silver hair matched the frost that seemed to coat every living thing. The locks covered his eyes as he leaned over the child he held in his lap with one arm, the other extended to his side as it oozed blood upon the ground from a wound.

Marcus hop-stepped with the help of his crutch to the man's side. The fellow's eyes were weary but there was a fire within them, and he clutched the shivering child closer to his chest with a defiant tilt to his brow as he took in Marcus's approach. He relaxed when he took in Marcus's hands, ready with bandages. Marcus knew that the man had reacted upon reflex. Marcus was sure there had been much to be afraid of in those mountains.

"May I tend your arm, sir?" he asked, half-kneeling, pulling a needle and thread from his bag and setting a roll of bandages in his lap.

"Please, tend the boy first. His foot is wounded. He fell as we were coming down the hill, and he rolled against a tree right hard."

"But, sir, you are bleeding. Perhaps I can at least wrap it first…"

The man pulled his wounded arm back and thrust the child forward with the other. "He gets tended first, or I won't be." The wince and flash of pain that overcame the old man's features did not go amiss to Marcus as he took the child gently in his arms and set him upon the rock beside them. The little lad could not have been more than six years old, and his face was littered with cuts from branches that had whipped his face. Silent tears fell down his cheeks, and Marcus reached a hand for the boy's feet. One ankle twisted at an unnatural angle, and both bare feet were bloodied and bruised, some of his toes gray and blistered with frostbite.

"You are such a brave boy. Your ankle is twisted, and I will have to set it right, which will hurt. Can you manage?" Marcus asked gently, holding the injured limb between his hands and waiting for acquiescence before he continued. The boy gripped the weathered hand that the older man gave him and nodded, clenching his little jaw, the bones jutting sharply on his thin, timid face. The brown eyes welling with pain were too much for Marcus, and with his stomach in his throat, he gave a calculated and skilled pull to the ankle. It clunked back into place, and the child slumped on the rock, caught by the arm of his elderly companion as a sob escaped his tiny breast.

Barely thinking, Marcus swiftly and deftly wrapped the ankle tight enough to hold its structure, but loose enough that it wouldn't cut off circulation. "There, now. Does anything else hurt?" He lifted a canteen up to the boy's blue lips, cradling his head on his arm.

The boy shook his head, but when Marcus went to adjust the child's position, he moaned and gripped his stomach. Marcus gently lifted the boy's shirt and caught sight of the large bruise forming on his abdomen. His heart sank. This boy might have internal injuries from his fall. He looked up frantically, searching for Everard.

"Everard!" He shouted over the din.

The large man turned instantly, his eyes searching the cluttered field for his friend. Marcus raised a crutch and waved it over his head. In just a few seconds, Everard's long legs had stepped over the wounded and broken till he was right beside them.

"Please take this boy to one of the houses prepared for them and tell Fendrel right away. I'm afraid he may have internal injuries and need an operation, but Fendrel must see him at once." He turned back to the little boy who was gazing at Everard with large, pain-filled eyes. "This man is safe. I promise you. He will take care of you and keep you that way."

The boy looked to his old companion for reassurance, and after noting the nod given him, he allowed Everard to gently scoop him into his arms. He gripped the thin leather cord strung around the man's neck in a tight fist and bunched his eyes closed as he shivered against the massive chest. Marcus nodded, praying that Fendrel would be able to care for the boy and give him what he needed to recover. "Now, we must see to that arm."

"Thank you for taking care of my grandson." The man's face crumpled a little now that he no longer had to be strong and care for his charge.

Marcus was already stitching up the gash on the man's arm. "Of course. I'm praying that you both recover well. What happened to your arm?"

The man's face went whiter than it already was. "Sword." He swallowed hard.

Marcus looked up with a flash, startled, and then went back to his quick, neat, even stitches, nodding to the man to drink from the canteen that his grandson had.

"Whose sword?"

"A Rusalkan soldier. They don't want us escaping over the border now that our countries no longer have peace. If that's even what you could call the treaty." He hissed through clenched teeth and took another drink as Marcus finished up the deepest part of the cut.

"They were attacking you?" Marcus, though he knew the intentions of the soldiers, was still surprised that they would take the time and effort to attack their own citizens and keep them from entering Elira.

"It was a free-for-all. No one was safe. They've been chasing stragglers like us over the mountains for the last few days, dogging our every step as we fought our way to the border. You must know…Elira was our only hope."

Marcus tied off the stitches and wrapped the bandages around the wound. He was nearly out of the supplies he had grabbed already. "Well, I'm glad you made it. If you can walk, make your way to that group of buildings over there." He pointed to the little cluster in the distance that was the village of Pranvera. "They are setting up lodgings and will care for you."

Standing, Marcus wobbled on his leg that had stiffened in the short while he had been on his knee.

The man gripped his forearm and looked up at him, eyes welling with tears. "Thank you. You have no idea how grateful I am to be here."

Marcus patted the man's hand. "Sir, I hope you come across more reason still."

A shout from off to his right sent Marcus scurrying toward the cry of pain without a second thought. His gaze roved over the injured that surrounded him, and nothing of dire circumstance caught his eye until he glanced up, catching sight of a woman clambering over the wall. Terror struck deep in his heart at the Rusalkan warriors that were fast on her heels. The last few stragglers were scurrying from the woods and making toward the rampart with anxious shouts of fear. They were closely followed by a group of kingsmen that fought to keep the Rusalkans, with their distinctive black leather armor, from getting any closer.

The woman fell to the ground on this side of the stone divider, and Marcus rushed for her as she scrambled up, moving further in with stumbling, weary steps. He wondered how on earth she could stand and watched in horror as her legs gave out and she collapsed. He drew near and fell to his knees beside her, dropping his crutch next to him. He pushed the hood of her cloak out of the way and lifted her head from the ground. Her face was pale as death, blistered with frostbite, and her clothes were blackened by drying blood. His heart beat loud in his ears as he pushed the matted brown hair from around her face, and her massive brown eyes flickered open.

"Please, save my son," she whispered with a heartbreaking moan before her eyes rolled back in her head once more, and her lids closed without a flutter.

Marcus looked around frantically for a child. She was so young, her son must be merely a toddler or an infant. He saw no child nearby who could be her son, and panic made his hands shake and his muscles cramp.

Where was this woman's son? And what had happened to her in those woods?

Four

WHEN LIVES INTERSECT

MARCUS HELD THE woman's hand as they moved her, though it felt far more like she was gripping his. Her frostbitten fingers held his like a vice. When Everard had returned, Marcus had told him to look for a missing boy, the woman's son, but the large man had shaken his head, sending the farmer to do so and picking up the young woman in his arms.

They carried her to the inn and tavern that had been set up as makeshift housing for the refugees who had escaped over the border at the last minute. While there had been a small skirmish between the Kingsmen guarding the border and the Rusalkan soldiers, it had been out of his sight, and Marcus had been far too busy to go out of his way to see what was going on. Everard wouldn't speak much, so Marcus would have to

41

wait until he could discuss it with Fendrel, they both were going to be far too occupied to do anything of the sort for some time.

Stepping sideways, Marcus held open the tavern door for Everard to carry the young woman through, noticing the imprint of a dove carved into the wooden surface. He glanced out at the sign swinging from the side of the building. *Dove's Tavern and Inn* was scrawled across the less than decorative, but serviceable, sign that swung from two rings below the wood support. Once Everard was through the door, Marcus followed on one of his crutches, his hand still holding the unconscious woman's. He'd have to figure out a way for her to release him once she was settled. From the looks and sounds of the wailing inmates scattered around the great room, he was desperately needed in more than one place.

A woman, ample of stature and with a scowl on her forehead, swung a wooden spoon their way and pointed them up the stairs before she turned and poured hot water into a basin, dipping the towel that was draped over her shoulder into it and handing it to an individual with large scratches on his face.

What on earth had happened to these people? They looked as though they had gone through a war themselves. Marcus swallowed hard. Except maybe they had. A battle of survival had taken no prisoners and left them with more mental injuries than perhaps a real battle could have.

Prying his fingers from the woman's, he scanned the room as Everard started up the stairs ahead of him. Making sure there was no one with more dire injuries than the woman, he followed at a more tedious pace, using his left leg to propel himself up one stair at a time, dragging his useless right leg behind him.

Completely out of breath when he finally reached the landing at the top of the stairs, he sagged against the railing before using it to help him into the bedroom that Everard had carried the young woman into. A fire, newly lit, crackled in the fireplace on the opposite end of the room, thick ice coating the single wood-framed window. A second and third cot had been prepared in the other two corners, both empty and ready for another occupant. The large man gently laid the wounded soul upon the bed as if she were a kitten, making sure her head was at a comfortable angle and straightening her legs, one foot bare and the other encased in a deerskin shoe. Marcus winced, noticing her toes were blistered from the cold. What had been chasing her in the night? Why had she not had time to search for the lost shoe? Had she not even realized she'd lost it? At what peril did a person run through snow without a shoe and mind it not?

"Thank you, Everard. Please send up any woman who is willing to help. She will need new clothes, and I need to assess her injuries." He hobbled closer, still gasping for breath. "Where is Fendrel?"

"With the boy you said needed tending. You were right about the injury."

Marcus pursed his lips, grimacing. "Would you see if he needs my help?" That poor boy. He prayed that Fendrel would be able to stop the bleeding, no matter how bad it was. No boy should have to lose his life, but especially one so young. Then again, Marcus had scarcely been any older when his life had nearly been taken from him. *Lord, please don't let him live out a life like mine. Be with Fendrel and strengthen him with Your skill.*

"And?" Everard waited at the door, glancing pointedly between the woman and Marcus.

"I'll need hot and cold water and bandages. We will need to get the blood back into her frostbitten limbs. If there is anyone available to be spared, I could use their help."

Everard nodded without another word and turned, his heavy footsteps fading down the stairs.

Marcus took a deep breath. There was already a pitcher of water on the wash stand, and he tested the temperature with a finger before pouring it into the basin and snatching the cloth from the hook beside it. Setting the dish on the bed beside the woman and dipping the cloth into it, he carefully bathed the blood and tearstained dirt from her face. The skin was wind beaten, but there were no frostbite blisters, and for that, he was grateful. They were painful enough on their own, but more so when on the face.

As his fingers touched her skin, he was stunned with her frigidity. It was only a moment before he shook his head and continued cleaning her face and neck, moving to her hands where he was more careful around her blistered fingers. He kept glancing at the unconscious face, red from frostbite but pale beneath it all. She was so much younger than he had expected. Barely older than a girl, or so it seemed. Her features were large for her petite face, and her long dark lashes brushed her chapped cheeks in slumber.

Scarcely more than the dead, her unconscious state concerned him but was not surprising.

Glancing down at the blood stains on her skirt, he then winced at the bruises and cuts that laced the skin on her lower legs visible below the bedraggled hem. He used the back of his hand to brush a lock of hair that had fallen in front of his eyes. *Lord, help this woman. Whatever her story...*

Fendrel entered the room, drying his pink hands on a towel. The sleeves of his shirt were pushed up past his elbows and his face focused as his eyes quickly scanned the figure on the bed. He was followed by a young woman carrying two basins, an arm layered with clean towels and bandages.

"What is your assessment?" Fendrel asked, doing his own nonverbal evaluation as he gently turned her face to inspect the chapped skin.

"She is not too severely wounded, no broken bones. I worry about internal injuries. She has clearly been bleeding, and I did not determine if it was from her monthly bleed or...something else."

The girl who had come up with Fendrel came closer with another basin, setting it down on the bedside table with a thunk. Water splashed over the lip. Her eyes were wide and her face suddenly pale.

"I'll step out unless you need me," Marcus spoke, wanting to leave their patient her dignity and allow Fendrel's more skilled hands and this young servant girl to manage.

Fendrel shook his head sorrowfully. "There are many wounded in need of stitches and some little ones in need of comfort below." He ran his hands down the woman's forearm, probing and checking at the bruises for any breaks.

Marcus nodded. "The boy?"

Fendrel looked up with a slight smile before going back to his work. "I was able to stop the bleeding. He'll take a while to recover, and we'll need to keep the wound clean, but he'll make it, Lord willing."

Drawing a breath of relief, Marcus rolled his head back and around, stretching the tense muscles that knotted at the back of his neck and shoulders. He suddenly felt weary. The adrenaline was wearing off more than likely.

He turned and nearly tripped on the way out of the room, but caught himself on his crutch, reaching back to shut the door behind him to afford them the privacy that they needed. He sighed. He was starting to feel the familiar pain creep up around his hip, causing it to cramp, but he shoved it aside, trying instead to loosen his shoulders that had wound up in defense against the pain. He needed to ride the wave of energy just a few hours longer.

But first, the stairs. He sighed. They never got easier.

Panic choked her, clawing at her throat like icy fingers. She fought it off, her blood running cold. She hated her life. Her existence. Every moment she lived she longed to see a different life. A brighter future. Fire tinged her vision, and the scorching orange, red, and light blue flickered nearby. Why did it feel so hot? She pulled her hands and feet from the fire, using them to drag herself free. Suddenly she was bathed in ice and the air was wrested from her lungs again.

She fought hard, the ice and fire taking turns, entrapping her in their ceaseless grip. She kicked, scratched, fought, and pushed her way through it all, dragging in breaths when she could.

She saw every one of their faces. Some evil, some longing. Painful, tortured, desperate, and vile by turns. There were so many faces. More than anyone should have to live with for their entire lives. She fought them away. She hated them all. Hated what they represented. Hated the way that they clung to fragments of her life like burrs cling to one's clothes.

She batted them away. They would not take up property within her mind, her spirit, her soul. They could not take more than they had already taken from her. She would not let them.

Never again.

"And with one stroke of the sword, the man freed the mermaid from her captor and set her free to swim the ocean for the rest of her life!" Marcus slashed his hand through the air, scattering his audience of tiny thespians with audible gasps of awe and wonder as he brandished his crutch like a sword in one hand and gestured broadly with the other, puffing out his chest like a hero of old.

"What happened to them after that?" piped a little voice, pitched even higher than its usual squeaky tone with excitement over the tale.

"Finish your breakfast, and then I'll tell you. I'm going to go change some bandages while you eat." He winked, trying to cover a wince as he readjusted his right leg and settled more comfortably on the stool by the fire. They had spent the night at the Dove's Tavern and Inn—what little was left of it after the flood of patients who occupied every inch of the place. He had caught perhaps an hour or two of sleep, and he was grateful that he knew enough stories to hide the fact that he was running on tea and prayers.

Trying to cover a groan, he stood to his feet, using both crutches today. All he wanted was to melt into a comfortable bed, but those were also in short supply around here with all of the injured and broken individuals who still needed care. Everard, the farmer and his wife who had come with them, plus the taverner and his slightly aloof wife were the only ones besides Fendrel and himself who were caring for these people. And between them all, they had around fifty patients in need of regular care and fifty others who were able to care for themselves but still needed shelter. About twenty-five people had been housed in the lower, main room of the tavern, which spread the entire width of the building, with the kitchen attached in back. The upstairs rooms were all spoken for, some injured lying on pallets on the floor, the beds being reserved for those with graver wounds and illnesses.

Marcus picked his way around the pallets strewn across the floor. It was a wonder there were enough blankets for them all. Some used cloaks to wrap themselves, though many in Pranvera had been willing to donate their blankets for use. Most of the fugitives had next to nothing to call their own. Marcus wobbled and drew in a breath between his teeth when the foot of one of his crutches got wrapped around a blanket. Adjusting his weight, he shook it free and continued on the hazardous trek across the massive room to the stairs.

His nemesis.

Along the way, he stopped at a table near the fireplace of the dinning hall, filling his leather bag with new bandages that the women had prepared and placing a few herbs in as well. Slinging the bag back over his shoulder, he let it rest over his good hip. It bounced against him as he laboriously climbed the stairs, one trembling step at a time.

Marcus was not one prone to tears, but a few almost escaped him when he reached the top, his limbs fairly shaking with exhaustion, the ache in his muscles throbbing with the effort. Wiping sweat off his forehead, he pushed back a lock of hair that had fallen near his eyes. Gasping for breath, he removed the crutches from under his arms a moment and leaned his back against the wall, staring down the stairs that now wavered in his blurry vision. His sight nearly gave out on him when that lightheaded feeling took over. He closed his eyes and leaned the back of his throbbing head against the wall, trying to steady his breathing. He prayed his knees would not give way.

A heavy hand on his shoulder jerked him out of a near sleep, and he looked up…and up some more to meet Everard's eyes. They looked as tired as he felt, and though they drooped, there was mirth and compassion on his face. He held up a finger in the universal sign of "wait a moment" before turning and disappearing down the hall. Marcus rolled his eyes with a slight smile tugging at the corners of his mouth. It's not like he was going anywhere fast enough to worry Everard.

The large man returned with a stool. Marcus quirked his head quizzically to the side, squinting at it and then back up at Everard. The blacksmith motioned to the first room on the right, and Marcus followed him through the doorway. Everard set it down near the bed, and Marcus sank into it gratefully, patting his friend on the arm. Everard's hand resting on his shoulder for a moment was one of the most comforting things he had felt in a long time, and he wanted to just melt beneath the subtle feeling of being cared for. Everard was a man who showed Christ-like love in a way not many did. And all with fewer words than it would take to explain it.

Marcus's weary bones thanked Everard more than his words ever could as he turned to the bed, pulling the strap of his pack over his head and laying it on the bed near the form that lay prone upon it. Glancing up, he caught the eyes of the old man from yesterday. They were tired, silvery blue in the dim light of the inn's room, his bad arm done up in a sling that hung from his neck. But his other hand gripped tightly the tiny, six-year-old paw that lay upon the bed.

"How are we doing this morning?" Marcus's words came out in a soft, hushed tone, loud enough to be heard but not loud enough to disturb any of the patients' slumbers. He reached out a hand and touched the boy's forehead. Cool to the touch. He drew a sigh of relief. The last thing they wanted was for the little boy to run a fever.

"A sight better than we were yesterday, much in part to you." The old man's words matched his tone, his eyes pools of gratitude.

Marcus only nodded with an accepting smile and lowered the sheet from over the boy's chest, revealing the bandages around his abdomen that he carefully started undoing. The wound would need to be redressed since the bandages had caught some extra bleeding throughout the night. All the while he removed the blood stained bandages, the boy slept like he hadn't in days…and Marcus supposed it was quite possible he hadn't.

"What are your names?" Marcus, though weary, made quick work of the bloodied linen and carefully cleansed the wound, then rewound the fresh binding.

"Jaromir." He pointed at himself, then motioned to the small boy who's black hair tufted at the top of his head in an unruly thatch. "Kahru."

Marcus smiled and ruffled the black locks gently, watching the boy slumber while he did so. Kahru's eyes flickered slightly under the closed lids. *Sweet dreams, little one.* "It suits him."

A slight smile lit the weary lines of the old man's face. "He's a fighter."

"A brave one, at that. How is your arm? Does it pain you much?"

The man shook his head. "There are others in more dire need than I am."

"Nonsense. To each their turn. When was the last time you drank any of the tea Fendrel recommended?"

The man grimaced. "The bitter one? Not since last night."

"Here." Marcus pulled a small bundle of tiny twigs from his bag and handed them to the man. "If you wouldn't mind making this into a tea, you ought to have a cup yourself, and the boy will need some when he wakes. The surgery will have left him with quite a bit of pain to overcome, but he seems to be doing well. Rest and peace will bring the deepest healing, I think. And he seems to be sleeping quite peacefully."

Jaromir nodded, setting the bundle on the bedside table beside two cups of water. 'Thank you. For everything."

Marcus smiled and nodded. "I'll be back in a bit." Carefully standing, he reached for the crutches and settled them under his arms. He could feel bruises forming from long use of the supports.

"May I ask?" The hesitant words arrested Marcus's hobbling steps halfway to the door. He looked over his shoulder to look at Jaromir, a question written in the lines that creased his forehead.

"Yes?"

"Your leg… You seem hardly able to stand yourself, let alone care for others, yet, you're here. Why?"

"I was injured when I was a child. It has never recovered, and my hip is not jointed correctly. But I've learned much at the instruction of Fendrel, and as his apprentice, I shall one day take over his practice as a medicinal. Though, I hope that is a long way off."

"But you seem to be in much pain."

Marcus sighed but smiled, even though his heart was aching. He hated when his apparently woeful attempts to hide his pain were unsuccessful. "The Lord gives me strength."

A cloud crossed Jaromir's face, his eyes darkening beneath their inner shadow. "I can't imagine how. He does not concern himself with the likes of us."

Marcus stalled. "What do you mean?" An inner prompting had him staying where he was despite the overwhelming amount of work that lay ahead of him.

"Perhaps God treats those of Elira differently, but He has never shown me any mercy." Jaromir's words were bitter—and broken.

Instead of immediately speaking out the remonstrances and some of the answers that came readily to his head, Marcus instead felt the urge to stay quiet. He could, in fact, relate with this man in more ways than one. He too had wondered where the mercy of God was. Why it was not shown to him sooner, more, better.

"He is no respecter of persons," was Marcus's thoughtful and quiet reply.

"Everyone is a respecter of persons. No two are created equal, and status matters to everyone. Even the Lord, apparently."

"What do you mean?" His legs were starting to get wobbly again, but he ignored the sensation, instead fixating on the conversation before him. He was on thin ice and felt the need to tread gently, in tune with the Spirit for every word.

"I know you do not have slavery here, so perhaps you do not know, but there are many different types of people, and not everyone has the same value. I ran away to save my son and his family from being sent to the mines."

Marcus drew in a sharp breath. He had never met anyone who had escaped the mines. Before now, that is.

The mines were a mysterious entity, never mentioned save in whispered words. They existed on the border of Rusalka and Elira, far to the north, and were often where they sent convicts and forced laborers. It had become a form of punishment in recent years under the chancellor's rule, and there had been several residents of Padlsey who had been sent there. They were never seen again.

Running his free hand through the stubble on his chin and then pushing back the shock of silver hair that fell over his forehead, Jaromir continued, "You do not know what it is like to live in constant fear of the whip, but even greater still, the fear that those you love most on this earth will be forced to join you in a hell of man's making."

Marcus's mind flashed back to the years of tortured pain, of never leaving a bed, to the feverish dreams and panic-filled nights that made his life its own version of a living hell. He had felt the scourge of affliction, and even now that prolonged pain was never far from him. It may not have been at the end of a whip…but it was at the hands of adversity and torment. Not the same thing, but they did indeed feel similar.

"I know you may not be able to understand or hear this now, but the Lord does love you. He does have a plan for your life. He says He knows the thoughts that He thinks toward you, thoughts of peace and not of evil, to give you a future and a hope. You have made it this far. Over the wall and into Elira, where you will experience a freedom I hope will be the best you have ever felt in your life."

Jaromir's lips pinched and he still looked bitter. "I appreciate the welcome, but pardon me if I do not rejoice in it. I have yet to determine if my son and his wife made it on the journey. We were separated, I with their son." He glanced at Kahru. "I just hope they make it over the wall and that they can be set free as well."

"I will pray for that, my friend." Marcus would have put his hand on the man's arm if he were closer and prayed for him on the spot, even if it was a silent plea. But silent prayers from across the room would have to do; his legs were on the verge of giving out.

He was able to step from the room, but his crutch faltered, snagging on a rough patch in the wooden floors, and he pitched forward. He tensed for the impact at the same moment he prayed for it not to hurt so terribly.

55

Five

NIGHTMARES AND NURTURING

SHE REMEMBERED THE day when she had been sold.

She'd been but eight. Her world was one of chasing rabbits in the runs and hutches outside, caring for the animals that were her family's livelihood. She remembered playing house in the woods outside their cabin. Her days had been filled with happiness—at least, all of the happiness that she knew. She had been too young to realize the hardships, too carefree to understand the trouble that plagued her home.

Until she had been the pawn that was exchanged for peace from that trouble.

She could see her mother running to her as she played in the woods, singing to her dolls made of twigs and pinecones and tending a fake fire and meal. She still remembered the scent of her mother—pine mixed with smoke from the kitchen fire. Mother's brown hair was done up in a kerchief, and the green dress that she wore had been soft with wear, the wool badly in need of a wash.

Her mother grabbed her arms, her face a poorly maintained cloak of panic and horror. Her nails had dug into the skin of her upper arms, the grip tight, grabbing her attention quickly and causing her to grow sick with fear.

"What is it?" Her voice had been small, too thin to echo in the glen where their forest home was nestled.

"You need to listen to me." Her voice was breathless, broken.

"What? Why?"

"We do not have time, Dilara. The man who is coming with your father…you must obey him. You are going to go with him."

"Why? When will I come home?"

"Your home will be with him." Her mother's voice broke, and a tear fell from her widened eyes.

"What do you mean?"

Her mother shook her; Dilara felt the muscles at the back of her neck ache with the harshness of it, and she bit her lip to keep from crying out.

"We do not have time for questions. But you must stay strong. You must know that no matter what happens to you or where you go that you will always be my strong girl. And do whatever he says. It will go easy with you that way. Do you hear me?" The pain streaked across her mother's face held her spellbound.

Dilara nodded, too confused to think.

She was suddenly clutched to her mothers bosom, and she felt the heaving, heard the heavy *thump, thump, thump* of her heartbeat, faster than when she would cuddle beside her mother at night. "If there is a God out there, I beg You, protect my daughter." Harsh and desperate, Dilara felt as though the whispered words cut through the strands of hair they were spoken over.

"Dilara!" The shout came from the direction of her home, and Dilara's own heart quickened in anticipation. Whatever was about to happen, she knew that her life was changing, even if she didn't understand how.

What she did understand was that whatever her new life would look like, it would not be a good one.

The man who stood with her father was dark-skinned, tanner than she or her family. His hair was straight and black, tied in a tail at the back of his head. His eyes were in a half-closed position that spoke of secrets to be kept. Dilara followed her mother out of the copse of trees, clinging to the maternal hand like a lifeline that she knew would too soon be ripped from her grasp.

"You will go with this man, Dilara." Her father stepped forward, and Dilara knew from that moment on that her father was not to be trusted. There was no sorrow in his eyes. Nothing but intimidation rippling from the man who stood next to him in almost visible waves. She sensed the power of the man with the black hair and knew her father was not comfortable in his presence.

The stranger held out a hand to her, and she simply looked between it and him, like it were detached from his body.

She felt her mother's hands on her shoulders from behind. "Remember what I said to you, Dilara. Take the man's hand."

It was calloused. Hard. Strong, with long fingers that wrapped around hers like a rope. She glanced over her shoulder at her parents. Her father wouldn't even look at her, and the sorrow in her mother's eyes made Dilara not want to hold her gaze. A sob worked its way into her throat, but with a quick look up at the man that she did not know what to call, she swallowed it, whole and unspoken. The howl of a wolf in the distance set her heart to trembling.

Marcus heard the howl of a wolf, and it sounded desperately near. Too near. He didn't think they usually ventured this far out of the mountains, but there was something strange about the sound. He had never heard it quite so mournful and…tender. He glanced at the girl in front of him and put a finger to the pulse in her wrist. Another howl met his ears, even closer this time. Her breathing, uneasy for the last hour, seemed to level, her pulse slowing. She was calmer, cooler to the touch than before. He relaxed against the back of the chair, his muscles knotted but trying to relax.

The girl moaned, curled to her side, and then relaxed again, her eyes fluttering beneath her closed lids.

Lord, bring her healing… He drew in a deep breath, letting it out through clenched teeth and leaning his head against the back of the chair. There were no beds available, but what he wouldn't do for one to lay on.

A small sneeze made his eyes fly open, and he spun toward the door. He couldn't help but grin, tired as he was. Three sets of the largest eyes he had ever seen stared at him from the crack in the doorway. His friends from this morning were back for the last half of the story, no doubt.

"We finished our breakfasts," one whispered bravely, glancing at the bed, then back to him with longing.

He smiled. "Is that so?" Reaching for his crutches, he used them to help him stand. He winced and bit down hard at the shaft of pain that sent quivers into his leg when he tried to move.

"Are you all right?" one little boy asked, probably no older than six or seven and clearly the oldest of this group. His thatched brown hair hung at odd angles over his ears and stuck up in the back of his head.

"Right as rain in the summer," Marcus quipped.

"My mother says it's not good to lie."

Marcus refrained from rolling his eyes at the young child's response. "And your mother would be right."

"So, what's wrong with you?" the boy pestered as Marcus shooed them from the doorway to leave the girl in peace, shutting it partway to dull some of the noise, but open enough to be able to hear if she were in distress.

Marcus sighed, leaning against the wall and stretching his bad leg out in front of him. He slid down to his seat on the floor, where the little ones joined him. He motioned to a few others who waited on the stairs. "When I was a boy, I did something that caused myself to get hurt."

"Who did it?"

Startled, Marcus turned on the child. His blue eyes were large in his freckled face, and Marcus saw himself in the features, though this child was far more inquisitive than he had been at his age. Though, perhaps such curiosity had been one of the reasons he had been hurt in his efforts to get at the kingsmen. He didn't want to scare the children or make them fear the Kingsmen, which were mostly good men now that Elgon had taken the crown. Some—though not all—still called into question their allegiance, but they were far from outrightly spiteful these days.

"I didn't tell you a person did it."

"You didn't have to."

The mouth on this child. "How old are you?" Marcus stared sharply at the young adult trapped in an eight-year-old's body.

"Seven and a half years, sir." In better circumstances, the puffed out chest would have made Marcus laugh, but he was fighting through the stitch growing in his back and the sudden bout of fatigue rushing him from behind like an attacker in a back alley.

"That's quite old, then. You'll be a man before you know it. And you know what men do, don't you?" Marcus watched with a keen eye as the child weaseled his way past the other two, effectively elbowing them from his path and taking a seat before them. "Men should be kind to everyone around them, but even more so to their women folk." The child was smart with his mouth, but was he quick-witted as well? Marcus looked pointedly behind the child and then back at the freckled face with an unmistakable meaning.

The boy glanced between Marcus and the other two tots, realizing his mistake and moving slightly out of the way…but only slightly. Marcus gave him an approving nod and leaned his head against the wall. The heat that was rushing up the back of his neck from his exhaustion was starting to creep up into his head, and he willed it away with little success. The last thing he wanted was to have a bad spell just now. He was needed at his best…not his worst.

"So, who did it?"

Good heavens, this child didn't let up. Marcus rarely was irritated with children, but this one was trying every ounce of patience he had been blessed with. "I got in the way of some men." Things were getting fuzzy. "What's your name again?"

"Matthias."

With his vision blurring and sudden nausea growing in his stomach, Marcus reached out a shaking hand. "Matthias, can you do me a kindness?"

"Of course, sir! If you'll tell us the rest of that story from breakfast! We would be obliged," he added in an afterthought, probably attempting to be more polite than he had been.

"Perhaps. Can you fetch the old man with the glasses or the tall one? And quickly?" Marcus hated asking for help. Especially now. Especially here. But the blackness and pain that was starting to pound in between his ears left him little choice.

"Yes, sir! The one with the large hands who doesn't talk?"

"That's the one." His own words sounded distant and stretched thin, even though he knew they had to have come from his own vocal chords.

The sound of footsteps was almost imperceptible behind the roaring in his ears.

A small, cold hand touched his face and soothed the fire that was spreading over his entire body. Whispers twittered in the background, and then there were arms around him. He forced his burning eyelids open and tried to speak.

"Hush, Marcus. You overdid it. Don't think or speak. Just rest. We will make do without you. Do not worry, or I swear, I'll tie you to the bed." Fendrel's voice was as close to a tender, cross growl as Marcus had ever heard it. But that was all he remembered before the blackness swallowed him whole.

"Dilara! You're needed." The voice was a raspy one, the words broken with a harsh accent.

Dilara melted into the wall of the barn, hoping her dark and dirty clothes, her brown hair, braided in lengths down her back, and her otherwise dirty and smelly appearance would blend into the shadows of the stable where she had been mucking out stalls. Hiding from her slave mother would either be the best or the worst thing to happen all day. It all depended on if she were caught.

She knew what they wanted. They treated her like brutes. The men they served were not men she desired to be around, and whenever she was called upon to serve the dining room, she hated every second with a loathing she had never felt before in her life.

There was so much that could be conveyed with a few simple words and a brutish touch.

"Dilara!" The words were sharper this time. "You better not be hiding from me, girl. The men won't feed themselves, much as I wish they would. Would serve 'em right." The last statement was spoken softer, grumbled to herself.

Dilara had nothing against Soria. She didn't hate the woman. But what Soria had come to represent and the better treatment she was given for keeping the girls in line had certainly bred feelings of ill-will in Dilara's heart. Much as Soria probably did not deserve them. She had been sold to these men even younger than Dilara had. And for that, Dilara wanted to bear compassion for her, but all she felt was disdain.

Soria didn't use her position to make the girls' lives any easier or to fill her own heart with compassion. Instead, she had been made harder, darker, and less caring by her life experiences. Dilara hoped with everything within her that she would never let herself get that way.

"Is that you hiding in the corner? Dilara, I swear, you are already going without dinner at this rate. Need I make your life more miserable?" There was a tired, resigned tone to Soria's voice, and Dilara's nearly empty stomach—and the thought of not one, but two, missed meals—made her step from the shadows with a bowed and penitent head.

"Good." Soria spoke gruffly. "Get your ungrateful bones back inside that hut and serve the men their mead."

Dilara swallowed against the nausea that gripped the back of her throat, trying not to gag at the thought of the moments that awaited her. A hard hit to the back of her head from Soria's knuckles sent her frozen feet stumbling forward. "Do as I say, or so help me, a missed meal won't be the only punishment you'll receive from me this evening," Soria growled, her patience clearly worn more than thin as she followed up words with a hard shove that nearly sent Dilara to the ground.

Stepping hard and fast for the kitchen, her heart beat loud in her ears, nearly drowning out the raucous laughter, obscenities, and crass comments that tumbled from the open doorway of the bordello like a barrel full of stones upturned.

She would do her best to avoid the eager hands, but somehow, her owner, Conri, always exhibited more anger toward her over the men's indiscretions than he did over those who perpetrated them. But he was not mad at her attempted self-preservation.

No, he wanted her saved. That much she knew. But for what, she didn't have a clue—and that filled her with the most fear, like an icicle straight through the heart. She just hoped she would be able to find a way out before his plans had time to bear fruit.

The sweltering heat and lurid scene filled her with panic as she knelt in front of the fire to stoke the coals and collect the warm mead in the pitcher on the hearth. She drew closer to the flames, almost relishing the heat and the sting they brought to her face. Perhaps if she burned herself, she would be seen as less desirable.

Six

FALLEN SNOW AND SOLDIERS

MARCUS FOUGHT THE haze that threatened to keep him buried beneath the surface of the fog and reached out his hands to grasp the daylight. They dug deep into the blanket that covered him, and he pried his eyes open. They blinked and burned against the daylight, but his headache didn't return with the effort, and he sank into the tick mattress, letting the muscles in his back relax as he intentionally rolled his neck to stretch it out.

How long had he been asleep? Looking across the room, he let his eyes focus before he realized that he was sharing a sick room with the young girl he had rescued and another wounded individual. The man was pale as a sheet and lay on a cot against the wall next to the door. Marcus blinked, focusing harder, then let out his breath when he finally saw the man's chest rise and fall in a shallow inhalation. The poor bloke looked to be at death's door, and Marcus's heart broke at the

67

sight. Tears rose in his eyes, and he pushed back the quilt that covered him, standing slowly on his good foot. He used the bed for balance as he tucked his shirt in a more orderly fashion, then used the nearby chair as a support to limp across the floor.

The fever had left him a bit weak, but the burning and tight muscles that had threatened to yank the very breath from his body were finally relaxed. Enough to allow him to function, at least. He needed to move and stretch and get the blood flowing to them again if he wanted them to ease up a bit more.

He always fought the pain. Every single day was filled with it, but he had learned how to cope and take each day as it came. Listening to what his body needed. Sometimes, he pushed too far or lived in denial of an episode that tried to break down the door and take firm root in his bones and muscles. For the most part, he could manage it, but on days like yesterday…or was it two days ago now? He'd pushed himself too hard. There was something in him that hoped there would be no consequences to trying to live a normal life, one closer to those around him, but so far, he always paid dearly for testing his limits.

He tried not to let self-pity consume him, especially right now. He needed to tend to this patient.

The pale man's dark, shoulder-length hair was tossed about on the pillow around him, greasy with sweat. His skin was clammy to the touch, whiter than it ought to have been. His tan seemed to lay like a film atop his skin instead of glowing from within. Marcus swallowed against the lump in his throat as he felt for the man's pulse.

The pain etched into the patient's forehead told him much, but the thready and weak beat that Marcus struggled to find in his wrist made the reality of the situation far more obvious. Suddenly, the hand turned and grasped Marcus's wrist. Startled, he let out a slight gasp, his bad leg collapsing beneath him as he sank to an ungraceful kneeling position beside the bed.

The dark, almond-shaped eyes were cold and almost unseeing as they looked past Marcus. Instinctively, Marcus reached out a hand and rested it on the man's forehead. He sensed the patient's fear, and his heart and soul rose to meet it.

"Did anyone ever tell you about Jesus?" The urgency in Marcus drove his heart to beating hard, setting his breath to coming in short gasps.

Tears filled the cold and faraway eyes. They tried to focus, and his Adam's apple bobbed once in an attempt to gather a voice.

"Have you asked His forgiveness and made Him your Savior?" Marcus's words were fervent, his hand gripping the other's tightly.

A small and nearly imperceptible turn of the head.

"Do you want to?"

A nod. The man's mouth opened, but nothing emerged.

"You don't even need to speak, just ask Him in your heart. He will honor your request. He is faithful to save, and He loves you more than you could ever know." Marcus felt his own fervency rising like pain in his throat, cutting off the words and making them raspy. The presence in the room was thick, like a warm blanket or tea laced with honey.

The man's eyes closed, and a rattling breath escaped the man's throat before he opened his eyes again, and a clarity overtook them as he looked Marcus in the face. Widening, tears rose in them like glassy pools, warming and deepening the brown color.

Marcus ignored the pinch in his hip and gripped the man's hand tighter, wrapping both of his palms around it and squeezing his own warmth into it. "Lord, be with this man. Let him feel Your Spirit and Your love. Cover him with Your feathers and give him a refuge from the pain and sorrow of this world. Thank You that You gave Your life that he might dedicate his to You in eternity."

The breaths became shorter and more broken, the rattle within them filling the room with the sound of the dying. Marcus gripped the hand harder and bent farther over the man, keeping eye contact and pouring every ounce of himself out in prayer that this man's last moments would be an encounter with His Savior.

The man's eyes closed, and one last shuddering breath sounded deep in his chest before the room was filled with a stillness and hush that sank into Marcus's heart like a stone sinking to the bottom of a riverbed. A shiver went down his spine, and the man's hand felt even colder than it had. No pulse jumped against Marcus's touch, yet the peace in the room shrouded him in the stillness.

He didn't even feel the need to cry. This man had met His heavenly King just now. Marcus was sure of it.

A soft moan from the other bedside startled him, and he gently lay the dead man's hand upon his chest, lifting the blanket over the now peaceful and smoothed face, so different without the caste of pain pinching the features.

He turned to the other cot. A medicinal's work was never finished.

The girl, her face pale, though now with a rosy glow of fever staining her cheeks, had a look of discomfort and distress as she rolled her head back and forth against the pillow, almost as if trying to free herself from the fever and pain that wracked her body. He limped to her side, which took longer than he liked. He propped his good hip against the bedframe and reached for the cloth that lay over the edge of the basin, dipping it into the cool water. He glanced out the small window that graced the wall and caught a glimpse of heavy, white flakes drifting softly in the gray world which wore a coat of white.

Marcus touched the cloth to her face, and she winced away from it, turning toward the wall. She seemed to be fighting to come back to consciousness, and he sensed the struggle she was in. The body often knew better than the mind what it needed, but when one warred against the other, it created more turmoil within. A moan escaped her lips, and her hands fluttered over the quilt covering her small frame. Marcus was short by most standards; even women were often taller than he was. Something having to do with his growth having been stunted after his injury, but she was even smaller than he was and definitely on the petite side. Her eyelashes were dark, nearly black against her white skin, and they fluttered against her cheeks like butterfly wings as she groaned again, heaved her torso in discomfort, then moaned deeper.

Placing a comforting hand gently on her shoulder, he felt her flinch away again, but she seemed calmer. Her eyelids fluttered some more, and she opened them at last with a gasp for air, like a drowning woman breaking the surface of the water. They were bleary and far from focused, but their deep brown depths reminded him of the heart of a chestnut.

"Shhhh," he cooed softly with a soothing motion on her arm that he always used to comfort children. Her eyes focused, and fear radiated from them before she heaved away and struggled against the counterpain, pushing herself as far against the wall as she could. His heart lurched into his throat at her sudden movement, and the twinge in his hip sent him to his knees.

Dilara wrestled against the fog and the pain that kept her in its grip, and she finally forced her eyelids open against the heavy bricks she felt rested atop them. Blurry forms in the shadowy room were all that met her gaze. Where was she? What was happening, and what was that gentle touch on her wrist?

Blinking hard, she dragged heavy breaths into her lungs, willing her eyes to focus. When she opened them again, panic clutched her throat in a tight grip, and her body reacted before she could settle her mind as she threw herself as far from him as possible. Despair beat down the doors of her heart, and a sob squeaked back the fear that held her in its grasp. Had she been taken back?

With her movement, a wave of pain washed over her abdomen and around her back, tightening her muscles into cramps and dragging a moan from her lips. It all came rushing back. The bloody snow, the tiny form, and the wolf's howls.

She simultaneously doubled over and turned closer to the wall, but she could feel herself slipping as the blood rushed to her head, and all she saw was a haze of red in front of her eyes.

Marcus gulped, still hissing breath between his teeth as the woman in front of him fainted. The poor thing had hardly opened her eyes before her flying panic had caused the pain to return more quickly than her brain could handle. He didn't want to touch her because she was obviously afraid of him, but her slouched over position against the wall couldn't be comfortable in the slightest.

He risked it, and with a quick motion, gritting his teeth against his own pain, he repositioned her shoulders to rest against the extra pillow he had placed behind her head so she could lay in a more upright position instead of flat on her back. When one was afraid and in pain, sometimes being completely recumbent created a greater sense of helplessness than was necessary. He also ran his arm beneath her feet and the blanket they were wrapped in, lifting them and placing a pillow beneath the bundle to help with blood flow.

Fendrel had said she had lost a lot of blood, and her light-headedness was probably a direct result.

A wolf howled outside again, and a clatter from downstairs distracted him from his care. The pain forced him to pay attention, and with a cursory glance around the room, he did not see his pack. He needed his turmeric and willow-bark tincture to help take the edge off and shake the lingering effects of his episode. The symptoms had beat a retreat but were still fighting for supremacy. He was no good to anyone if he was in pain himself.

Where had they put his crutch? With a deep breath and gritted teeth, he used the bed frame and then the wall to make it to the door and step out into the hallway. With the assistance of the wooden walls and then the stair rail, by some miracle he made it down the stairs with minimal effort and less pain than he'd expected. But going down was the easy part.

Fendrel was speaking with the innkeeper, Rensen, and both of them used animated words and body language. Neither looked angry, though Rensen's face was pale, and there was fear lurking in the wrinkles at the corners of his eyes. The apron around his thick, though not rotund, abdomen flapped with his movements and was stained with dirt and probably leftover food and ale. Some of the pallets had been folded up against the wall, but the children were grouped in the corner, vying for a spot at the window as they clamored and climbed over one another in their efforts to see through the small glass panes.

Windows were kept small to keep the cold out, but large enough to allow some light in. Marcus would have been glad if they were larger. Natural light was just as important as insulating in more warmth. At least in his personal opinion.

There seemed to be a clamor outside, and he wished he could see out the window, but even if he wanted to risk walking across the room, there were ten small faces he would have to fight with to see out.

"Fendrel." He called across the room, still staying at the stairs to utilize the railing he was gripping to keep his balance. He knew better than to try to walk without his crutch, especially in his current condition. On a good day, he could make do with a cane, but this was far from a good day.

Fendrel's head turned, and his gray beard trembled, his brows dipping down in a V of disapproval that Marcus could feel the effects of all the way across the large room, even without any words being added to the look. He paused and decided to let Fendrel make his way to him instead. That would probably smooth the lines of worry out of his face. He was feeling rather winded as he rested a hand on the back of a chair and another on the table top.

"What on earth are you doing out of bed? I thought I left distinct instructions that you were not to overdo it, and I—" Fendrel's grumpy growl was cut short by Marcus's hand on his shoulder when he drew close enough for him to finally reach out.

"I'm doing fine. The fever is gone, and while tired, I am much more readily able to function."

"But I—"

"No one was upstairs, Fendrel. I need your help, and I had no one to send in my stead. And it appears that someone divested me of my crutch." Marcus's tone was pointed as he narrowed his eyes at his mentor.

Fendrel seemed to swallow the last of his remonstrances, rolled his eyes heavenward as if petitioning for help, and reached forward to slip his shoulder under Marcus's. Marcus knew Fendrel only became grumpy when lacking much-needed sleep. God had given the man a supernatural ability to turn from normal to nocturnal in an instant, but even that grace wore thin after more than a few days. And unless he had been out longer than he remembered, it had been at least four.

"What do you need? What was so urgent that you had to come fetch me yourself?"

Marcus ignored the snide comment about his activity and pulled Fendrel toward the stairs. "It's the girl. She woke up. But the other one…the man passed."

"Ugh." Fendrel picked up his pace, half carrying, half dragging Marcus with him. There was a look of sorrow on his face. "So many lives already… The poor girl has been through much, I can tell, and I must speak with her to further ascertain the extent of her injuries. She lost a lot of blood."

"That explains her passing out after being upright for maybe thirty seconds."

Fendrel's pace redoubled as he growled a prayer under his breath, heaving Marcus up the stairs with him. Marcus tried to be of use and utilize the railing, but Fendrel was moving much too fast, and the two of them had grown used to Fendrel becoming Marcus's crutch in a pinch. It didn't happen often, but they were capable of moving in tandem when needed.

Marcus was a bit more than out of breath when they reached the room and stepped in. He sank to a seat on the foot of the bed, gripping the corner post that nearly touched the ceiling like a man grasping the mast of a wayward ship. He squeezed his eyes shut and dragged air into his burning lungs before he raised his gaze to Fendrel.

The older man had his fingers to the girl's wrist and was staring at the ceiling, counting intently for a moment. The girl's eyelids fluttered, and Fendrel released her wrist, folding his hands in front of him in a place that she could see.

A moan escaped her pink lips, and her pale face contracted in pain before she opened her eyes again. Those massive brown orbs—so large for her petite face—widened in fear, but Fendrel stepped back, his hands still folded in front of him.

"I will not harm you, my lady." He spoke with the same deference that he would to any woman in his care, but the girl's eyes widened still more, and Marcus marveled at how that was even possible.

She blinked hard and threw her gaze back and forth between them, pulling the sheet up to her chin and shrinking into the pillows.

"Who are you? Where am I?" Her words were raspy, and two pink apples formed on her cheeks as she grew flushed. The pink stood out harshly against her white skin beneath the freckles that were scattered across her thin nose and trim cheeks.

"You are in a town called Pranvera and have been ill for some days. My name is Fendrel, and I am the medicinal who has been taking care of you. This is Marcus, my assistant."

She stared at them, her chin trembling a little as her eyes took on a glassy look. "What did you—" Her voice gave out, and she caught her breath, a look of resignation coming over her as she seemed to look past them.

Fendrel's voice was gentle and his movements nonexistent. "My lady, nothing has been done to you. The innkeeper's wife bathed you, and we have simply administered herbs to help ward off infection, fight your fever, and slow your bleeding."

Her eyes blinked back to life, a spark rekindling some internal flame as she looked back at Fendrel. "Bleeding?" Her hands loosened on the sheet somewhat, and Marcus barely dared to breathe. He felt that he was too close, impeding her space, even at the very foot of the large bed that was made to sleep men much larger than she. But he also dared not move.

Fendrel swallowed, and Marcus could tell he was weighing his words.

"You lost a lot of blood. With time and the herbs we administered, it did slow. But you were unconscious for some days." He hesitated, and Marcus saw the compassion come out in his gaze as his voice grew quiet and huskier. "Do you know how far along your pregnancy was?"

Dilara's heart stuttered before resuming its heavy pulse. The pain seared through her entire body, a numbness cloaking her foggy brain and bleary eyes. She felt weak; perhaps it was the blood loss. But the realities of her condition still came to her mind as if by rote. "As best I can figure, three months and three weeks."

The man named Fendrel nodded, and she glanced between him and the younger man who sat at the foot of her bed. She had seen the blond-haired, blue-eyed face moments before she passed out. Even though fear at the thought of anyone near her overwhelmed her to her very core, there was a gentleness in his eyes that was as unfamiliar as it was comforting. Both of these men had a peace to them that seemed at war with the fear and guardedness that usually drove her interactions with men.

Men had always used her. Been the boot that kicked, the hand that hit, the infliction of every pain she had ever experienced. Men had made her what she was. Had sold her into it, bought her, beaten her, and made her a mother…only to take that from her, too.

The older man's thin gray beard twitched a little as he rocked back and forth on his heels, still not making a move toward her in the slightest. Her trust for him grew. But she still held it warily away from her, not letting the trust get too deep or place too strong a hold. Trust could be broken, more readily when given, and often when it was least expected.

"Do you know when it happened?"

She shook her head. She still did not know how long she had been unconscious, but the days filled with pain, weariness, and endless snow had blurred together. She shut it from her mind, the broken place too raw for her to visit just yet. She caught herself picking at the sheet with her fingertips in nervousness, and she gripped them in her other hand, folding them in toward herself to still the outward sign of fear and weakness. Sitting up was suddenly becoming more of a chore than she had felt it at first, and her head felt too heavy for her shoulders. But the anxiety that gripped her throat set her heart to beating too fast. It was as if it had come out of nowhere, and the same feeling of being chased and worrying if she would make it to the border in time slammed into her like a wave of cold from an open door.

It had no warning, and she knew no trick to harness it into a stop. She felt her head growing heavier, and she gasped for breath.

"Here." The deep voice was gentle but oh, so far away. "Drink this." The clinking of a spoon against pottery echoed in the recesses of her mind as if she were in a cave, every sound echoing against a cavernous wall.

"It's hard"—she gasped—"to breathe." Each word was punctuated by a helpless inhale as she desperately tried to fill her spasming lungs with enough air to survive.

A cool glass was held to her lips, and with a splutter and cough, she fought through her unsteady breathing and racing heart to swallow what was in it.

Vision clouding further, her heart rate slowed, and she felt her head touching the pillow before she closed her eyes. The darkness was more a friend to her than the light.

Marcus was equal parts relieved and disappointed that she had fallen back asleep. Her body needed the rest. Her loss of blood would give her need for much of it in the coming weeks. Based on what he could surmise about her and where she had come from, the realization of what she must have gone through to get to the border squeezed his heart. He pictured her alone, in the woods, her only motivation for running through snow while with child, or having recently lost one, coming from a fear he could hardly fathom.

Such desperation and brokenness pulled at him with sorrow in a way that brought him more pain than his own did. He watched as Fendrel smoothed back the girl's brown hair from her pail and restful face. "Praise God she will sleep now. It's much needed if my conjecture is right." He shook his head, sadness pulling his face into long lines that Marcus could tell were mixing with weariness.

"You should get some sleep, too," Marcus urged in a whisper so as not to disturb the slumbering lass.

Fendrel shook his head. "Not yet."

"Why? Surely I and Everrard can care for the patients? Even for an hour or two, Fendrel—you need rest."

"I need to speak to the Kingsmen first."

"Soldiers?" Marucs felt a shiver creep up his spine.

Fendrel led him from the room, handing him his crutch from where it had been resting against the wall in the hallway. Marcus swallowed the remonstrance to Fendrel for putting it out of his reach. He could discuss the medicinal's attempt to keep him off his feet soon enough.

Fendrel didn't respond until he shut the door softly behind them, leaving it unlatched and a sliver of light between the frame and the door. "The Kingsmen are on their way."

Marcus felt his breath catch in his throat. That word still made him quiver inside, though he knew now that under the control of Elgon, the army was much more civilized and protective of the Eliran people than they had been under Enguerrand's rule. Though, occasionally, he caught a malicious gaze that seemed to smolder from within, and he wondered if there would come a time where it would be allowed to burst into flame again.

"Why are they coming?"

Fendrel gripped his shoulders and let out a sigh as he locked eyes with him. "Because, lad, the Rusalkan army seems to have decided that it wants its citizens back."

Marcus shivered, his eyes widening as he thought of those that had been in his care for the last few days. Their broken bodies and desperation when speaking of the evil that had forced them to give up everything to escape. He swallowed hard. Did this mean war?

Seven

TO SERVE A KING

MARCUS NEEDED FRESH AIR. Something to clear his head. He threw his cloak around his shoulders, pulling the ends together around his neck as he fought with his crutches. He hated to think how his muscles would seize up if he didn't prepare himself for the cold that awaited out of doors. His brain was muddled, the ginger and turmeric helping take away some of the pain, but his appetite was still missing. The idea of food made him shudder.

The heavy wooden door of the tavern slammed shut behind him as the wind caught it and threw it into the jam. He winced. Hopefully it didn't disturb too many of the invalids.

Taking a deep breath, he let it out slowly through pursed lips, his eyes growing wide. With as many people as filled the tavern, there were still so many outside. Makeshift tents had sprung up on the frostbitten ground, their green and brown canvases scattering the field and the valley butting up against the wall. Marcus drew a breath. So much destruction and pain.

A branch cracked off to the side, and he spun to look into the woods, his nerves on edge at the thought of Rusalkan soldiers so close.

He froze. A white wolf, gray coloring her coat, stood in the inky shadows that bled between trees. He didn't dare blink, though the cold wind stung his eyes mercilessly. A man and animal, gazes locked. A small cloud of fog puffed from her nose and filled the brisk air around her. Neither of them moved until a shout off in the distance shattered his focus, and he glanced away, toward the source of the noise, then back again.

She was gone.

Brow pinching, he searched the gray-brown shadows of the frosty forest, looking for a sight of the magnificent creature that stole the breath from his lungs and filled him with just as much dread as exhilaration. Nothing. He shook his head. Was he seeing things? Perhaps he *did* need to lie down again.

A tremor started in the ground at his feet and worked its way up his spine, jarring him. He sucked in a sharp breath.

Horses hooves. A lot of them. Coming this way. Clenching his jaw, he turned toward the inn. He needed to tell Fendrel. What if the Rusalkans were forming an attack? All of the men, women, and children, derelict and broken in the field below, would be in danger. The strength within them had barely been enough to reach safety, let alone fight. He nearly tripped over his own crutch in his hurry.

Marcus's heart was beating so loudly in his ears that, as the thundering horses all came to a halt before the tavern, it took him a long moment to realize that they were kingsmen, the Eliran symbol of a lion surrounded by a crown of thorns upon their crests, and not Rusalkans come to wage war. Never in his life had he thought he would be so pleased to see kingsmen.

But it was with a healthy mix of apprehension that he took in the fact that it wasn't just a group of kingsmen, but the King's convoy. The sea of horses parted to make way for Sigeric, Elgon sitting astride the beast. Elgon dismounted, striding down the snow-covered pathway before Marcus was enveloped in a fierce hug.

"Marcus!" Elgon held him tightly before he slapped him gently on the shoulder, likely remembering his infirmity. He stood back, a smile on his face as he gripped Marcus by the shoulders. There was a strength and fortitude amongst the weathered lines on his face that spoke of hours of patience that had been worked into him. Somehow, the prince turned farm hand turned king looked older than he had the last time Marcus had seen him, and it brought a smile to his face. The look suited Elgon, and every bit of resentment Marcus might have been harboring slipped away.

All was right with Elgon and Violet, and Marcus knew they belonged together. He could no longer begrudge them that. He could miss his best friend without feeling the need to envy their life.

"How are you, old friend?" Elgon asked, holding his gaze steadily with inquisitive and honest eyes.

He knew the needs of the many were desperate…yet Elgon took the time to look him in the eye and ask how he was. As if he alone mattered in that moment.

"As well as can be expected, your majesty." Marcus bowed his head, unable in his current state to truly bow to a knee as he would have wished.

But from the way that Elgon still held his shoulders, keeping him upright, he was not sure the king would have let him. "Don't be ridiculous," Elgon muttered, a grin pulling at his mouth. "You needn't call me that. Malcolm, my first knight, would say you must when in the company of the court, but out here it's just Elgon. Violet told me to pass on a message to you if by chance I were to see you, and I must say, I'm terribly glad you are here. This world needs your skill, my friend." He nodded at the field of broken people.

Marcus felt a smile spread on his weary face at the words— ones he'd sorely needed to hear. "What did Violet say? How is she?"

Elgon's face beamed, so bright it might have eclipsed the sun. "She's expecting our first child. She wanted me to tell you and ask what you thought it would be." The grin on his face, though tempered with the gravity of the moment, was enough to make Marcus's heart take wings and fly away.

Marcus, despite the pain and suffering that surrounded them, caught the flicker of hope from the joy in Elgon's face, and he clung to it. The promise of new life, however small, was a beautiful thing to be celebrated. When all else had been hard, a struggle, wrought with pain, fear, and sorrow—the glimmer of light at the end of the tunnel, the whisper of spring at the end of winter—it was more bliss than he dared hope for.

In his mind's eye, he had a vision of Violet with a daughter. It just felt right. "You may tell her for me that I am overjoyed at her news, and that for some reason, I can only think of her first child being a girl." He grinned up at Elgon, his pain forgotten for the moment.

Elgon smiled at him. "She will be glad to hear it." He sobered then, leaning closer to say in serious tones, "She misses you. Know that, Marcus. I would be glad to take you to the palace, should you want to go."

Marcus was already shaking his head before the words were out of Elgon's mouth. There was a magnet that clung to him and tied him down to this corner of the kingdom. For what purpose, he might not know, but it was there nonetheless. "I am afraid my place is here, your majesty, though I am grateful for the offer."

"Ah, none of that if you please." He waved his hands and rolled his eyes. "It doesn't seem fitting for two friends, I must say, and it feels even stranger on your lips. God go with you, my friend." Elgon squeezed his shoulder, his voice husky.

"And with you, my brother." Marcus spoke the words, though they felt bold, reminding them both of the bond they had in Christ.

Elgon's eyes grew misty, and he clenched his jaw, giving one last meaningful look and a pat to the shoulder before he let go and strode over to the kingsmen who were asking for his attention at the wall.

Marcus drew a breath. He now had another soul to pray for in addition to the ones littering the spiritual battlefield nearby.

He hoped the physical field before him would not hold a battle as the days drew on, but he could sense the restlessness of the Rusalkans who kept hidden on the other side of the wall and within the edges of Pranvera Forest. He heard a wolf howl in the distance, and it brought a chill across his skin. Perhaps it was the one he had seen. Swallowing, he rubbed his arms before adjusting his crutches and heading back into the inn, swarmed instantly by children begging for another story.

The world of snow was slowly caving in on her. A wolf howled in the distance and shattered her quiet stillness. A heavy weight pressed on her chest, ice crystals scraping her lungs with every breath. Cold closed down on her like the force of a tree trunk, fallen across her body.

But the intense spasm rippling across her middle flung her upright with its force, her body tensing, every single muscle focused on one task—delivering her baby.

But it wasn't time yet.

All of the panic flooded in again, the weight on her chest lifting in between contractions.

Birth was supposed to be a joyous event, wasn't it? Those that you loved gathered in support around you as you brought the child you had borne in your body for nine months into the world, the pain somehow worth it.

But the dread that filled her soul and the way she was fighting with her entire being to keep this baby inside of her spoke a different tale. One of desperation. She begged anything, everything outside herself to let her keep her baby just six months more. Her lips quivered, numb, likely blue from the cold and the snow that swirled around her with every breeze, the massive trees that spun above her head, swaying with the wind as it howled its mournful song, a dirge she didn't want to hear. A song that she didn't want to be true. Her heart broke in two as she bit down hard, shuddering into another contraction as she did everything she could to hold on.

Perhaps if she fought it hard enough, she could keep her baby. She drew a deep breath, the wrap-around sensation of the labor pain bearing down and around her spine like a snake squeezing the life out of her baby. Every ounce of anger at the man who did this to her filled her with firm resolve not to let her baby enter this world until it was time.

But the pain that slammed into her was the most intense, crushing torture she had ever experienced. The words of Soria came to her foggy mind as she gripped handfuls of snow in tight fists. "Don't fight the pains when they come. They will be easier that way."

But Dilara had no choice. And fight she would.

"No!" She screamed long and loud into the darkening wilderness. Everything in her willing her baby to stay. To live.

Another wolf's howl joined her own cry as sweat poured off of her freezing body. Her chin trembled as if it had a mind of its own, and she gasped for breath. The edges of her vision blurred, and she doubled down, her teeth feeling as though they would shatter with the force. The cloak she wore around her neck was a harsh reminder of the hand that had choked it nearly four months ago in the back of a dirty and rank tent.

Her eyes were full of water that froze in a trail down her face and into the folds of the cloak at her neck. Every ounce of her focus was poured into survival, and removing the cloak wasn't even an option.

"God, if You're there, save me. Save my baby. Please…" She gasped again and let out a wail into the lonely and dark woods of the Kaira mountains, her cry echoing off the snow-encrusted cliffs and through the woods, bouncing back at her with the even nearer howl of a wolf.

Another pain climbed up her spine, wrapping its icy tendrils around her swollen middle. More tears coursed down her cheeks, and her head fell backward, then jerked up again against the spasm. "Please don't let us die."

Another keening howl shattered the forest one last time as she shut her eyes against the pain. She had already lost so much. Losing the soul inside of her that had comforted her with its kicks and flutters over the last few weeks, reminding its mother that she was not alone, would be her end. She couldn't survive it.

With one last scream that felt like thunder from her belly, she cursed the night, the cold, the wolves that circled nearby. She cursed the man who had made her what she was, who had given her the life inside of her…only to snatch it from her grasp before it could even live. This life of hers was being stolen. Taken from its place beneath her ribs. And then a sudden hollow realization struck… There was nothing she could do about it.

But still she would fight. To the death.

The clash of weapons, metal, and the broken shouts of those at the wall arrested Marcus's attention from the poultice he was making for one of their wounded patients. The poor chap had been clapped over the head by his attacker as he fled.

What concerned him was how loud and overpowering the sound was. It crashed through the inn walls and could be heard even at this distance.

The muscles in his neck knotted up as he swung his head to see out the window and catch the scene as it unfolded before him.

As if frozen in time, the battle was relegated to slow motion as the dark-clad and gray-covered Rusalkans streamed over the low stone wall and clashed with the Eliran Kingsmen who rose to meet them. Though not without the sacrifice of a few men who had been stationed closest to the wall and had swiftly fallen under the hand of the enemy's long, curved blades.

Marcus seemed to catch a snapshot of every face of each soldier within his view, like colors splashed haphazardly on a canvas, every shade of fear, resignation, and brokenness spread across the frosted field. All the refugees were turned toward him, icebound in what felt like stillness as their feet made one step in front of the other in their effort to flee the field.

The riding guard notched arrows to their bows and sent them whistling into the bloody fray, striking many in the Rusalkan battalion. More men fell as the Kingsmen swooped down over the field, their swords raised, voices loud, their horses' hooves thundering across the plain and near the wall, cutting off the charging Rusalkans who were on foot. The enemy's eyes were barely visible above the grayed masks that covered their mouths and noses. Only by lore did Marcus know that they wore their scarves in such a way to fend off the cold of the mountain passes from freezing their lungs and causing an internal hemorrhage. But their eyes were mere slits, whether in anger or determination he would never know.

"Marcus!" Fendrel's voice. Urgent. Forceful.

It was enough to pull Marcus's attention back to his own tasks. He turned and started gathering up as many bandages as he could carry. The turbulence and pain continued around him. So many wounded, and already another attack beating at their doorstep. These people had given up much to try to taste some freedom…and now, the Rusalkans were attempting to wrest them from its grasp yet again. Adrenaline was setting his nerves on edge in the steadiest of ways. It's what Fendrel said made him a good medicinal—the gift from above to channel his fear and stress into steadiness and usefulness rather than panic.

It was similar to the way God had made Marcus to feel knit together and steadied in times where others were shattered by fear. It was a gift.

"Lord, protect them all. Keep every hand safe. Every life untouched. By some miracle, bring victory to our soldiers. Let the Kingsmen fight with You on their side, and keep the people safe. Let them make it to safety and keep the injuries to a minimum. Father in heaven, pour out Your mercy."

"Amen." The chorus of voices surprised him. He hadn't realized he had been praying out loud, but it was just as well. Hopefully the rest of them would take heed and do likewise.

Muttering under his breath, Marcus continued to pray in the Spirit as he gathered the last few medicinal supplies he might need and headed out into the gathering shadow of night. The sounds of battle grew louder as he drew near to them. A kingsman was coming up from the valley with his arms dragging another soldier, the injured man's uniform bloody and his gait as shuffling as Marcus's own. The hand not wrapped around his comrade's shoulders was holding a gaping wound on his abdomen.

Marcus swallowed hard. The curved sword of the Rusalks could be deadly. "This way!" he commanded without a second thought.

Waving a hand in a clear motion at the tavern, Marcus caught the kingsmen's attention and directed them inside where he could care for them. Fendrel passed Marcus with a nod of approval and a look of steely focus. Fendrel would care for those on the battlefield below who were far too injured to make their way up the hill. Marcus would receive them here and tend to the worst of the wounded who made it up to the tavern.

But this young kingsman would need his help immediately. If he didn't sew up the wound in his gut, the soldier wouldn't last the night.

Peasants and refugees were pushed to and fro, frantic to get away from the valley. Remaining soldiers and townsfolk with their own distinctive weapons of choice, such as pitchforks and axes, in hand ran in the opposite direction, creating a chaotic explosion of activity that felt like two mighty rivers colliding. Marcus would have lost his footing if Everard hadn't suddenly appeared like a mountain looming amongst the forest of wavering humans and grabbed his arm with a supporting hand.

Marcus drew a breath of relief and tried not to let it turn into frustration at not being able to manage on his own. With his hands and arms occupied with either crutches or medical supplies, Marcus let Everard do the heavy lifting and set him on his feet again at the doorstep.

Everard's dark eyes, high above Marcus's own, caught his gaze for a burning moment of understanding and silent encouragement before he was gone with the speed of a wolf on the prowl.

Marcus turned to enter the tavern after the kingsmen, and he nearly tripped over Kahru. The boy shouldn't be out of bed, but the wild fear that pinched his pale face and widened his dark eyes set Marcus's teeth on edge.

"What are you doing out of bed?" He dropped a crutch and leaned against the doorframe to lay a hand of comfort on the little boy's shoulder.

Kahru gripped his gut with one arm and pointed shakily with the other. "Grandfather is down there! He left to look for Ma and Da." His little voice shook, and he grew paler still at the sight of another bloody kingsman heading up the road. His little legs gave way, and he fell over in a faint.

Marcus let out an exasperated breath, "Father, help us all." Then louder, "Someone! Come help me with this boy, please!"

The taverner's wife hustled over, her serious demeanor overcome with a steely resolve and a stern, but motherly, air. She scooped the little boy up in her arms like he was a feather and strode toward the stairs. Mothering spirits, it seemed, dwelt within every woman, no matter how deeply buried.

Throwing another prayer for Jaromir heavenward, Marcus pulled out his tools and prepared to operate on the pale, gasping, and writhing kingsman who had been laid on one of the tavern's tables. The Lord would have His hands full tonight.

As would Marcus.

Eight

INVALID MATES AND BATTLE SCARS

DILARA WOKE WITH a gasp and sweat on her brow, her hands like ice and her memories sharp as knives. Shaking her head, she hoped her mind would clear of its own accord. But it was like hot, sticky cotton, swollen and immovable. Much like her throat. She reached across the bed, a sharp pain stabbing across her middle as she did so, and grasped a cup and the pitcher of water.

Her hands were numb and shaky, and some water spilled to the floor and onto the bed. What remained in the cup, she brought to her lips, downing its entirety.

She lay back, taking deep, measured breaths, trying to calm her fast-beating heart and the uneasy feeling that didn't leave the room after her departure from her dreams. She hoped that with some calculated thinking those pesky images and intrusive thoughts would leave her alone, but the room itself—

nay, the whole building—felt as though it was steeped in a sense of unease and trepidation.

Afraid to close her eyes, lest her nightmares visit her in broad daylight, she stared at the ceiling. Her eyes grew watery and dry at the same time due to their long exposure to the light.

A tiny, cold hand slipped into hers, and she let out another gasp, pulling away from the touch, her heart, which she had desperately been trying to calm down, now thundering hard in her chest again.

It was a child.

His nearly black eyes were large in his little face, and his dark thatch of hair was awkwardly cut and sticking up at odd angles around his head. She felt the simultaneous feeling of wanting to smother him comfortingly in a hug, but also the sharp sting of sorrow that she quickly pushed from her mind.

There was something about this child's eyes. So old for such a small and young face. So full of the world and its pain. Had her eyes looked like that when she was his age? Had she been the gaunt, broken girl with ages in her eyes and the weight of the world on her shoulders?

The little one said nothing, clutching one arm close to his belly, a fistfull of the long tunic undershift that he wore gripped tightly in his fist and the corners of his mouth pinched as if he were in pain. He couldn't be older than five or six. There was a buzzing in the back of her ears, but the need to comfort and coddle him pulled at her heartstrings.

"Would you like to come sit up here with me?" Her voice was raspy from the depths of her shadowed dreams, and her ears still buzzed as if from something in the distance. Her skin began to crawl, but she didn't know why.

The child nodded and, before she could help him, was already clambering over the side of the bed with more determination than skill. He moaned softly when he rolled atop the quilt that covered her legs and clutched his belly with both hands, rocking forward and back with his eyes squeezed tightly closed.

Sorrow burrowed deep in her being. She knew his pain.

Dilara felt suddenly helpless, devoid of any strength and grasping desperately to help the small child. His feet were wrapped in bandages, one splinted. How had he gotten into her room in this condition? Reaching out a hand to touch the boy's shoulder, she looked up and toward the door, open only a crack, to see if anyone was without the threshold. Surely this boy had a caregiver somewhere. "Are you all right? Where do you hurt? How did you get in here?" she asked, realizing as the words left her lips that she was asking too many questions at once.

He pointed at his foot and made a hopping motion with his hand then placed the hand on his stomach again, his face a little grayer than she thought it should be.

"Did you get hurt?"

"Hurt, like you." His words were in a soft baby voice that simultaneously sounded older than it ought and yet bore the tone and inflection that a young child never loses until they simply grow out of it. He pointed a finger at her stomach and then back at his own.

Dumbfounded, Dilara froze. How could he know that it was her stomach that hurt? "But where are your parents?" she mumbled.

A broken look came over his face, and instant tears filled those massive eyes. Before she could fumble out an apology, the boy scooted near her and nestled under her arm, his little head resting over her heart.

And it stopped, frozen in time. Her breath barely left her lungs.

A wave of sorrow washed over her at the same moment that instincts kicked in, and her hands caressed his hair, smoothing back the unruly cowlick and holding the shuddering shoulders close to her chest. Tears fell freely from her eyes, and her throat closed around them, holding back a choking sob. She squeezed her eyes shut, willing them to hold back the rush of water, and rested her chin on the little thatched head.

A loud cry of pain from downstairs made her snap back to the present, and the cacophony of noise that had been an underlying buzz in the background finally came rushing to the forefront. There were noises down those stairs she wished she couldn't hear. Sounds of pain. Sounds that had mirrored her own in the forest. Guttural, pleading, filled with panic.

She covered the little boy's ears and started humming deep in her raspy throat. A tavern song she had picked up from the men at the bordello. She kept the words from her lips and merely hummed it, keeping it slow and letting it drift into mournful sounds so that it sounded more like a lullaby than a rousing dance tune filled with legends of men dancing with women in the foundations of the world. Its pagan nature was not one she would speak in words over this child, but it was one of the only melodies that she knew. She hoped, too, that it would keep the dreadful sounds from downstairs from rattling her ears.

She didn't know how long they sat there, her back cushioned with pillows, her chest and arms cradling the little boy. The shadows were suddenly lengthening, and she realized she must have drifted off to sleep. The little child still slept on her, his breath moving in and out in little puffs.

She tried not to move, even though her arm was numb, but she startled when the man from before burst into her room, his crutches thudding on the floor and his face panicked until he caught sight of the little boy who now sat up, rubbing the sleep from his eyes.

"Kahru, I was worried sick when I couldn't find you." He stumbled wearily to the bed and glanced at Dilara as if asking permission.

She nodded, and he sank to a seat at the foot of the mattress. Gratefully, far enough away from her that she felt some ease, though there was still an uncomfortable air to the room.

"My name is Marcus." he spoke softly.

"Dilara." She didn't fear him; as a cripple and with eyes that were kind, he seemed unlikely to hurt her. But she didn't trust him. Kind eyes could hide dark secrets, and people with broken bodies could have minds just as broken.

But the little boy—Kahru, Marcus had called him— crawled over her legs to the foot of the bed, dragging his splinted leg behind him and snuggled against the lanky side of the medicinal who she knew had helped her in her sleep. She caught herself gaping at them. Seeing children so trusting of men was something new to her.

The medicinal seemed surprised as well. Though, there was a weariness to his gaunt face. "You sure can get around just fine, even with one and a half feet out of commission." He shook his head, allowing himself a small smile that still spoke of pain and sorrow.

What had been going on all this time? This man looked positively worn to the bone, and his eyes were full of sorrow and a simultaneous peace that was an enigma to her. How could one feel both at the same time, let alone display it?

"What happened?" was all she asked, her words a whisper.

The medicinal shook his head and nodded down at Kahru who was playing with the buttons on his vest. Dilara noticed a splatter of blood on his collar she hadn't seen before, and her stomach jumped in queasiness at the realization of what must have been going on.

"Is my grandfather going to be all right? Did you find him, Marcus?" Kahru's eyes were questioning as he looked up at the medicinal—at Marcus. The name seemed to suit him, and she tilted her head, watching their interactions.

Marcus's eyes dropped as he lifted a hand to rub the boy's head, petting it soothingly as he shook his own. "Not yet, Kahru."

Kahru wilted and sagged against Marcus once more, gathering a fistful of his shirt and burying his face into Marcus's side.

The man looked heavenward, his reddish-blonde hair matching the disarray of Kahru's and the eyes blinking hard against what Dilara realized in surprise was tears.

She looked between them, wanting to ask more questions to distract her from the throbbing pain deep in her stomach that was starting to wrap around her back again, but instead she merely changed positions, trying to get more comfortable against the pillows.

The silence stretched. A particularly sharp pain made her breath hitch, and she tried to cover it with a sigh. But Marcus's blue eyes were on her in an instant, and she shook her head, then ducked it toward Kahru with a questioning tilt.

The little boy had collapsed entirely against Marcus, his limp hand falling off of the button on Marcus's vest and into his lap, his mouth hanging open and soft puffs of peaceful breath escaping with every exhale. She smiled. If only sleep could be so comforting. But for her, it served as a reminder of the nightmare she had lived as she was forced to relive them again in slumber.

"What happened?" she whispered as Marcus shifted, cradling the child against his side with an arm around his back, and used his other hand to guide the fluffy head down to a resting spot on his lap.

He swallowed and wouldn't look at her as he raised his now free hand to rub his face and softly rest his other on Kahru's shoulder. "There was a battle."

Her breath caught in her lungs again and a sharp pain dug into her stomach like a dagger till she shifted again, her head feeling a little fuzzy. "Battle?"

He nodded, the rhythmic movements of his hand petting Kahru's head starting to lull her into a more restful state simply by his own proximity. "The Rusalkans came over the wall to drag the people back, but the Eliran Kingsmen held them at bay." He gulped again, clearing his throat softly. "They paid dearly for it."

Dilara felt her blood run cold.

She could picture *his* face. The absolute disgust that was etched into his features and the explosive anger that he would burn with at being bested by a "slip of a girl with no more mind than a rabbit." She gritted her teeth to keep them from clinking together as she could remember the feel of his hand clamped around her throat. She swallowed again, hard, trying to erase the memory. But Conri was just one man, and she knew there had to be others. Most of the people who would have made a break for Elira when word of the treaty spread were those who stood to lose the most at the hands of the tyrants who ruled over them.

People like her. Their lives were not their own until they made one mad grasp at freedom, like a drowning man reaching for the sun and gasping for air as the cold water closed around him with its clammy grip. The worst that could occur if they failed was the same life they had been leaving or perhaps another welcome alternative—a death that would remove them from this pain forever and set them free entirely.

"Are you all right?" Marcus's voice felt far away and echoey, as if the room had suddenly grown larger and emptier.

"I'm fine," she croaked, reaching for a cup with a trembling hand that knocked the stoneware from the nightstand instead of gripping it in her weak fingers. It clattered to the floor, and she couldn't see it through her blurry eyes, but it hadn't shattered. "I'm sorry," she stuttered, wrapping her shaking arms around her aching middle.

"You should sleep." The words were even farther away, and before she even knew what was happening, a pillow had been removed from behind her shoulders, and she was eased into a recumbent position. Her screaming back muscles welcomed the different position, and she closed her eyes; keeping them open was more trouble than it was worth since she could hardly see anything out of them anyway.

With one last burst of strength, she fought to stay awake, the darkness gripping at the edges of her consciousness with the ugly reminder that sleep brought nightmares. Dreams that only brought her living hell into sharper focus. But then it was too late as another pain stabbed her abdomen, and the darkness swallowed her whole.

Marcus rested Kahru's head on the foot of Dilara's bed and used a blanket rolled into a sausage to wrap around the little one so it would be harder for him to fall off the bed. The tavern's tick mattress was large enough to accommodate a married couple if necessary, so there was plenty of room for the two invalids, both of whom were smaller than the average adult.

After settling them comfortably, Marcus rested a hand on the bedside table and reached for the cup on the floor. His hip caught, and he stumbled, catching himself on the side of the mattress with a groan. Dilara barely shifted in her sleep, though her eyebrows dipped together, and he was grateful he hadn't disturbed her further. He hated the haunted, terrified look in her large brown eyes. They reminded him of a deer caught on the path, her lithe figure like that of a fawn who had lost its way.

With a groan and a pain so sharp it made his eyes water, he righted his leg and shoved himself upright, using the bed for support as he hopped toward his crutch. Cursed infirmity. The fact that it had grown worse in the cold weather and now prohibited him from doing such a simple task as picking up a dropped cup from the floor sent heat roaring through his insides.

"Forgive me, Lord." He huffed as he wrapped his arms around his crutches, gripping the handles Everard had shaped from a hollowed-out wooden spindle and suspended from the frame of the crutch with wire left over from his forge. "I know you have given me so many gifts and things that I can do, despite this pain, but it sure would make things easier if climbing the stairs didn't take years off my life." He glanced back at his two patients and smiled sadly to himself. Sleep was their best medicine, and he was grateful to see them resting peacefully. With what they had been through and seen, peaceful sleep was certainly something to be thankful for.

It had grown dark outside, and he had been tending the wounded in the tavern for several hours before he used what felt like the last ounce of his strength to take the stairs and check on the others who were resting up in their rooms. He swallowed the sick feeling at the back of his throat when he thought of Jaromir. The last he had seen of the man was his veined hand caressing the little one of his grandson and soothing him in his sleep. Why had such an old and needed man gone down to the encampment?

With his mind full of questions, he settled a foot on the first step at the top of the staircase and leveraged his crutches and the wall as three points of support to get him down.

But Marcus knew exactly why. A man would do anything to find the family he'd lost, even if it meant putting himself in the way of certain death. He gulped. An image sprang to mind of the man who had sacrificed his life for him, and his chest ached. He swallowed hard.

But the guilt that made his heart beat with a bitter echo was enough to blur his vision and send fire coursing through him. *Lord, why did You have to take him? I wish You had taken me instead.* Thud, thud, thump. One crutch, then the next was lowered a step before he slid his feet down to join them. *I know I oughtn't to question Your will, but I know Your will is never for Your children to suffer. So, even if it was Your will that I somehow live, why couldn't it have been at the hands of any other circumstance than taking the life of the only man I had to be like a father to me?*

"For My thoughts are not your thoughts, neither are your ways My ways, saith the LORD. For as the heavens are higher than the earth, so are My ways higher than your ways, and My thoughts than your thoughts."

Thud, thud, slide, thump.

But why did it have to be me? How can I live with the truth that, because of me, Violet lost her father?

"And we know that all things work together for good to them that love God, to them who are called according to His purpose."

Thud, thud, slide, thump.

Marcus tried not to grumble. Sometimes his passion for Scripture came into his head more as an argument to his own thoughts instead of the comfort he'd prefer. What kind of believer was he if he still questioned the God who knew all?

It was one thing to know the verses front and back as if they were a part of him. He had spent enough time reading and re-reading in the years and months and weeks he had been bedridden. The words had become such a part of him that they sprang to mind unbidden, often in argument to his very own thoughts.

Thud, thud, slide, thump.

"Do not put the Lord your God to the test."

Marcus gulped.

He knew the things that rankled in his heart were contrary to the surrender he should be living in. He knew they didn't align with what God's Word said. But it was one thing to believe the things he knew to be true and another to truly live that belief. Especially when the words of others, the pain of those he loved, and the guilt and shame in his heart all seemed to scream the contrary.

Thud, thud, slide, thump.

The sounds from the floor below—the smell of sweat, the cries of pain—all were like a punch to his gut as he turned the final corner of the staircase, making his hands shake from weariness. So many wounded. Kingsmen with families of their own, their bodies broken and bleeding in the sacrifice for others.

He couldn't seem to get away from sacrifice.

And then his stutter steps stopped, nearly throwing him off balance. Because the pain was suddenly filled with a beauty that transcended the agony of this mortal realm as it reminded him of the One who had sacrificed himself to ensure that all humanity could attain the Kingdom of Heaven.

Those in the room below had sacrificed themselves and were now in an agony that mirrored that of the Son of God, who had died to give them a place with Him, away from the pain and sorrow they now experienced.

His heart ached with the sadness and beauty of it, the two emotions mingling into a masterpiece that surpassed the physical and settled on his spirit with the subtlety of an ox and the gentleness of a butterfly.

Marcus's leg was shaking from the strain of the descent. Elgon's brown eyes rose to meet Marcus's as he sat amongst his soldiers, a kingsman as he had once been, returned again, this time to set the captives free. His uniform matched those of the soldiers around him, and none would have known of his highborn status if not for the marked pauldron on his right shoulder with the king's seal pressed into the leather.

Elgon had his right arm gripped in his left hand, a bloody rag held to a cut. He nodded at Marcus. He shifted in his seat upon a wooden stool, his back to the stone wall of the tavern and his face contracting in pain at the movement.

"Are you all right?" Marcus hobbled over to Elgon, pulling out a clean cloth from the messenger bag that hung over one shoulder and leaning his crutch against the wall to make better use of his hands.

"I'm fine." Elgon waved his bloodied right hand, then winced again. "Though, that was a rather idiotic move." He raised his eyebrows in the universal sign of distress.

"Let me tend your wound." Marcus reached for the bloodied rag on Elgon's arm and pitched forward when his knee locked up. He caught himself with a hand on the wall behind Elgon, while Elgon's left hand grasped Marcus's shoulder. His face heated, and he almost stammered an apology, but Elgon had already maneuvered around on the chair to allow Marcus to use the wall for support while tending the wound on his arm. The king didn't say a word, and Marcus swallowed back his embarrassment, grateful for the unspoken compassion.

Elgon winced again and dragged in a hiss through his clenched teeth as Marcus cleaned the long gash left by a Rusalkan's curved scimitar. It was deep.

"This needs stitches."

Elgon rolled his eyes. "Great. Violet's going to kill me."

Marcus smiled. He could imagine the tongue lashing that Violet would give her husband. He had been on the receiving end of her well-intended concern many a time. "I'm sure she'll understand the circumstances."

Elgon rolled his eyes. "Right. I doubt that. You should see the state she's in with her emotions running high these days."

A chuckle escaped Marcus, and it felt good. It had been a while since amusement had comforted him like a warm blanket on a cold evening. "It's the pregnancy."

Elgon shook his head. "Whatever it is, it's setting *me* on edge. You'd think after all we've been through, she could handle me taking a trip to shore up the border, but she reacted worse than I expected." A flash of concern crossed Elgon's face.

"She didn't want you to leave?"

Elgon squinted past Marcus, his gaze fixed on something beyond him. "I don't know. It was strange. She felt worried by my departure and even told me she didn't know why. Just that something wasn't right."

Marcus swallowed back the bitter taste in his throat. "You'd be wise not to disregard it. Violet's been right more often than not, and her entire family has always seemed to have feelings—er, premonitions, if you will."

"Some call it second sight. Perhaps it is in a way." Elgon nodded and drew a deep breath as Marcus tied off the last stitch in a perfect row on his bicep. The king then grinned. "Mighty fine stitching. Want to sew up the hole in my shirt sleeve while you're at it?"

Marcus snorted and rolled his eyes. "I'm sure you have plenty of servants to do that for you, my lord."

Elgon straightened his arm and looked at the stitched cut with admiration. "They could all take lessons from you and be the better for it, I'll wager. Well done."

Marcus faked a bow, using the wall as support so he didn't collapse. "Perhaps I'll add that to my list of qualifications. I can just see it now, my wooden sign hanging from my home: 'Marcus, the medicinal and teacher of fine sewing.'"

Elgon smiled. "The opportunities are endless."

"How did everything go?" Marcus asked, nodding his head over his shoulder at the room full of kingsmen. He remembered a day when the thought of a roomful of the king's soldiers would have set his teeth on edge, but in the hands of the capable ruler before him, those fears had been transformed into a healthy respect.

Elgon drew a deep breath and sighed as he stood, stretching his back out before handing his arm to Marcus to wrap in a clean bandage. "Better than I expected."

Marcus's eyes widened in a question.

Elgon shrugged. "Rusalkans are fierce fighters, especially if they have the upper hand, which they did. I would have preferred to have had time to get more people away from the wall before they attacked, but all things considered, we still own the ground we stand on, and they were forced back into the woods on their side of the wall." Sorrow filled his eyes, darkening their color and pulling at the corners of them. "I do wish…" He swallowed on a crack in his voice. "I do wish that our sacrifice had not been so great."

Marcus patted Elgon's shoulder after the wrapping was complete. "You did what you could."

Nodding, Elgon brushed the back of a dirty hand across his eyes. "I'll be leaving in the morning."

He sank onto the stool Elgon had vacated, wincing at the pinch that wrapped from his hip to his back. "So soon?"

Elgon turned around, a tired smile back on his stubbled face. "I remember a time when you wished me to leave."

Marcus didn't respond, his heart too heavy to speak.

"What's the matter, old friend?" Elgon rested a hand on Marcus's bony shoulder, the weight bringing more comfort than Marcus felt he'd earned.

"Will you do me a great kindness?" His stomach flipped at the audacity in his own request as well as the nervousness he felt at expressing his pain so vulnerably.

"Anything." Elgon's voice was husky, his eyes compassionate when Marcus looked up.

"Will you tell Violet that I'm sorry?" He swallowed the lump that tried to close off his throat. Tears filled his eyes, and he willed them back with a clenched jaw and tight fists. "Sorry for being the cause of her father's death."

He didn't expect his hand to be enveloped in the calloused one of his king, nor to have his ruler stoop to a knee so that he could look up into the downcast face of a simple healer who had no right to ask anything of his majesty. And he certainly didn't expect the warmth of compassion and depth of feeling that accompanied the look.

"Marcus, she does not blame you."

Marcus bit his tongue. He could not speak. The hand tightened on his shoulder and held him upright against the burden pressing down on his back.

"That burden is not yours to bear, my friend."

"How could she not blame me? If I hadn't been there…" His words broke off, too weak to speak the rest of his thought into existence.

"A better question would be how *could* she blame you? Marcus, you are her brother in every respect except blood, and even that is transcended by the spiritual bond you share. You must not carry a burden that was never meant for you and, furthermore, is bound to you by nothing but the enemy's lies. Violet's love for you knows no bounds and is not hindered by any unforgiveness. Certainly not for the tragic loss of her father that was set in motion by far more than simply your actions."

The weight still lingered. "How do you know?"

"She told me everything. Marcus, do not let this pain come between you and her in a way that she does not wish. Any and all forgiveness that you could ask or desire from her has already been given long ago. Don't burden yourself with the weight of guilt for something that no one but yourself holds against you."

"But…"

"That isn't God talking, nor is it Violet. So who is telling you that you are to blame, Marcus?" The words came out with a strength of emotion and purpose behind them that could have been construed as frustration if it were not for the empathy that filled Elgon's face as Marcus again met his gaze. The authority in the king's words transcended the weight of guilt on his back, and it lifted, ever so slightly. He swallowed, some of the strength returning to his spine and pushing back against that burden.

"Only listen to voices that are true, Marcus. You are not your past guilt and shame. Take it from someone who has to continually fight that lie every single morning that I wake."

"He should have let me die." The words tumbled out of Marcus's mouth of their own accord like stones dislodged from a cliff-face and falling with the inevitable weight of gravity.

But he sucked in a breath as Elgon's strong fingers snaked around his arm and squeezed…hard. He looked up with a remonstrance that died on his lips at the sight of those brown eyes, burning from within like golden flames of a torch, the intensity of Elgon's gaze holding Marcus like a climbing rope tethering him to the mountain face, buffeted by wind and snow as he was.

"Don't for one second think that." Elgon's words were barely above a whisper. "You have so much, and you've given it freely. Your hands heal and touch not just bodies, but minds and spirits. Your purpose is so evident to everyone but yourself. Your life is the Gospel personified. A life laid down for those around you. In every single moment. Marcus..." Elgon's voice cracked, and the fiery eyes started to swim.

Marcus fought to drag a breath into his contracted lungs.

"You were the Gospel to me. You were one of the reasons that I saw a Savior. That I reached out to grasp Him. That I realized He wanted to save *my* life." Elgon blinked rapidly, clearing his throat, but never once losing the line of connection between them. "Had you not been, I would not be a child of God. Your life has value. No matter how hard and worthless it may seem. Your worth stretches far beyond anything you could possibly see and into eternity. Do *not* forget it." With each word, his grip shook Marcus slightly, the very foundation of his thoughts shaken to the core in a mighty earthquake that left little but humility in its wake. Each word was a dagger into the heart of every aching fear, struggle, and lie he had believed. Because that's what they were—lies.

Elgon released him and reached a hand to pat the small volume of pages that rested within Marcus's vest pocket and never strayed far from there or his hand. "You inspired me to read this. You and Violet. I do everyday, but perhaps you ought to read it a little closer with a lens for yourself instead of others." A small smile pulled at the corner of his mouth, and some of the heat ebbed away, cloaking the king in a softness that felt like freshly fallen snow on scorched earth. "You might have missed a few things."

Marcus wanted to match the smile, his heart taking in the subtle and well-intentioned joke, but his spirit was so deeply shaken by the encounter that he didn't have any words to break the stunned spell cast by Elgon's words.

Elgon stood and pulled him into a manly embrace, his large hand patting Marcus's shoulder with a gentleness that was aware of his infirmity but had the strength of a brother in arms. "Thank you for how you have allowed Christ to live in you, my brother. I wish we had more time."

Marcus's words finally returned as he tried to blink back the witless tears that gathered in his own eyes. His greatest desire had always been for family. From his earliest recollection of the little waif with nowhere to call home, his hunger and thirst for a heart to call his, be it father, mother, sister, brother… It had been a long wait for the fulfillment of that wish, and it finally stood in front of him in the unlikely pairing of a king and an orphan boy, joined together in the bond of brothers who served the same Savior. "God go with you, my brother."

"And also with you." Elgon's hand squeezed his shoulder one last time before he gathered his kingsman's cloak from the floor where it had fallen, swung it over his shoulder with the majestic swoosh of a man born to royalty, and strode across the room and out the door into the lantern-lit night that was punctuated by the sounds of men's pain, a wolf's howl, and the whistling wind.

Brothers indeed.

The evening had worn down to a dull roar, and Marcus sighed upon reaching the top of the stairs. "Thank the Lord that Fendrel's home doesn't have these monstrosities," he muttered under his breath, leaning heavily against the wall. "And thank You, Lord, for the strength to meet every step."

He drew in a deep breath, trying to calm his pounding heart. A moan from the room off to his left snapped his head up, followed by another wolf howl outside.

The creature seemed to be settling in closer which was strange in light of the chaos from the battle and the amount of Rusalkans who had flooded the woods over the last few days. Wolves usually ran in packs, so it was strange that he only heard one and with such frequency. He wondered about the wolf he had encountered in the woods earlier. Perhaps that was where the howls were coming from.

But then came the moan again.

He hobbled into Dilara's room, hoping she was perhaps just having a nightmare. He swallowed. The gravity of the situation was clear when a nightmare was the preferable alternative.

He didn't even have to touch her forehead to know that she was burning with fever. Her skin was flushed over a pale pallor, her cheeks flaming despite the chill in the room. "Lord, please, bring Your healing." He gently wiped the perspiration from her brow with the back of his hand.

Another wolf howl punctuated the whispered prayers that fell from his tongue that would have made no sense to anyone but the Lord. In stark contrast to the ice crystals coating the window panes, her skin burned with a fire that would be hard to quench.

He dipped a cloth into the basin beside him on the table, doing his best to fight off the intense feeling of dread that started to overtake the room like a black shadow grasping at him with dark fingers.

Through gritted teeth, he fought through his own pain to sponge the girl's feverish face. Hadn't she been through enough pain already? "In the name of Jesus, I speak healing and peace in this room. Father, I know I haven't even the faintest clue of how much this child of Yours has gone through, but let her strength not be wasted in this hour. Do not let her die."

He gripped her twitching hand that seemed to have a mind of its own with his free one and dipped the now warm cloth back in the cold basin.

He wouldn't let this fever claim her. Not if prayer and faith could push back the pain that threatened to take over the atmosphere in the room.

Marcus was a firm believer in faith. It had yet to steer him wrong, and he doubted it ever would.

Nine

A BATTLE OF THE VOICES

THERE WAS NOTHING LEFT. Everything had been spent. Dilara lay in the snow, her body having given up all its strength to get her to this point. With one last contraction, Dilara leaned forward and caught her stillborn child in her hands. She stared at the little face—immovable, precious, tiny.

So small.

There was nothing left within her to even weep. She wrapped her child in the red scarf from around her neck. It had been the last remnant of her short but happy childhood, and it felt fitting to wrap around the little body, as if it could somehow impart to her son the happiness and few good memories she possessed.

With a sigh that seemed to exhale everything from her lungs, her aching spine curled around the tiny, still form, as if, even in exhaustion, her body knew to protect her child at all costs. Her womb, now empty, still longed to protect and shelter, holding on like weak but determined fingers to a cliff face, daring to hang on. To survive. To make it through this.

She wanted to scream, but there was no air. It was thin up in the mountains, and every muscle had spent itself into exhaustion. A whispered "Why?" floated out and was swept away by the howling wind.

Everything. They had taken everything. Even a life, all to serve their selfish desires. And the gaping wound within her womb mirrored that of her aching heart. Flayed raw beyond pain to the depths below it. Filled with the darkness that comes when a wound is too deep to even scab over. Too painful to bear. Too wretched to desire to go on living.

A wolf's howl was near.

Too near.

But she didn't care.

Come and take me, she taunted it silently. After all, this was all her fault. Now she had the death of another on her hands.

A footstep crunched in the snow behind her, but she couldn't move to look for its source. What did it matter?

Her body heaved with one last effort to remove any remnant of the means for life it had contained. Dilara swallowed against the bitter taste in her throat. The metallic taste of blood. The smell of it filling the air. Coating the snow. The red steaming as its warmth dissipated into the ice crystals beneath it.

Another step sounded. Snow crunching loudly, shaped like crystals, pummeled by the wind into the tiniest and sharpest of fragments, grating against each other at even the lightest touch.

Take me.

Snuffling came from behind her, and with it a throaty hum. Almost human in its tones of gentleness. The hum turned into a soft chirping noise with nearly a whistle at the end of each chirp.

Dilara shut her eyes. Perhaps this was the end. But the desire to fight came over her. Was she really willing to let all of it go and submit to death? But what else was there to live for? How could she possibly fight a wild animal of the mountain forest?

A warm, damp nose pressed into the back of her neck, soft chirping still echoing as it nuzzled her sweaty and snow-matted hair from off her neck. Suddenly a warm body nestled at her back, and the chirping slowed, a rough tongue licking her cheek, warming the tears that had oozed from her eyes and frozen to her face.

Alone. Abandoned to the forest. Broken and bereft. A creature of the wood had settled beside her and offered her comfort. Still clutching her own child close to her chest, she turned her head and was stunned to see the gray and white coat of a wolf and two black eyes like coals, glimmering with the last dying shades of the light of day. Warmth spread through her aching back. A warmth she had never expected to feel again.

She closed her eyes. The land of the living seemed just a bit closer than it had a mere moment ago.

Thank you. She was still too weak to speak the words, but they formed in her mind. It was moments like these that she wondered if the God that the traveling Eliran had spoken of was real. She wondered if it was His presence that she felt hovering over her or if it were simply a trick of her grieving and exhausted mind.

Her eyes slid shut. The wolf could destroy her for all she knew, but somehow she felt peace in its presence. Almost as if it too understood her plight.

And perhaps it did.

A wolf's howl sounded yet again, and gooseflesh prickled Marcus's arms where his sleeves had been rolled up. Fendrel was still needed downstairs, and Everard had been so busy tending those outside, Marcus hadn't even seen him once today. Keitha, the taverner's wife, had helped him multiple times over the last few hours as they had worked throughout the night to keep Dilara's fever down, praying that it would break and leave her in peace.

Instead, it tossed her to and fro like an anchorless ship in a winter storm, and Marcus feared it would sink. The taverner's wife sat on the floor, snatching a few moments of sleep, her head leaning back and her mouth open in a soft snore. She had a strangely gruff exterior and somewhat belligerent tongue in her head, but Marcus saw the mother beneath. The woman who still had a compassionate heart beating somewhere beneath the tough shell. She was like a hardwood tree, a rough bark covering the beautiful strength and purpose of the core.

But he was alone at that moment. Alone with tormenting thoughts that seemed to weigh him down like the wet snow that sometimes covered the mountain passes with its heavy coat, stifling any movement.

This was his fault. He had let Dilara do too much today. Perhaps if he hadn't let Kahru—who had looked so comfortable curled up at her side—stay when he had, she would not have overexerted herself, and perhaps the fever would not have returned.

Another moan escaped her dry and cracked lips. The frostbite had touched her skin in places, leaving dried marks that marred the pale smoothness of her still partially bandaged hands. Some patients spoke in their feverish dreams, replaying past experiences or circumstances that seemed to haunt them, but her lips were pressed tight. Nothing but a few moans escaped her, and he couldn't help but be a little disappointed.

He wished he knew more about her. Wished there was a way to peel back that outer layer, the quiet distrust she wore like armor. There was something about her that pulled on his soul, called out to him, as if there was something he felt called to do for her or in her life.

But he didn't know what.

He had that sometimes. He always had that connection to Violet, though this time it felt different. He could sense things others missed with certain people he was close to. Fendrel had always said Marcus seemed to have the gift of discernment. As if there was some sort of second sight he possessed toward those he was in tune with.

Granny, rest her soul, had always seemed to know, too. Her mind, though broken in the physical world, seemed to have the ability to see into the spirit world with a keenness that often unnerved him while it simultaneously amazed him. She would look at him with those knowing eyes of hers, give him a nod from across the room, and then return to her knitting.

There was something to knowing the thoughts that others wouldn't look at themselves. It was like peering into a locked box, catching a glimpse at the treasure or the monster that was kept there, a box that was locked to all but him and the Lord. Locked, even from the person whose box it was.

"What do you see?"

He jumped slightly at the sound of Fendrel's voice in the doorway. Marcus wrung out the rag again and frowned as he tried to soothe away the redness of fever from Dilara's face, but to no avail. "What do you mean?"

"I know that look; you see something in her." Fendrel stepped forward. One would never know, unless they had been with Fendrel through the best and worst of times like Marcus had, that he was tired. His face held the same immutable, calm expression it usually did. But his step lagged, and his shoulders slumped forward more than usual.

"I see something in everyone." Marcus shook his head, trying to get rid of the feelings of pain that cluttered his mind. "It's like a curse."

"Perhaps it feels that way. Curses have a way of turning out to be blessings in disguise. It's a wise man who will see the first and recognize it as the other."

Marcus sighed. Feeling the burdens of others was a blessing, though it did often feel like the opposite. Especially for a cripple who could barely carry his own weight. And not even that some days.

Fendrel's face gathered dark shadows as he examined Dilara. Changing out a few of the bandages and looking over her frostbitten hands carefully, he hid it well. He always had to be the picture of steadiness for his patients, but Marcus recognized the growing worry.

"How is she?"

Fendrel scrubbed a hand across his stubbled face. "We need to pray."

"I already have been."

"Well, don't stop. I don't want to have to operate. In her state, it would do more harm than good. But I'm worried there is an infection internally. We need to make tea from Motherwort and nettle. If only we had some wild yams. I didn't think to bring them."

"What about cedar and coneflower?"

"We could try those as well. Both would fight off infection while also strengthening her against whatever is making her sick. And the sooner the better. You look like you could use a break. I'll take over here for a time. Why don't you go ask the taverner if they have any stores of herbs here."

Marcus heaved himself to his feet, reaching for his crutches. He would gladly take the stairs again. He needed to get some tea for himself as well to help himself stay up tonight. Dilara needed not only his care but also his prayers.

The stairs took less time than usual. He found the taverner still up and tending the kitchen, despite the lateness—or perhaps the earliness—of the hour.

"I think Keitha has nettle and yams about, maybe even the coneflower you asked about. Ah, here..." He pulled some dried purple flowers from a rack overhead. "Here's that last one."

"And cedar?" Marcus took the coneflower, pulling the heads of the flowers from the stems and dropping them into a mortar and pestle that rested on the large oak kitchen table.

"Them's the trees just outside."

"Do you have a knife? I can fetch some." Marcus looked around for a sharp implement and blinked when, within a second, the taverner had pulled a dagger from his belt and flipped it, offering it hilt first to Marcus.

He glanced up at the larger man who, based on his size, seemed to have some shared ancestry with Everard. There was a twinkle in the man's eye as he gestured with the knife. "I wasn't always a taverner." He winked.

With a smile that took longer than usual to make it to his lips, Marcus grasped the dagger, tucked it into his own belt, and swung himself across the kitchen with his crutches. He hung a lantern from the extra crook of his right crutch which he had carved himself for such a purpose.

The air outside bit him with a sharpness that could rival the shining blade that rested at his hip. He sucked in a breath. He coughed on the bitterness, remembering that they were closer to the mountains and the air was thinner and colder than he was used to. Slinging the corner of his green cloak over his face and across his shoulder, he pulled on his hood and traveled through the thin layer of crystal snow that coated the frozen ground. The snow was thin and light. The kind made from intensely low temperatures and thin mountain air.

Glancing up, he studied the branches towering overhead to ascertain the cedar. These were some of the largest he had ever seen. They had big trees in Raintamount, but these seemed descended from otherworldly giants. Their limbs towered so high into the sky that the tips were lost to the fog, though the darkness ate their remains with its inky shadows. The sprawling clumps of a cedar met his eye after some searching, and he eagerly hobbled toward it. The bark and even some of the needles could be incorporated into a tea that would hopefully bring some relief and assistance to Dilara's body as it fought the battle it was waging.

With the dagger, he scraped off some of the bark, using his crutches to steady him while still managing to use both of his hands. An edgy feeling crept its frigid hand up his spine, and he stilled, the sound of his scraping too loud for his ears. There was danger near. He knew it. Sensed it.

Even his breath whistling into his lungs was too loud, and the creaking of the branches in the wind threw his heart into beating faster than a galloping horse's hooves. The moon's light threw a pale silver hue over the world, and he almost felt as if he were living in a painting, distant from reality.

Snow crunched off to his left, and he swung around, losing his precariously placed balance and falling into a heap at the foot of the cedar tree. Everything he had been holding or that had been holding him up clattered to the ground with a crash that echoed through the trees with a din that could have woken the dead.

He had really done it now. If the creator of that sound was a lurking Rusalkan warrior, Marcus was done for. He wouldn't survive that encounter, not without a miracle. *God, help me*, he cried inwardly. His eyes struggled to adjust to the inky blackness of the forest shadows since his lantern had been snuffed out from the fall, and he blinked rapidly, hoping to increase his night vision quicker than usual.

A gray blur passed off to his right. He strained to catch another glimpse of it. A low growl met his ears, and he scrambled backward, gasping in pain as he scraped his bad hip against a rock. The object moved closer, filling every fiber of Marcus's being with dread.

In the puddle of moonlight breaking through the trees, the gray and white face of a wolf met his gaze. A low rumble started in its throat.

Marcus hadn't realized he had been holding his breath. He trembled and tried to push farther away, but his limbs wouldn't move, frozen to the ground.

It took a step closer.

The rumble didn't reappear, and instead, it dropped its head lower, its black eyes still burning holes into Marcus as it brought its nose closer to his foot.

Marcus didn't dare move.

Another wolf howled in the distance, it's sharp, three-pitch call chilling his bones. Was this one alone or with a pack? He was about to be this beast's next meal if he or God didn't do something quickly.

A sniff, followed by a chirp, came from the wolf in front of him; its haunches would have reached his mid-torso had he been standing. But that wasn't the sound a wolf made when it was about to devour its prey, was it?

Taking a step closer, it continued to watch him, sniffing his bad right leg as it did so. Marcus's body heated through with panic when it pressed its nose into his leg.

They stared deep into each other's eyes, unmoving. For how long, Marcus didn't know. His heart resumed its steady beat, and his hands grew numb from where they were buried in the snow. He hadn't noticed until this minute. But there was something about the wolf's gaze. Something…otherworldly. It was as if those gray eyes didn't belong to a horrible beast, but to something deeper. Almost…heavenly?

The blood rushed to his head, and he felt dizzy, but still he watched it. Her. It was a she-wolf. What was it about him that kept her interest? Why didn't she behave as other wolves?

Another howl in the distance broke their locked gaze, and her head came up as she stepped tentatively backward, her feet effortlessly pressing into the paw prints she had previously made in the snow.

In awe, Marcus exhaled sharply. Another howl caused her to shake her head, and in the time it took for him to blink, she had disappeared.

He gasped for a breath, rolling off the rock that had been pressing into his side, and pushed himself into a more upright sitting position. He dusted the clumps of snow from his trembling hands. The trees tilted around him, and he felt his eyes filling. More from the sharpness of the cold and the shock than anything else.

The encounter had rattled him. Down to his very core.

Reaching for his crutches, now half buried in snow, he heaved himself to his feet. He winced, letting out a ragged breath. That rock would leave a bruise. But he needed to gather the cedar bark for Dilara. She needed to get well. She had to. It was his fault she was worse; the least he could do was try to help her get better. Fear, too, now drove him to hurry and return indoors.

Frantically, he carved off enough bark to make up for what he had dropped and gathered it into his leather bag. Tucking the second crutch under the same arm as his other one, he doubled them up to leave his left hand free to hold the dagger should an enemy come upon him.

Every snap of a twig and creak of the woods sent his heart thundering harder against his ribs. Perhaps the wolf had left him because he was of no use. He wasn't exactly covered in much meat. Perhaps she had realized there was next to nothing but skin and bone and left him for better prey. He shook his head, still dizzy from the mad rush of adrenaline.

Using both crutches as one slowed him down even more than usual, but it was worth it to feel the slight protection that the knife offered him, resting easily in his palm, the blade glinting in the moonlight. Everard had taught him to carry it underhanded against his wrist, but with his crutches, he felt more comfortable with it pointed outward as his range of motion was limited. A step crunched in the snow behind him, and he spun, his crutches catching on the ground; he fought to stay upright, brandishing the weapon toward the figure that had crept up on him.

"It's me." The deep voice was scratchy, and the looming form betrayed Everard's identity.

Gasping for breath, Marcus let Everard reach out a slow hand to take the blade from him.

All of this for some bark. He swallowed against his dry and frozen throat, then coughed. He wasn't used to how dry and frigid this air was, especially at night.

Everard grasped Marcus's arm with one hand, steadying him while he gathered his crutches under his arms.

As they made their way toward the inn, Marcus coughed again, this time starting to choke on the dryness of his own throat.

With a few more painful steps, he was inside the inn, in front of the kitchen fire, a tankard of hot tea in his numb hands and some warmth seeping into his bones.

Everard simply stood over him, arms folded, staring. Or maybe it was closer to a glare. Marcus tried not to roll his eyes. Between Fendrel and Everard, he felt like he was being fussed over by a couple of mother hens. And Everard didn't even have to say anything to get his point across. Just stood there and looked down his crooked nose at him.

"I know," Marcus grumbled, feeling compelled to respond as if Everard *had* spoken.

Everard grunted, but still didn't move. Marcus lifted trembling hands to his shoulder. They were nearly frozen as he fiddled with the leather strap of his bag. After a moment of struggling, he successfully removed it and handed it to Everard. "Can you make tea? Fendrel needs it for Dilara. And yes, I would be grateful for your help bringing it upstairs."

Everard shook his head with a glance heavenward as if asking for mercy, and then went about following Marcus's instructions for making the tea with the cedar and other herbs the taverner had gathered from their stash and Marcus's own.

Everard still pierced him with a glance every now and then with his sharp gray eyes.

"I know, it's colder here than in Padsley; I just didn't plan on being out there so long. I thought I heard something, and it ended up being a wolf, and I tripped and…" Marcus rubbed his hip where the bruise from the rock was already blossoming into existence. "Scared the life out of me. I kept thinking I heard something in the woods after that, so when you came up behind me I was worried it was a Rusalk, so…" He coughed, the crackling heat from the fire finally starting to sink into his bones, though he still felt stiff. Why did he feel like an old man all of the time?

Everard's hands froze in stillness over the earthenware teapot he had been stirring their concoction in.

"What?"

Everard was staring down at him, unnervingly so, with the look of a bear about to defend its cubs.

Some people went on a verbal rampage when they were angry or protective. Everard just…stared and cracked his massive knuckles out of nervous habit.

"I won't go out alone, I promise." Marcus was quick to reassure him. "At least not in the dark," he muttered under his breath.

Keitha strode into the kitchen, tying an apron on as she did so, her hands behind her back and a sleepy, but good-natured look on her face. She wrinkled her round nose at the sight and smell of Everard's brew on the kitchen table and leaned over to take a look. She grimaced. "What in Rusalk is in that witch's brew? Good heavens, it smells strong enough to wake the dead."

Marcus winced at her turn of phrase. Hopefully that wouldn't be necessary. "Maybe add some honey to make it more palatable," he directed Everard, taking a sip from his own tankard of tea. And suddenly, tiredness seeped into every limb. He felt weary and worn like a piece of linen that had seen too many washings. His shoulders slumped forward as he rested his elbows on his knees.

God, please make her well.

"He healeth the broken in heart, and bindeth up their wounds."

He sucked in a breath. *Let it be so.* Taking another draught of his tea, he let it soothe his spirit as well as his tired body.

"And heal the sick that are therein, and say unto them, 'The kingdom of God is come nigh unto you.'"

He choked on the sip when those words sprang to mind. He coughed, his eyes watering. *Lord, was that you?* The words felt like a dagger to the heart. As if they were made for him. Spoken to him. Burning in his very soul like a brand.

"And in every deed for this cause have I raised thee up, for to shew in thee my power; and that my name may be declared throughout all the earth."

Tears burned his eyes, and he tried to cover them with another cough. The purpose of the words spoke so deeply and aligned with what Elgon had spoken over him the day before.

Had this not been what he had been doing? What he had indeed been doing his entire life? Had he been so blind that he did not see it? With as much passion and purpose as he had in serving those that his Heavenly Father placed in his care, how had he not seen it all this time?

He dashed a falling tear with his fist, turning his body as if he were staring moodily into the fire and hiding his face behind his tankard. He still carried the thoughts of bitterness, the pain of uselessness and a broken form laid to waste. He hated that Everard and Fendrel had to coddle him. He hated the life that he had and how it was a burden to those around him. Those things still overwhelmed him. They still rankled like a burr stuck between clothing and skin.

Just because he knew the truth didn't mean he lived by it every moment. *God, help me be that. Help me be Your instrument, the ointment that You use to heal and comfort and speak life. Don't let my life be an empty vessel. I feel so small. Violet is in the capital doing big things for Your Kingdom, changing the world with Elgon from their seats upon the throne, and here I sit. Tending wounds, making tea, mixing herbs. Sleeping through more days than I walk through.*

His shoulders shook, and he pulled his cloak tighter, staring harder into the flames as his eyes burned with repressed tears.

It feels as though my life is full of nothingness for You. A waste. Like just one tiny insect in the face of the whole world. What do I have to offer? To bring to a King? I don't want to die and have done nothing for You. Nothing for Your Kingdom. Father, give me Your hands and Your purpose. I feel so empty in mine.

He held his cloak close like a defense against the world, against the thoughts that battered him into worthlessness.

He almost didn't hear the soft creak at the door, but the sudden rush of cold air that wrapped around his ankles, the crash of pottery, and the sudden shriek that pierced the air from Keitha set his blood running cold again. Whipping his head around, he caught sight of a massive gray blur that slunk past the kitchen table and through the doorway into the dining hall without hesitation and before Everard could move.

The wolf.

Ten

GRAY PAWS

MARCUS STOOD ON wobbly legs, using the table to hold himself upright. Everard dashed from the room, his long stride taking him enviably far in a matter of seconds.

The sounds of confused and worried exclamations from the dining hall full of wounded men grew like the rumbling of thunder before a storm.

"God, please protect us all." Marcus pulled himself toward the door. A wolf in a room full of men, too injured to defend themselves and all smelling of blood and death, could not be a good mix. And certainly not in the beginning of winter when the beasts had just started to run out of food.

By the time he made it to the doorway, the wolf was nowhere in sight, just soldiers and peasants alike, attempting to gather themselves into a defensible position should it return.

"Where did it go?" Marcus felt his heart rate slow again. This didn't feel wholly wrong. Or at least not as wrong as it should. Why was he suddenly feeling that cloak of peace that liked to settle its comforting hands around his shoulders when it was needed most?

A few fingers pointed him toward the stairs, and instead of feeling the intense dread over the women and children who populated the rooms above, he grew calmer. The Lord had a purpose in this. He didn't know why or how or what on earth a wolf had to do with God's divine plans, but there was a reason for her journey through the tavern and up the stairs.

Dilara.

Her name was like a warm spring breeze that blew through his mind, spinning his thoughts. He knew better than to question those gut feelings, because they usually came from outside of himself and were more often right than wrong.

It took him longer than he would have liked to make it to the stairs, and even longer to climb them. If only stairs could move of their own accord. The chill had left his body in its entirety by the time he made it to the landing at the top of the staircase. The uneasy murmurs from the patients downstairs over the wolf in the building could still be heard in snatches. A few arguments about how they should kill the beast or protect the others started, the echoing voices, broken and harsh with pain, sounding irritable and groggy.

The door to Dilara's room was open, and his heart led him there first. Everard's broad shoulders were blocking the doorway, but he shifted when Marcus tried to enter. The sight that met his eyes was not one he would soon forget. His heart lurched into his throat.

The wolf, seeming larger now that it was in a confined space, settled back on its haunches, its nose resting on Dilara's forearm. The animal's ears were turned toward the feverish girl, and it's dark eyes, glinting in the candlelight, stared straight ahead at the flushed and pain-filled face.

Everard's hand descended on Marcus's shoulder, resting softly, but with enough weight to settle his fast-beating heart. For some reason, this creature not only knew Dilara, but it had resonated with her in some way, sensing her pain and feeling the need to comfort her in it.

Marcus could not wait to ask their patient the story behind such a phenomenon.

But the Lord worked in mysterious ways, and with a small smile of relief, he felt at peace in the presence of the wolf. It reminded him of the verse that spoke of entertaining angels unawares. His knees started trembling like jelly, and he moved his crutches to accommodate, leaning more weight against them. The adrenaline spikes had plateaued, leaving him with very little in the way of reserves. Had it been just last night that the battle had taken place?

Elgon would be gone in the morning. And though he had Fendrel and Everard standing right here in this room, Elgon's departure felt like a tie being broken. Marcus's knees wobbled even more, and Everard, barely breaking his watch from the wolf, slowly moved a chair to the foot of the bed and maneuvered Marcus by the shoulders into it. Marcus stretched out his hand to rest upon the quilt, relaxing his torso into the foot of the mattress, taking some of the weight off his right hip.

He knew he was exhausted. Hence why the sudden loss of the only tie Marcus still had to Violet seemed to overwhelm him so.

Rensen, the taverner, entered the room warily, the tankard of the 'witch's brew,' as his wife had called it, clutched in his hand.

"Well, I'll be," he whispered, his voice gruff and soft in the quiet room. "I've never seen the likes of it. That wolf must be domesticated; she's as gentle as a lamb." The breathless remark brought Marcus's eyes back to the wolf.

A truer word had never been spoken. He drew a breath, feeling his muscles relax a little in the hush of the sick room. But then he froze. The wolf's eyes were on him. Black as coal, with a tiny flame flickering within them.

That wise gaze held his own. The animal of the wood had seen far more than he, and he knew there was a different spirit about it. This was more than a wild beast. More than an animal. More than a huntress of the forest.

This was a protector. A healer. And as strange and confusing as it may be, Marcus felt at home, safe in her presence. He did not doubt she had been sent for some purpose to them, to Dilara. This she-wolf, the predator of the mountains, was also a mother. He could see it in her eyes.

Perhaps that is what had drawn her to Dilara. They shared the same walk of life. And every mother had need of being mothered themselves at some point along the way.

She could feel the wolf's presence. Its heat radiated into her back through the flimsy excuse for a coat that hugged her slender frame. She blinked, her eyelids burning in the cold, stinging wind. It was as frigid as her heart felt at the moment. Numb, without life. How far could one cease to exist while still existing? So much of her was void of any feeling that she almost wondered if she was dead. And if this was heaven, what mad trick of fate was this? And if it were hell, where was the fire?

White flecks dotted her cheeks, their sting the only feeling that registered. Their soft whiteness whispering down to the ground and reflecting the moonlight dizzied her sight, making her blink again. A tiny puff of steam came from her nose on her next breath. Good. She was alive.

A howl sounded off in the distance, and her body convulsed in a phantom cramp. No, a contraction. She felt empty.

Void.

Barren.

She tried to move her head and caught sight of a hollowed out log off to the side. Its bark protected the interior from filling with the snow that was raining down on them with the persistence of a mountain stream. She tried to swallow, but her tongue was dry.

As empty as she felt, she needed to do something. Anything. Even with the warmth of the wolf, she would die here on this mountainside. If not by her own negligence, then by the savage hands that would find her if she lingered for too long. Opening her mouth, Dilara caught a few snowflakes on her tongue. Their frozen water turning to life-giving droplets within her mouth. She turned her head, using her tongue to scoop up some of the snow that rested on the ground next to her face, the ice crystals scraping against her frozen and tender skin.

The animal at her back shifted, another howl in the darkness of the forest sounding again, closer this time. A whisper joined it, and her heart thudded harder in her chest. There was life there after all. Pulling in a larger breath, she gulped in the frigid air like it was her lifeline. This move would take everything in her, but she needed it to survive. She had to.

Gripping a fistful of snow like it was an anchor, she rolled from her side up onto her knees, her stomach clenching with the effort and her gaze whirling in a blur of spinning, barren treetops and evergreen pines. Her eyes squeezed shut along with her hands, grasping at the thin threads of reality that were humming like a harp, whispering a lullaby through the wind whistling in the treetops. Sleep had never sounded so good.

But no. She blinked into the dim light from the nightly celestial being casting a compassionate gaze upon her and met the eyes of the female wolf in front of her. They were wide, staring, open, trusting, and dark. Understanding lit the space between them with its slow, burning heat, giving her a breath she wasn't sure she could take.

A few steps—if only she could crawl just a few steps to the log, tuck herself within its open center. It would be the perfect place to hide out of the elements and out of sight from her captors. If she knew Conri at all, she knew he would come after his prize. He had poured too much into her over the years to let her go without a fight.

She remembered the God that a few of those she had met in her life insisted was real. He was her only chance. She had none on her own, so what could it hurt to ask?

"Help…me." The words, a raspy whisper, were torn from

her tongue by the winter blast. The wolf whined, standing beside her as she wavered on all fours herself, leaning its head into her shoulder with a soft nose. Nuzzling her, the she-wolf reached her head under Dilara and bore some of the immense weight that her body had suddenly become. Strength seemed to flow from the creature into her very bones, and she moved a few paces in a crawl.

Her heart suddenly puttered to a momentary stop, and she glanced around her in the dim light, frantically searching. Her baby. Tears fell unheeded from her eyes, freezing to her cheeks. The blood had been covered by a soft layer of snow, and her red scarf was missing. A sob wrenched her gut, and she reached out a hand to start digging in the snow, searching for the child of her womb. The remaining link to the only thing that had ever been hers and hers alone. But with the effort, her arms collapsed, dumping her onto her face in the snow, her arms shaking as she tried to rise again.

Something gripped her tattered coat between her shoulders, and she had just enough support to crawl to the log as another deafening blast of wind rattled the tree branches, their crashing and clacking a sickening sound. Tumbling inside, she realized how small she was and how large the tree was that had breathed its last and tumbled to the forest floor. It must have been standing dead for quite some time to be so hollow. A shiver wracked her small form as she curled up inside the unlikely shelter.

She had been much like this tree, standing, dead on the inside, broken within, hollowed out and empty as daily life moved on around her. Tears fell unchecked down her cheeks as the she-wolf crawled in beside her, her body nearly larger than Dilara's own. Her nose touched the tears falling from Dilara's face, and she wondered that she wasn't afraid of the beast.

It was hard to fear something when you had lived through worse. And this creature clearly wished her no harm. Dilara's body shook and trembled by turns as some heat from the soft, fluffy gray coat of the wolf soaked into her skin, and her tears continued to fall. When would they end? Would they never dry up? Or would they flood the log she used for shelter, drowning her alive in their depths?

She rested her head against the cold bark, welcoming the rough patches against her face as the darkness deepened and a soft guttural chirping sound came from the wolf at her side. She shuddered in a breath. Not only had her baby's life been taken from her, but she had even lost the opportunity to bury him.

Heat coursed through her body, and a shudder shook the bed frame, making Marcus cringe. It had been a long night; a frozen dawn was just on the horizon, and he glanced again at the icy patterns that brushed the window with their artistic fingers, tracing patterns with his eyes as they took on shapes such as flowers, trees, mountains, and rivers in his mind's eye. The wind howled, and a wolf echoed it in the distance. The gray-coated creature at Dilara's side barely moved, but her ears twitched, never once taking her dark-eyed, intense gaze from the girl on the bed.

There was a darkness circling the room. Toying with them, drawing nearer. Even the wolf seemed ill at ease, though it didn't move. Fendrel's tired, worried eyes and his shake of the head every time he checked Dilara's vitals made Marcus's chest feel heavy. There was something about this girl he had rescued that he felt drawn to. He didn't know what it was, but there was something more than just his usual hope that a patient would survive beating away in his chest. He could sense the pain trying to overcome her, the panic in her movements, the unsettled fluttering of her hands over the quilt as her eyelids flickered with dreams, restless even in sleep.

There was a deeper battle at stake in this room than merely that for health. It was life or death, and perhaps for more than just her physical body. The snow pounded at the window with a gust of wind that rattled the wooden shingles of the roof above his head. A chill shivered down his spine. So he did the only thing he knew to do in times like these.

"When you lie down, you will not be afraid; yes, you will lie down and your sleep will be sweet." His voice was tired but grew with strength as the words flowed from his memory like a stream trickling downhill. "Do not be afraid of sudden terror, nor of trouble from the wicked when it comes; for the Lord will be your confidence and will keep your foot from being caught."

Dilara's white-knuckled grip on the quilt released slowly, her eyes still fluttering beneath their lids.

"He that dwelleth in the secret place of the most High shall abide under the shadow of the Almighty. I will say of the Lord, He is my refuge and my fortress: my God; in him will I trust. Surely he shall deliver thee from the snare of the fowler, and from the noisome pestilence. He shall cover thee with his feathers, and under his wings shalt thou trust: his truth shall be thy shield and buckler. Thou shalt not be afraid for the terror by night; nor for the arrow that flieth by day; nor for the pestilence that walketh in darkness; nor for the destruction that wasteth at noonday." The remainder of Psalm 91 rolled from his tongue as it poured from his heart, filling the little room with a warmth that could not compare to the flickering fire on the hearth.

Darkness retreated to the corners as the words continued to flow. So much of Scripture was buried deep within him that he didn't even need to take the small book from the pocket of his vest in order to recite it. Psalm 23, then Psalm 103 added a certain light and amber warmth to the room that hadn't been there a mere moment before.

His voice grew raspy, and he reached for a glass of water on the bedside table. His pause made the wolf turn her head to observe him, almost as if she was wondering why he wasn't still speaking. Dilara moaned upon the bed, more agitated than she had been over the last space of time. Both she and the wolf settled the minute he resumed his recitations, and he smiled. Hope had a healing effect.

A warm hand on his shoulder woke Marcus from his slumber. He lifted his head from where it had fallen on top of the foot of Dilara's bed and shook the sleep from his fuzzy brain. Fendrel smiled down at him, his wizened hand still resting on his shoulder. After quoting and singing psalms and hymns to Dilara all night, he must have dozed off.

Winter sunlight streamed in through the window, lighting the room and making the shadows of the night before seem lost to everything but his memory. He wondered if he had simply imagined it.

"Dilara?" Marcus winced at his own raspy voice and tried to stretch out his shoulders at the same time that he stretched out his right leg. He grimaced. His leg was asleep. A sigh tumbled forth. He knew the numbness would give way momentarily to sharp pain and then a muscle ache for the rest of the day, but it would have been worth it if it helped Dilara recover.

"Her fever broke in the night. She is weak, but I think she will do well. She is young, and it won't take her as long to recover as she might think. Encouragement will be key over the next few weeks. As it will be for all those who crossed the border. Internal wounds are more numerous and deeper than those we can see. And many need to be healed still, but the Lord is already at work." Fendrel's silver eyes sparkled in the sunlight.

"Perhaps you should get some sleep." Marcus could tell that his old friend was reaching the end of his physical resources. Fendrel was probably running on nothing more than the grace of God and tea.

Surprisingly, Fendrel nodded. "I may just do that for a spell. Everard is downstairs tending the wounded again and helping move everyone around to accommodate our landlady and her need to serve meals to the guests. I'm sure she is none too pleased that her dining room has been relegated to an infirmary. Now that you have gotten some sleep, you should do your best to move around and get some blood flow going, or you may regret your decision to sleep in a chair."

Marcus nodded, accepting Fendrel's assistance with an arm

about his waist to leverage him to a standing position where he rolled his hip joint with a groan and stood taking deep cleansing breaths as the blood returned painfully to his crippled leg. When the dull ache was all that remained, Fendrel handed him his crutches and patted him on the back. "Get some nourishment and even step outside now that it's daylight. You could use the fresh air."

The medicinal retreated from the room with the first yawn Marcus had seen him indulge in over the last few days. He smiled and shook his head. It was a wonder how Fendrel survived. It could only be the Lord's sufficient strength and grace, but it never ceased to be a marvel. Fendrel could run for days on no sleep in an emergency, and only when the last patient had been tended to and all was right again, then—and only then—would the exhaustion catch up to him, only to be slept off in a manner of eight hours or less. A wonder indeed.

Dilara was slumbering peacefully, the heavy flush gone from her pale cheeks, and the nervous hand movements lost to death-like sleep. The best thing for her under the circumstances. The she-wolf was no longer staring worriedly into her patient's face but now reposed, curled upon the carpet that rested next to the bed. Her eyes were closed, and her face laid over her crossed front paws. When Marcus moved toward the door, she opened one of her eyes before huffing softly and returning to her slumber.

Marcus felt a chill go down his spine. There was something of God in the way that wild animal had not just taken to Dilara but had seemed to put aside all beastly urges and acted as a spoiled guard dog. "The Lord works in mysterious ways."

Dilara woke the next morning with the gray eyes of her wolf protector staring into her own. She reached out a hand and patted the large gray head timidly, but the animal simply chirped low in her throat before turning her head to accept the affection with appreciation.

For the first time, Dilara was hungry. She felt as though she had merely awoken from a long sleep and desperately desired food and water, but had forgotten—or perhaps she only tried to forget—the dreams that had plagued her. She was surprised when Marcus told her she had been asleep for two days.

The taverner's wife, whom she learned was named Keitha, bustled in with a bowl of delicious smelling soup and a steaming wedge of bread covered in goat cheese. That plate was possibly the most glorious thing Dilara had seen in her life.

"Well, isn't it just a happy sight to see your beautiful eyes winking at the world! Here, dear, let me help you sit up a bit. It's about time you ate something delicious instead of whatever those two medicinals have been trying to give you with their witch's brews of tea concoctions." Keitha made a wry face and wrinkled her nose while she fussed with Dilara's pillows and quickly but gently moved her into a more comfortable, half-sitting position. "Awful smelling things, those. I can't possibly understand how you abide them. Excuse me," the woman spoke in an aside to the wolf who had opened her eyes to watch the woman. "I'll do my best not to get into your way, majesty." Then in a conspiratorial whisper behind a hand to Dilara, "The thing acts like she owns the place. Like she's the queen or some such nonsense."

Keitha stirred the steaming bowl and held a spoon to Dilara's lips, which she blew on, then swallowed with relish. Chicken stew, the broth warm, rich, and flavorful with a touch of salt and sage. Her tongue sang with delight.

"But that animal of yourn has another thing coming if she thinks she can intimidate me. I, a taverner's wife who has recently entertained the very king of Elira himself. Can you believe it? Wolves can make nice pets. My sister-in-law raised a pup when she were a little one, and it was the most faithful guard dog anyone could ask for. Did you raise yours as a pup?"

Dilara had taken as many mouthfuls of the soup as Keitha could ladle in that short monologue, but her mind was whirring. It still felt like it was a wagon with stuck wheels, and the woman's words were more or less flying past her mind without truly being processed. "I—"

"Never you mind, dear. Just eat your soup like a good girl and get some rest. If you keep this down well, I'll get you that bread and cheese. It's been a big hit with the soldiers and refugees alike downstairs and up. We haven't seen a full house like this in years."

"How are you, well—" Dilara nodded out the door. She had seen the large swarm of people who had crossed the border before she had collapsed, and the idea of them all dwelling in this inn astounded her.

"We have plenty of room. Always have. It's a blessing, ain't it? Truly seems like providence that the Lord would give us the capacity to take all His children in during their time of need. The neighbors are helping, of course. Pavlin has seen its share of hard times under the chancellor's reign, but now that King Elgon took back the throne, we have started to see brighter days.

"It may take a while for the Kingsmen to earn back my trust, but they went a fair piece toward it the other day when they fought back those Rusalks like their very lives depended on it. I won't forget the sights and sounds of that battle very easily." Her voice faded, and she swallowed as she scraped the last few vegetables from the bottom of the soup bowl with the wooden spoon.

Dilara noticed tears had gathered in Keitha's eyes, and while she had no idea what the woman was truly talking about, she knew that whatever had happened in the last few days had taken this woman farther into a place of trust than she could have ever expected.

Eleven

MOUNTAINS OF MEMORY

THE DAYS THEREAFTER moved somewhat swiftly while also feeling unearthly slow at the same time. Dilara felt some comfort in the nearness of the she-wolf that had adopted her and seemed to never leave her side. Sleep visited her fitfully, but sleep brought back the darkness of the forest with a force she dreaded. With so many people floating in and out of her room like ghosts, there was very little opportunity for her to let any of the pent up feelings loose. Nor did she want to. There was some comfort in locking her scars away and walling them off from the world with bricks that were about as impenetrable as the border wall. It seemed fitting. Perhaps if she could pretend that she had left all of the old scars, brokenness, and pain behind the stone wall when she crossed over into Elira, the land of freedom, then she could survive over here without them.

After all, she had yet to meet anyone with the same evil

look in their eye Conri or any of his cronies had worn. Even Soria's tired eyes and broken heart that had been masked by violence and betrayal was not to be found in this place. Maybe the whispers of Elira that had come in the form of gossip from the other girls she had lived with had been true. Maybe there were less men like Conri here.

Marcus and Fendrel certainly seemed to be cut from a different cloth. She was wary of them, eyes open at all times. Fendrel reminded her of an energetic grandfather with his snapping and vibrant silver eyes, and his swift but gently moving hands. He never seemed to grow tired. There was a large shadow of a man who lurked in the hall and never entered her room, but Marcus had told her his name was Everard. He had said the man did not want to alarm her and chose to stay in the hall so that she might be granted her privacy. She was curious but also grateful for the unexpected courtesy.

Getting to know two men and trusting them with her care was hard enough. Every other man she had come in contact with had either betrayed her, or she had wished they had. Most of it felt like a dream. Too good to be true and too pure for this world. Marcus, especially, intrigued her. She saw a brokenness behind those cornflower blue eyes that reminded her of summer days spent picking wildflowers in the mountains as a child. The pain mirrored hers. But there was also a peace that rested on his shoulders like a light summer cloak. She couldn't discern what it was, but she felt as though she could—or should—trust him.

Yet while one should never trust a stranger, the feeling was there all the same.

Dilara always felt herself thrill a little inside when she heard the thumping of his crutches. She was unsure as to why she felt disappointed when they passed her door, and she would relax into her pillow again, wondering what he was doing, what other patients he was tending, and what words of comfort and encouragement he was speaking over them. For the words that tripped off Marcus's tongue as if breathed from the deep caverns of his soul were inspired, always positive, and speaking of a God she wished she could know.

But Marcus's God was not the One she knew. No. The One she knew of was distant, turned a blind eye to the pain of mere mortals, and let unspeakable things happen to those that Marcus swore He loved.

The large wooden door creaked open, and she startled, shifting her back against her pillows and smoothing out the quilt in an effort to hide her trembling hands as Marcus entered, a box balanced expertly between the crook of his arm and his crutch. He stopped and used his foot to move the door out of the way, and she marveled at the ability he had to balance and complete mundane tasks in creative ways that made allowance for his infirmity.

"I brought something to keep your hands busy. I'm sure it gets tiresome staring at the wall all day. Though this beauty seems to be doing quite the job of keeping you company. Aren't you?" Marcus nodded to her protector, setting the box on the foot of the bed and adjusting his crutches so he could bend and give the she-wolf a pat on the head.

The animal stared at him with unblinking dark eyes; the only emotion she relayed was a slight flick of the tail and a gentle chirp in the back of her throat.

"'Atta girl. I don't know where you picked her up, but I bet she was a godsend getting over the mountains. Protection and all that."

Dilara didn't say a word. She didn't want to remember the flight over the mountain, and the moments spent with the wolf had been her most devastating. But something he said hooked at the memory, jostling it forward. It was strange that this animal should appear in her hour of need and not leave. No matter how strange for a wild wolf to turn tame, guarding a human as if it were her own pup. Godsend...

"If you don't want to do them, I'm sure I can find someone else."

Snapping back to the present, her vision flickered a little, reminding her that she was still an invalid. "Oh." Her voice broke. "I'm sorry. I would love to help if I can. You're right—it is tiresome not being useful. And, of course, I must earn my keep."

He shook his head, and she would have sworn that if his feet could have moved he would have stepped backward away from her.

"No, no...I—that's not what I meant. Of course you don't have to work to earn your keep. That wasn't it at all, I just...I don't know. You seemed lonely, and I—"

Silence filled the room awkwardly until the wolf nudged Dilara's hand on the coverlet, and she raised it absentmindedly to pet her. Dilara cleared her throat. "I would love to help. Please show me what you need."

He heaved a sigh of relief at her truce, the fear leaving his features as he pushed the box across the quilt toward her. Opening the small, carved wooden lid, he pulled out some scraps of soft, cream-colored muslin, a small set of sheers, and a few cloth sacks stuffed full with something that crinkled when touched.

"If you are able, I wondered if you might make these herbal sachets? They have been helpful to the invalids. Willow bark." He touched each of the sacks. "Ginger, and this is coneflower. Just put a pinch of each into a small square of this material, and use the string to tie them off. They should be small; we'll use them to brew tea to help with fevers and pain."

She nodded, using her hands to explore the tools and various items. "I can do that. Do you do this often? Prepare herbs?"

He nodded. "Fendrel showed me how when I was a little boy, and I've been working at it ever since. I wish it wasn't winter out now; I'd go explore the local plant life and see what new herbs I could add to my collection."

She gave another nod as she started cutting the squares of fabric with the sheers. It felt good to be useful, her hands moving almost without her needing to tell them to.

A giggle at the doorway and a clatter of small feet promptly followed by a "Shush!" met her ears, and Marcus's face blossomed into a smile that almost took her breath away.

"Well, I'll leave you alone now." His voice held a stage seriousness, and he spoke louder than necessary. "I have some very urgent patients to see, if you'll excuse me." He threw her a wink that she was entirely unsure what to do with; it surprised her enough to make her slip in her cutting and snip thin air. She shook the cobwebs from her brain with a frown as she watched him gather his crutches beneath his shoulders, pat the wolf on the head one last time, and head for the giggles and whispers that congregated just outside her door.

He flung it wide with an "Aha!" and squealing came from without and the clatter of feet as they tore down the hallway. Little feet. Dilara felt a small smile rise to her lips. Even when experiencing the harshest of pain, a child's giggle could always bring a smile to one's face. She strained to look through the crack in the door as she heard Marcus growl like a bear and clump after them. She bit her lip. If only she could watch the tableau unfolding outside her room.

The sachets were done sooner than she expected, and she laid them out in neat rows back in the box, tying off the diminished bags of herbs with the drawstrings sewn into the top. She shut the lid and ran her hands over the top. While there were certainly a few carved decorations near the corners, it was a plain box. An open space waiting to be turned into something beautiful.

Her fingers itched with inspiration, and she reached for the burnt stick that had been used to light the candle and that rested on the wax-covered dish. The black, charred side would do nicely.

Brushing a hand over the box to clear off any dust or herb fragments, she used the coal to brush a few strokes onto the smooth and well-worn wood. The peace of the Kaira mountains rose on her wooden pallet, and she added a few of the fir and cedar trees that dotted the cliffs. Next came her cabin, her childhood home where it rested snugly in a little valley, perched just before the river carved deep into the mountains. Her hand trembled at the remembrance of her last time there, but she drew a breath and instead thought of the happy times when she would get lost for hours, playing make-believe in the forest and making flower crowns out of the cornflowers and daisies that dotted the valley.

The Kaira mountains, full of promise, majesty and beauty, but hiding ugliness deep within their crags and crevices.

Marcus chased off the children with a playful roar, grateful he could get a break while they enjoyed some of Keitha's delightful soup. Many of the soldiers who had been too injured to travel back to Niran with Elgon were now mending nicely. The last few weeks had given them enough time to gain some strength back and be able to engage with those around them, their pain having lessened. A few more dire cases still fought infections in the rooms upstairs, and Marcus felt the smile fall from his lips as a prayer winged heavenward from his heart. He was grateful he had the Lord and His Word to rely on, because, by worldly standards, there was little hope for those who fought for their lives in the rooms lining the tavern's second-story halls.

A loud giggle escaped from the table along with the clatter of cutlery as a soldier made a face at one of the children, who exploded in laughter, causing soup to come out of his mouth and land back in his bowl. Marcus grimaced at the sight and then chuckled.

It felt good to laugh.

The people of Elira were resilient, and it seemed as though the people of Rusalka would fit right in.

"Lord, protect Jaromir." The old man was still nowhere to be found after the attack. Some of the kingsmen thought perhaps some Rusalkans had captured him and taken him back over the wall. Whatever the case, it left little Kahru in Marcus's and Fendrel's care, and as the boy regained his strength with the quickness and agility of a young child, it was becoming increasingly difficult for Marcus to answer the child's inquisitive questions of when his grandfather would return.

Everard stomped into the room, a child on either shoulder and another clinging to his ankle, the latter child's small bottom resting on top of the man's large boot.

Marcus shook his head. Children were a blessing and a gift from God, that was for certain. He whispered a prayer of protection over Elgon and Violet's little one and smiled as he thought of Violet as a mother. She would be majestic and protective, and it made his heart sing to see some of the restoration and gifts she was receiving after having lost so much.

Sighing, he gathered his crutches again for the trek back upstairs. He winced, then glared at the staircase which was proving to simultaneously be the death of him as well as strengthening muscles he didn't know he had. As was evidenced by the soreness that plagued him the more he climbed.

Huffing and out of breath when he reached the top of the stairs, Marcus clenched the handles of his crutches and stretched out his hip before stepping back into Dilara's room after a furtive knock to signal his entrance.

Dilara startled despite his effort to alert her, those wide eyes reminding him more of a startled deer than they had before. He caught his breath. Those eyes would haunt him to his dying day. "I'm sorry, I didn't mean to startle you."

"I'm so sorry," she murmured, trying to clean something in front of her.

"What on earth for?" He stepped closer, hobbling with his three-legged stride across the wooden floor. The wolf took this moment to slink from the room, obviously deeming Marcus fit company for her mistress and probably headed for her twice-a-day turn outside.

"I wasn't thinking. I'm sorry." Dilara pulled her sleeve down over her hand and started to swipe at the lid of his herb box.

"Don't! Wait." Marcus held up a hand, confused by why hers were shaking and at the obvious fear in her eyes when she froze in obedience to his command. He berated himself internally. He shouldn't have spoken so sharply. He remedied it with a softer tone for his next words. "May I see?"

She swallowed, her hands still trembling as she handed him the box, and he noticed the black coal smudging her fingertips.

Taking the item, he looked down at the lid and his eyes widened. How she had been able to capture the Kaira mountains in such a beautiful and recognizable way with simple charcoal on wood boggled his mind. A little cabin nestled in a valley, and trees hugged the crags of the mountains, their cedar and pine like sentinels on the cliffscape.

"Did you draw this?" he said with wonder, his eyes loath to leave the drawing as he glanced up at her face. Freckles dotted her nose. Color flooded her cheeks, and she dropped her gaze to the quilt that she was nervously picking with her fingertips.

"Yes. I'm so sorry."

"You have no reason to be sorry, Dilara. This is beautiful. I almost wish that it was painted so it would stay forever. I'll be sorry to see the drawing smudge off with wear." His eyes traveled the mountains on the box again, and he drew a sharp breath at a pang that shot through his heart. She had used charcoal. He glanced at her, but not just at her, instead seeing through her. Into the wounded heart beneath the frail and delicate shell.

He didn't know the details, but her spirit cried out in pain. He knew the look. He had tended to hurt and wounded things since he was a child. Once so little that he barely knew how to string words together when he had cared for the first bird he'd discovered with a broken wing. He had learned and cultivated a discernment that somehow knew the depths of pain in another's heart.

And with that discernment, he knew Dilara carried much. The scars were so fresh they had yet to scab over. Seeing her create something so beautiful out of something that most would call black and dirty held divine meaning. As a medicinal, he knew that charcoal was used as a purifying agent and for purging of impurities. And the idea struck him as inspired.

What if creating pictures could be Dilara's way of purging the pain and darkness that held her soul in such tight shackles? He swallowed, feeling so right about it deep in his gut. This discovery could not be an accident.

"Have you always had such a gift for creating pictures?" Marcus kept his voice low as he set the box back on the bed and reverently ran a finger around the edge of the wooden frame.

"I haven't really had a chance to before. I've always toyed with charcoal when I had the time and no one was looking, but I've rarely been able to draw pictures in such detail." She glanced questioningly between him and the box, almost as if shocked he was taking such an interest and yet confused as to his meaning.

"What if I procured parchment for you? And more charcoal? Even paints. Have you tried painting before?"

"I—I haven't. How does that work?" Life and light, hesitant and timid, but there nonetheless, colored her voice.

His brain was spinning with excitement and ideas. Praying silently, he gathered the tea sachets she had made, admiring her work on them. "I have flowers and herbs in my wooden chest. I brought many to be used while tending the refugees, but I can spare some. We can make a paste from them of different colors, and you can draw in more than black and white. Would you like to try?"

She shook her head. "I don't want to cause you any trouble."

"Tsk." He bit his tongue before he told her not to be foolish, cringing at how terrible that would likely sound to her sensitive heart. "'Tis no trouble. I'd be happy to do it, and I think...I think it would do you good. It might even go a long way to making you well again." He clamped his lips together, feeling an urging to hold back any further thoughts from her.

Her eyebrows scrunched at his cryptic words, but she nodded. "Thank you. I think I would like to try, if you think it would help."

He smiled. "Absolutely. I'll bring this back downstairs and see what I can find. I think Keitha should be headed up with some soup and tea for you soon."

Dilara nodded, and he could sense a hesitant trust blossoming between them. The smile on his face widened. Even frightened deer soon grew to be comfortable near those that tended them.

Stepping from the room, he crossed the hall to visit Kahru. The child was mending so quickly that Marcus was going to let him out of bed today for a walk across the room. Happiness wriggled in his stomach like butterflies, and he felt some of the weight release from his shoulders. More than a few patients were improving today, and it was a dose of hope to his weary soul.

Setting the box down on the foot of the bed, he scolded Kahru for jumping up so quickly and bouncing on the tick mattress with all the pent up energy that a five-year-old could muster. "Now, now, take it slow, I said. We must get you well so when your grandfather returns, he will be happy with the care you received and not give me any trouble for letting you get up before you are healed. Slow, slow…" Marcus shook his head. The little boy had been feverish and languid for so many days, he couldn't help but grin and shrug at the sudden energy he exhibited. It was a good sign, though he would have to be careful. Hopefully Kahru would stop when the pain caught up with him. Better to let a patient's body dictate the needs of sleep, rest, and movement.

He hobbled alongside Kahru's slow journey from bed to fireplace and back, his little limp mimicking Marcus's own as he hobbled on with his broken leg in its sturdy splint. Glancing out the window, Marcus drew a breath at the magnificent sight of the Kaira mountains visible over the lower treetops on this side of the tavern. It was just a few snowy mountain caps, but it was finally clear. The snow storm that had lasted for a few days had lifted, for the moment at least.

Dread filled his soul, and he stumbled, catching himself on his crutch. Swallowing back the suddenly bitter and dry feeling on his tongue, he drew a shuddering breath and started muttering prayers under his breath. Something was wrong. He could sense it. But prayer was the only tool the Lord had lent to him at this time, and it would have to be sufficient.

He drew a calming breath to still the trembling that had hit him at the sudden sense of doom he had just encountered. Prayer might just be the mightiest weapon of all.

Twelve

PAIN UNBURIED AND RAW

MARCUS DREW A DEEP breath, that painful feeling deep in his gut nearly slicing him in two. He was on the verge of panic at any given moment, but he shoved it down, rewrapping the injured arm of the kingsman he was tending and reassuring him that he would be recovered soon. He whispered prayers under his breath, asking the Lord for safety for Jaromir every time he came to mind. Something was amiss, but there was nothing Marcus could do but pray. Kahru asked after his grandfather every time Marcus stepped foot in his room, but there was no news to give him.

Today, Fendrel had carried Kahru into Dilara's room, and Marcus had left them both drawing on parchment pieces together.

Dilara had taken to art like a deer to the forest. Life flooded those deep brown eyes when there was a piece of charcoal in her hands, and the pictures she drew took his breath away. Mountains, streams, forests—but it was the dark pictures that haunted him. The ones that felt like the blackest soul with the most haunting memories drew them.

Black, deep shaded corners, shadows falling ominously across the page, and a wolf, always lurking. Not a gentle one like the she-wolf who had taken up residence within the tavern as Dilara's self-proclaimed protector, but an evil, frightening menace with fangs bared and ears flat on its head.

A childish giggle came from his right, and he pretended not to have heard it as he gathered up his supplies. "You should be all set for the journey, captain. I wish you and your men Godspeed."

"Thank you. The king was right." The kingsman stretched his arm and rolled his wrist, admiring Marcus's neat bandage that covered the gash which, had it been a fraction to one side or the other, would have severed his arm from his body. Marcus paused, winding a scrap of a bandage around his hand neatly and without thinking. "What do you mean?"

"The king said you were the best healer and medicinal on this side of Elira, perhaps in the whole of it. That you have a true talent for the healing arts and that you would do everything within your power to ensure your patient got well. He was right. You *do* have a gift."

Marcus paused, the scrap still tangled around his fingers, and met the studying gaze of the kingsman. The man didn't waver—almost as if he spoke truth, which caused a whole other kind of pain to form in Marcus's chest. Like a salve over an open wound, hurting only because it was healing.

He had often wondered what place he had in this world and why God left him here to do so little for His kingdom. Elgon was serving the entire country; Violet had become queen and now served so many in her capacity. Word had already reached as far as Pavlin of the queen's good grace and her kindness to her subjects. People awaited the birth of their child with utmost delight, and they spoke of her with joy and reverence. All, at least, but some in Padsley it seemed. One often was without honor in their hometown.

Fendrel was the true master, teaching Marcus everything he knew. And Marcus often doubted whether anyone would feel any great loss over him if he were to disappear from the earth. What did he truly do that another could not?

He startled, realizing that the kingsman was asking a question and pinching his brow. "I'm sorry," Marcus said. "Thank you for your kind words; I do appreciate it."

"You seemed to fade out for a moment. Perhaps you are working too hard and need a rest." The kingsman patted Marcus on the shoulder. "You can't take care of everyone else and not take care of yourself. You told me that." He smiled kindly behind his beard and brushed a lock of hair off his forehead.

"Did I? Well, you might be right. Godspeed, captain."

"Aye. And to you." With a another friendly slap on the shoulder between them, the captain waved an arm at his subordinates and a handful of kingsmen strode out to the front of the tavern, letting in a gust of cold wind and snow crystals that skittered across the floor before they melted in the heat from the fire.

Another giggle penetrated Marcus's confused and addled brain a second before he was rushed from three sides, and tiny arms wrapped around his knees. His legs buckled beneath the weight.

Giggles turned to gasps as his crutches slid on the wooden floor and he slipped backward with a sharp intake of air. His surroundings blurred together as he fell to his back, his head thumping against the floorboards. Shockwaves shuddered through his vision as it clouded.

No air met his lungs.

Three little faces congregated above him worriedly, smiles gone from their faces as their mouths moved. Marcus couldn't hear their voices beyond the roaring in his ears and the panicked, internal screaming for air that sought to consume him. Pain seared from his hip, and involuntary tears leaked from the corners of his eyes before he finally gasped enough air to cough. A gasp and cough followed each other in quick succession before a groan escaped him as he tried to roll to his left side and off his blasted, aching right hip.

Thundering footsteps echoed through the room, and the small worried faces parted as Fendrel's own broke through the crowd. "Are you all right? Lord in heaven, Marcus, say something."

"I'll—be fine." A lie. Probably the worst he'd ever told, and by Fendrel's shake of the head, the medicinal knew it.

"Go get Everard." Fendrel commanded the oldest of the youngsters who looked thoroughly cowed and contrite before he ran off, brushing a few tears from his eyes. "Don't move,

Marcus." His hands sped over Marcus's form, checking for breaks.

Marcus pushed them away. "I said I'm fine." He wasn't entirely lying. The pain had subsided to a dull roar, and he wanted to move. *God, please.* He prayed that no lasting damage had been done. He wasn't prepared to spend weeks in bed as an invalid. Not again. Not now.

"You should spend the day in bed."

There it was.

"I'm truly fine. Just give me a moment to breathe." He tried to pull himself into a sitting position to regain some of his dignity, at least, but Fendrel held a hand to his shoulder.

His silver-brown eyes were full of concern, and his graying hair fell around his face like an oval frame. "Please, just lay there for a moment while you catch your breath. You can do that just as well lying as you can sitting. There's no hurry."

No hurry but to get myself off this floor. Begrudgingly he obeyed, despite his annoyance. He drew deep breaths in through his nose while trying to take his mind off the numbing pain that seemed to dance throughout his muscles to determine where and if he was actually hurt. His hip seemed to have taken the brunt of it, as usual. But the ache from it was sending muscle spasms through the rest of his spine and even into his shoulders. Sometimes the use of the crutches started to irritate his muscles, and he had been using them exclusively for some time these last few months. He couldn't wait to get back to just using his cane, but right now, that seemed further off than ever.

Everard appeared over them like some lurking shadow on a mountain peak. He didn't say a word, as per usual, but his looming presence grated on Marcus's frazzled nerves. He hated that he had to be watched over by these men like two mother hens.

"I'll be fine. I swear. Just let me up." He forced Fendrel's hand away, wincing at the sharpness in his own tone as he pulled himself into a sitting position. Bad mistake. He tried to straighten his right leg to the side to stretch out his hip and alleviate the pressure, but only successfully wrung a guttural moan from his lips.

Panting for breath, he looked desperately to Fendrel. "I think it's out."

Fendrel sighed with a compassionate shake of the head and maneuvered to Marcus's right side, where he swiftly and deftly, without a word of warning, placed a hand on Marcus's hip and another on his knee and rotated the leg back into position. The cry of distress that it dragged from him scared even himself.

Then he saw their little faces. His pain was mirrored on those of the children, coupled with fear. He felt tears sting his eyes at what they must be feeling. With sweat beading on his brow, he tried to smile at them. "I'm all better now. See, Fendrel fixed my leg. No harm done." His reassurances made their countenances brighten somewhat, but they looked back and forth between Fendrel's still worried face, Everard's impassive one, and Marcus's.

"He's right." Fendrel kept a hand on Marcus's shoulder. It was trembling. "Marcus will be fine. But he does need a rest now. This was no one's fault. Accidents happen. Now, run along and find something to play. I know you could play a game of straw pile if you just ask Mrs. Keitha; she'll be sure to assist you with the findings you will need for such a game."

They hesitated a moment, then dashed off to the kitchen like a bunch of rambunctious and disorderly puppies.

Marcus dropped his pretense of being all right and groaned. "Lord, that was a hard fall."

"And it's the reason you are going straight to bed."

Marcus scowled. "But I—"

"No objections, Marcus. You disjointed your hip. There will be plenty of work to be done later."

Marcus heaved a sigh. Back to the invalid's couch he would go. "I don't even know why you brought me along. Clearly, I'm more trouble than I'm worth."

"Never. My boy, you are exactly the right amount of trouble. No more and no less."

Marcus shook his head at Fendrel's cryptic attempt at humor. But it worked. He smiled a little, then grimaced again as Everard scooped him up like he was a child.

Fendrel went up the stairs ahead of them, and Marcus was surprised when they turned into Dilara's room. "You can keep each other company," the medicinal said.

Heat set his ears aflame and worked up his neck as Everard carried him in and set him on the bed on the opposite side of the room. He was grateful to be near the fire, though, as a chill crept into his bones.

"Thanks," he whispered to Everard. Everard sent him a slight smile—the only kind he seemed to give—in encouragement before leaving the room without saying a word.

"I'll have some tea brought up." Fendrel pinned him with a serious look. "You stay in that bed till I give you leave or I'm sending you back to Padsley."

Marcus knew it was an idle threat, but he nodded anyway. "I promise. Turmeric, right?"

Fendrel rolled his eyes. "I know how to mix your tea, Marcus. I taught you how, remember?"

Marcus felt a weak grin spread across his face. "I know. Just keeping you on your toes. You have a lot of patients to tend."

"Which I'll do with pleasure." Fendrel winked to Dilara before striding from the room.

Marcus didn't want to meet Dilara's eyes. He felt wholly exposed and vulnerable. It wasn't often that the patient had to see the medicinal in such dire straits. He closed his eyes with a wince as he shifted on the pallet, trying to find comfort on his tender hip.

"What happened?" Her voice was soft, carrying a slight rasp with it, and he opened his eyes, shifting upright against the pillows as well as he could.

He hadn't noticed the deep cleft in her upper lip before. With some more color in her cheeks, she was…well, stunning. She didn't look any different, but with the ravages of pain slowly taking a departure, she had a beauty about her that felt almost divine in nature.

He blinked and cleared his throat. "Some children rushed me, and I lost my balance." He grinned. "I wish I could say I had defeated some stalwart enemy, but no, I was taken down by three children who don't even make it to my waist in stature."

A smile brushed her full lips—possibly the first one he had ever seen from her. "You like children, don't you?"

"Of course. They are blessings and gifts from God. You?"

Pain swallowed her features, and she almost seemed to cave in on herself. Marcus mentally bashed himself for saying something so heartless. He had forgotten. She had lost a child on her journey.

"They have such entertaining personalities." He rambled on, not sure if that was the right topic to press into, his voice wavering with his indecision.

He saw her swallow, blink, and try to recover with deep breaths.

"What was your childhood like?" He hoped changing the focus would take her thoughts from her loss.

She shook her head. "Short."

He hesitated.

"Too short."

"What do you mean?"

Her eyes flashed. "Like everything else in my life, it was taken from me before I had a chance to experience much joy in it." Bitterness laced her words, so harsh it felt like singed ashes burning out at the touch of oxygen and then floating away, dry and useless.

He threw a prayer heavenward. *Give me the words to say. Help me to know what to speak and when to speak it. Let Your words flow from my tongue.* "I won't tell anyone if you want to talk about it. It might help." He kept his tone gentle, casual.

"Like my drawings?" She fluttered her hands around her, motioning at the sheets of parchment, different sizes, shapes drawn in charcoal scattered across their surfaces.

"Perhaps. Or you can ask me questions."

"What happened to your leg?"

Straight for the jugular, that one. He cleared his throat again. Blinked. His own rawness bubbling to the surface with that one question. He hated the pain that reliving the moments brought forth, but if telling his story helped her discover the grace of God in hers, then he would tell it a million times over.

"When I was a child, my parents were sent to the mines, and I was on my own. My friend, Violet, was like a sister to me, and her father treated me as his own son. I got in the way of some kingsmen one day. They were evil men in that day, ruled by black desires. The king has purged out the evil ones as best he can at this point, but then they lived by their own rules, especially in Padsley, where I'm from. It's the farthest town south of the capital, and there was a lot more leniency given to the captains and outpost there. They started beating on me. I've never been the same since. It's an infirmity that I have to live with. My hip isn't jointed correctly, and there is something wrong with my spine. Some days are worse than others, but by God's grace I can live with it. Even with these moments of setback when I'm forced to take a break from daily life, it's hard, but I get through it. I like to use these moments to get closer to Him and spend more time in His presence and in His Word." Marcus's hand instinctively moved to caress the book in his pocket.

Silence filled the room, the only sounds the winter wind and the crackling fire on the hearth. He pulled a card, wax, and thread from his leather pouch at his belt and started waxing the thread for later use. Perhaps if he had something stealing his attention, it would take away any pressure she might feel.

Then her whispered words floated across the silence to him, the she-wolf cocking her ears as if straining to hear her mistress. "I was on my way to the mines when I escaped."

He caught his breath. The mines were still somewhat of a mystery, especially to those this far south of them. Many people over the years had been sent for forced servitude there, and none had returned. Not a one. Either it was a life sentence, or there wasn't much life to live upon arrival.

"Why?" Marcus was far-fetched to think of even a remote reason for a young, beautiful, and strong girl like Dilara to be sent to the mines. Though, he wouldn't put much past a Rusalk.

"I had outlived my usefulness to them. They had already taken the one thing from me that provided the most value. And I would no longer heed their commands." Her face was emotionless. Stoic, almost without feeling entirely, and Marcus felt his heart lurch into his throat as his spirit instinctively burst into prayers. There was something deeper and more amiss than he had at first thought. He kept silent. There was nothing he could contribute, nor did he feel at liberty to say anything. *Lord, let her words be a release and bring healing.*

The pain was buried. Somewhere deep inside the caverns of her soul, coated in inky-black shadows, their memories so deep she couldn't call them to the surface...nor did she want to. Perhaps that was why even finding words felt like she was speaking around a throat that had been frozen solid, her vocal chords sealed.

Pressure built in her middle. Something bursting and aching to escape. The truth. The reality of what she had been through.

There was a trust in this room. A peace that she did not carry or match. It called to her, pulled at the chains shackling her suffering inside like a beast playing tug of war with its enemy. It begged her to speak, to release, to open her heart and let it explode out like a demon caged within. She started to tremble, the very act of holding it in exerting her beyond her physical limit for strength.

His pain mirrored hers. He could understand. His suffering was an image of herself staring back at her. The stolen dreams, body, and hopes of a child desperate to be loved. Desperate to be made whole. Broken, irreparable, and burdened with a suffering beyond their control.

The story poured like hot magma into her throat, scarring it like the rock, scorching her heart black, pouring up and out with a force she could not contain.

But peace met it. Was it compassion? What did compassion even feel or look like? How could she ever receive it again?

"I was sold."

Silence met her response, but it wasn't horrified, stunned, or even judgemental. Instead it was comforting. Compassionate. Open. Available. But all of the self-loathing boiled up inside her. It was her fault. She should have been a better child, a better daughter. More, right, perfect.

"My father sold me when I was eight. I was kept with other girls until I was deemed old enough. Conri, my owner...he kept me longer than the other girls, and I considered myself fortunate. But—it was only to— He wanted me for himself.

"When they found out I was pregnant, they didn't want me to keep the baby. They tried to get me to—to kill it." Her body was shaking harder. Anger roiling now. She was no longer a damsel in distress, but a blazing firebrand of bubbling acid and scorching flames. She didn't know where it came from, and it scared her. It felt so right but so wrong, pulling her soul apart and rendering it broken between the two. "I couldn't. The first time I felt him kick, I knew it was bone of my bone and flesh of my flesh. He was mine. Something I could hold onto. Something that they could not take from me." Anger lashed her words, leaving them bleeding, raw, and harsh. It tumbled out now. Unrestrained. Broken. Scalding tears burning the skin of her face like embers flying from a roaring fire.

"On the march to the mines, they gave me a poison. I didn't know until the pains started. I don't know how, but I was able to get away. I escaped in the middle of the night. Climbing the mountains in a blizzard. There had been talk of an escape, and I knew several others who disappeared from the slave train that night. I knew they were coming. I don't know why, but I knew I had to survive the night. To live. To go on. I shouldn't have lived." She shook her head, the tears flying off her face like a spring rain.

"But you did." Soft, soothing, like a balm upon a burning soul.

"But then the baby came, and there was nothing I could do to save him." A sob escaped, and she realized she was holding her arms in a cradle position. Empty. Woefully void. The flames licked higher. "I should have known better than to think I could be a mother. What kind of mother loses her own son?" She gasped for a breath, the shame of losing the one thing she should have been responsible for above all else. He had been her responsibility. Even in that she had failed. Had not been good enough.

"It wasn't your own fault."

Never had a greater lie been told, and the shame buried her deeper. She should have seen it coming, should have known of the poison, should have escaped earlier. Should have, should have, should have… "I should have—"

"Dilara, you did not cause this." Cool water to a dying child of fire, suffering of thirst.

"You don't know that. You weren't there. I could have stopped it."

"You did what you could; you escaped. You ran for your child. You stayed alive. You could have died on those cliffs. It's a miracle that you are alive."

"I feel like it is my anger that has helped to keep me alive." She tried to tamp down the flames that threatened to consume her, drown her without water.

"Or perhaps the Lord gave you the strength that you needed to meet each moment."

Dilara glanced at this man who was an enigma. A man who had no strength, but carried the strength of a thousand men within his heart like a torch aflame. "Perhaps. But then why did a God like that let these things happen?" Her heart broke, and the tears stung her eyes as she dashed them away from her face. Angry. She had been numb for so long that these tears, these sobs, felt like a betrayal, a reminder of a suffering she could have stopped.

"Why are you here?"

"What?" Her heart thudded with shock and confusion at the sudden change of topic.

Marcus set down the suture thread he had been waxing and winding around a card and looked her in the eyes. "How did you come to be here?"

Her eyes widened, and she caught her breath, understanding his meaning. "I would have never come to Elira..." she whispered, trailing off.

He nodded, his blue eyes deep pools, rippling with compassion. "What else?"

She thought for a moment, and the tears redoubled. "My...my son."

His eyes were locked to hers like the chains that had bound her at night after the first time she tried to run away.

"And...you."

He did nothing but blink; it was as if their breath was held in a collective attempt to keep the atmosphere even, the same...unchanging.

"I would have never met you."

"I know it's hard to understand now..." Marcus murmured, his voice barely above a whisper, his eyes still drilling past her face and into her very heart. "But your story knows no bounds with how God will use it. Your life was not a useless emptiness or waste of pain. Your life is full, meaningful, purposeful. Every breath you continue to take has a reason, and who are we to assume that to end it would be in the best interest of the world around us? Dilara..." His voice caught.

"To have never been or to change any part of your past would be to rob the world of who God created you to be and what you have become as a result of the sorrow and pain that has shaped you. What you will become. While it seems underwhelming to say 'how can we know His plans and purposes,' the reality is, they are far deeper, long reaching, and more impactful than we could ever imagine." He leaned forward as more passion filled his voice. "Just think about Jesus. His brokenness and sacrifice is still spoken of today, over a thousand years after he lived and breathed. And that was just one man. But God's plan was so infinitely greater than Christ's own that he willingly laid down his plan every single time it rose within Him to change the course of what was ahead.

"Dilara, even Jesus wished to change the life that was set before him. But I am infinitely glad that He did not."

"But—" The rawness grated in her throat. The effort to hold back the rush of anger and brokenness beating the walls to get out exhausting her. The worry of if she said too much, should even have talked of it at all, and that Marcus was not someone she could trust… The fear started to clamp its dark hand over her soul again. "How could a God who knows all and can use it all abandon me? Again and again?"

"Perhaps He didn't. Perhaps He was there all along, but you were without the eyes to see Him."

The weight of Dilara's story was like an anchor around his neck, but one that he felt given the strength to hold up. A story she had trusted him with, that God had given to him, and the responsibility was heavy. She had cried herself out and had drifted into an exhausted sleep. He could see the pain lacing her beautiful face from here. He saw it now. The stunning beauty of her full lips with the dimple on top. Her small, thin nose, those heavy lashes on eyes so wide and deep one could drown in their walnut depths. He shuddered. The things that had been done to her and taken from her were beyond understanding, and a greater thankfulness for those who had made it into Elira filled him.

But so did the pain over Jaromir. He prayed he was not abducted back into slavery. That his family could be rescued. That God could provide the miracle He had for Dilara to His other children. That Kahru would not be without his family forever. Marcus drew a faltering breath and tried to release each burden to the Lord, keeping his hand busy with the suture thread as he shifted on the mattress. Though still in pain, it had subsided considerably, and he felt sleep pulling at his own eyelids.

Stories of suffering were exhausting whether you told or heard them. But keeping hands busy was a great distraction from that pain and suffering. It eased the ache when instant gratification of productivity could be procured.

Marcus didn't know how many hours had passed when he was startled awake by a slamming door and loud chatter below.

The snow had picked up speed outside, and the window was a blaze of white swirls with not even a shadow of a tree limb making it through the white-out of snowflakes and blustering wind. Even the fireplace danced with an extra flare as the sound of a rush of wind rumbled down the chimney every few moments.

He glanced at Dilara who was sleeping, dimly visible in the faint glow of the fire. She simply stirred, tucking her hand beneath her chin as she curled onto her side. Her face carried the most peaceful look he had seen on it since she had arrived, and he smiled softly to himself. Letting out the pain and turmoil of one's story of struggle eased a burden people often didn't know they carried.

The chaos downstairs grew, and Marcus glared at his hip, simultaneously feeling the urge to jump out of bed but knowing that he shouldn't move too quickly so that he didn't cause any more trouble. Besides, Fendrel had told him not to move until he returned. But the noise grew louder, and with gritted teeth, he swung his legs over the edge of the bed, stood on his left one, and let his right foot dangle instead of putting weight on it. No sudden stab of pain followed, so with a scowl at the crutches placed so far away from him by Fendrel, the scheming old hen, he dragged his foot as he took a step that was more of a shuffle toward his crutches.

The wolf whined deep in her throat as she stood, watching him with her dark eyes. Sweat beaded on his forehead, and he felt his muscles tremble beneath the strain. Each limping step seemed even harder than the last, and he gripped the corner bedpost with a white-knuckled hold.

Marcus swallowed hard, trying to force back the rising frustration. He should be past this. Past the annoyance. Why hadn't he learned to live with this yet? It had been over a decade and still his infirmity came up to mock him, taunting him with his weakness, his inability to do the smallest of things for himself. Why had God left him on this earth if he were only a burden to those around him who were forced to carry it with no recompense or reward for their work?

"Lord, You made the lame man walk, so why do I remain lame? What did I do wrong to deserve this pain? To suffer and cause those around me to suffer with it? I know You can heal. I've seen You do it. I've witnessed the comfort You give and the life-changing capabilities of Your Spirit, but why do I still remain void of it? An empty vessel with nothing to pour out?"

"You are not empty. Your life is not an empty waste. Your story is not complete."

"But why don't you just heal me?"

"Why did Lazarus remain in the tomb for four days?"

The tears came faster than before, and Marcus's knees wobbled with the prolonged weight upon them. A soft, furry head snuck beneath his hand and took a portion of his weight with a low churring sound. Through blurry vision, he caught sight of the she-wolf at his side, her eyes still taking him in and her throat chirring with a high-pitched, comforting sound.

He let her take more of his weight, and like a miracle, she helped him to his crutches which he quickly placed beneath his shoulders in order to give her a better look. He never thought he would be this close to a wolf, let alone a wild one. But this animal was more than just a beast; she was an angel of comfort sent by the Lord's hand to those who needed it most. He patted her head, timidly at first, running his fingers over her soft ear, thick with fur. She leaned into his touch, her eyes seeming to never blink as she gave him a strength he didn't know he could receive.

He brushed away a tear that ran down his cheek. "Thank you for being who God made you to be," he whispered to her. She cocked her head a fraction of an inch and stared up at him.

His heart ached. Another layer of surrender of his hopes, frustrations, and pain laid down again at the foot of the cross. "My life for Your glory. Even the pain and the struggle. Even every frustration." His throat choked up, and his stomach ached with repressed emotion. "Though you slay me, yet will I trust in you."

Shouting voices echoed up the stairwell, and Marcus drew a deep breath, biting his lip as he angled toward the door, trying to keep his thumping crutches quiet so as not to wake Dilara. She had earned her sleep.

Another rush of wind rumbled down the chimney.

The door opened before he could open it himself, and he threw up a finger to his lips to warn the intruder to be quiet a second before he recognized the hurried and snow-bedecked gentleman in front of him.

"Jaromir?"

As if in a daze, Fendrel was at Marcus's side, whisking him out the doorway, into the hall, and closing the door of Dilara's room before Marcus even had a chance to blink.

Marcus drew a breath, his heart beating fast in his chest as he gaped at the grinning old man in front of him whose eyes were full of tears as assuredly as his beard was coated with ice crystals.

"Grandfather?" The tiny voice from the doorway across the hall was hesitant and hopeful. With a blur of blond hair and green tunic, Kahru had limped across the hall in his cast and jumped into Jaromir's arms. Laughter and tears mingled as the old man clutched the child to his shoulder with a grip that was tight enough to bar out the whole world as his hot tears cut rivers through the frozen skin of his face. Steam rose from the shoulders of his equally frozen cloak, and Kahru dug his face deeper into Jaromir's neck, his small hands holding fistfulls of the material as he giggled with joy.

Marcus was so transfixed by the reunion before him that he couldn't think or dare to move.

Two faces came up the stairs, their eyes hungry, desperate, hopeful. The man had Jaromir's eyes and nose, and the woman at his side had chapped lips and strands of hair frozen in tendrils around her face.

Kahru fairly lunged over Jaromir's shoulder with a heartrending cry of joy and was caught in the man's arms as all three of them sank to the floor, hugging, kissing, and crying. Marcus noticed their gaunt and trembling frames and their sunken cheeks, but the joy burning from their eyes was enough to melt the snow and ice that clung to them like burs from their past life melting away in the rays of a blazing sun.

Marcus was suddenly gripped in a hug that he felt would squeeze the life from him, crutches and all. His heart ached with a joy he hadn't felt in months, and tears trickled from his own eyes.

"Thank you, my friend. Your prayers have performed a miracle," Jaromir said.

Marcus patted the man's shoulder, a throaty laugh tumbling from him, laced with emotion. It was obvious what God had done. The image of a family reunited was enough to melt the hardest of hearts.

After the frenzy had died down, Jaromir gripped Marcus shoulder in his hand. "Remember how you told me that even if I wasn't ready to hear it yet, you knew God loved me? And that He had a plan for me, no matter what I could see with these tired old eyes?"

Marcus nodded, far too overcome to even attempt to speak at the moment.

Jaromir's grip tightened affectionately, and his eyes met Marcus's. "I see it now. He rescued my entire family and brought us out of a broken land and into a life of freedom. I couldn't have done or survived what I did without Him, and I see Him. I believe in Him now. Will you help me become like you? I want to believe in Him the way that you do."

Marcus blinked hard to clear his vision. He laughed around a choked sob. "You are already on the right track, my friend. And all you need do is ask Him. He's listening. Always and forever, He is near. He has given us His spirit to dwell in us that we may be in communion with Him every single moment of our lives. Would you like to invite Him in?"

Jaromir's eyes filled with tears, and his hands trembled under the weight of emotion. "We all would." He gestured to his children and grandchild as they gathered close, Kahru still grasped in his parents arms with a grip Marcus was sure would never let go.

Dilara listened to Marcus tell the story of Jaromir's family reuniting as she sipped the soup Keitha had brought to her for dinner. She had never seen a man bare his emotions in such a way before, and the extreme joy and passion that brought tears to Marcus's eyes equally surprised and unnerved her.

She shuddered when he spoke of Jaromir reentering Rusalka in order to find and rescue his children if he could. After three days of wandering in the forest, trying to find the trail, he had discovered their slave route heading back north on this side of the Kaira mountains. Nearly starving and weak from days spent hiking through the forest, he kept a close watch for his son and daughter-in-law as he huddled behind a copse of trees.

After a few hours, he finally saw them, and it was all he could do not to immediately rush to them. But they were under close guard, and as the moon drew closer to the skyline, he knew it wouldn't be long before his opportunity to help them escape would be gone. Desperately, he had prayed to the God whose love and mercy He didn't believe in, and shortly before dawn, the drunken guards fell into a deep, stupored sleep.

Jaromir had been able to sneak undetected into the camp and free his children and the rest of the slaves from their chains and escape into the woods. Their ragtag band had made it over the foot of the Kaira mountains and back into Elira by heading south. It took them six days just to reach the border as they fought through hunger, thirst, frostbite, and blizzards.

Marus soon realized that the night he had grown ill with worry had been the night that a pack of wolves had surrounded them. The refugees had nearly given up, but a mysterious sound had startled them off just in time, saving them from a horrific death in the jaws of the wild beasts.

So obviously had they seen the hand of God over their life and the miracle of them not only escaping, but surviving, the mountains in their malnourished and frozen state, that they could deny God no longer. The entire band—Jaromir, Kahru's parents, and the three other slaves they had freed—had accepted Christ and His Holy Spirit, declaring and committing to serve Him all their days, and they were celebrating over bowls of Keitha's broth downstairs this very moment.

Dilara tried to smile around her soup, but her heart ached harder than ever before. *Why do you only rescue some? If you are truly who Marcus says you are, why is your hand only used for some and not for another? You could have rescued me before Conri put his hands on me. Or even before Papa sold me to him. You could have stayed the hand that gave me poison, taking my son. But no, You did nothing. Why?*

"Dilara?" Marcus's voice echoed into the forefront, and she blinked, her wooden spoon clanking down into the bowl.

"I'm sorry. Did you say something?"

"You seemed a million miles away. Are you all right?"

She shook her head, then nodded. "I was thinking of something else. I'm fine."

His blue eyes seemed to pierce her soul, and she looked down, using her napkin to dab at the droplets of soup that had splattered from her dish. She couldn't meet that gaze. Couldn't abide the look of faith and joy radiating from his eyes like a summer sky. It burned her, sizzled against her frozen heart and the bitterness locked inside it. She wished she could trust as easily as Marcus, Jarmoir, and Kahru.

But her heart had been torn in two and nothing, it seemed, would mend it.

"I think I'm just tired. I seem to crave sleep even though it seems that's all I do of late."

He nodded, his eyes never once leaving her face. She started to feel the itch in her finger tips, memories too poignant to speak but begging to be released. "Do you think I could have some more paper? I don't want to keep using it, but…"

"Of course! I'll call Keitha and ask if she has more." She noticed him wince when he stood, and during his few steps toward the door, there was a hitch in his step accompanied by a sharp intake of breath. She saw his shoulders tense from behind, the muscles in his neck spasming for a moment as he let out a breath, taking a few deep ones before shaking his head and continuing on. Sadness overtook her at the sight of him. As if a young man of promise had been locked inside a broken body. The tears started to her eyes. She saw him anew. Chained to a fate he would not have chosen, a prisoner against his will, shackles holding him inside a cage of pain and infirmity.

She wrung her hands as he spoke to a child outside the door. Her fingers ached and trembled, begging for paper and a medium to spill the pain inside of her onto the page with its inky blackness. Flashes of memories assuaged her vision, and she took a deep breath, letting it out with a shudder as her own shoulders drew up with a tension she could not relax.

Something felt dreadfully wrong. She hadn't felt this raw, ugly, and broken since being here. The intensity of it was unmatched, and she felt sick to her stomach.

"Are you all right?" Marcus's voice was far away, echoing, and she couldn't see through the foggy lens of her vision to discern the shape of his expression.

She fought it, her body trembling and washed with heat all over. She drew in another deep breath, then another, feeling as though she were drowning under the weight of the darkness pressing in around her.

"Dilara, you are safe here. Nothing will harm you, I promise." His cool hands touched her spasming hot ones, and she jerked away.

She desperately wanted to grab hold of his hands. Hold onto something, anything that would allow her to trust. To break through the dark memories that threatened to bury her beneath their sharp sting of cold, frozen inside, locked away from any love. Was there a way she could feel that again? Feel the soft glow of spring on her face and the tender love of someone who chose her before themselves? What did that even feel like?

A wet tongue licked her hand, and she opened her eyes that had been squeezed shut, some semblance of reality returning as the room came into focus. The she-wolf had edged Marcus away and was standing at her side, dark eyes meeting Dilara's unwaveringly, and Dilara saw love for the first time since she had been a child. Felt it in the tender lick on her hand again. She raised her trembling fingers to comb through the thick winter coat of her rescuing angel, and a soft chirp from deep in her throat escaped the wolf, followed by a sympathetic whine as she jumped up on the bed, avoiding Dilara with her feet, her weight making the tick mattress creak. Curling up on the other side of Dilara, the wolf laid her head in her lap.

Tears spilled from her eyes, and she suddenly realized Keitha stood in the room, Dilara's discarded tray of dinner resting by the carved wooden handles in the woman's hands.

A look of wonder was on her face, and her words were soft and warm. "Mother wolves make that sound to their cubs to comfort them."

Dilara wrapped her arms around the wolf's head, burying her face in its fur, all fear of the animal gone in that moment as she accepted a mother's love from an animal, a love that her own mother had somehow been unable to offer her.

Thirteen

FROZEN HEARTS AND THAWING SPIRITS

DILARA BRUSHED A clump of hair off her forehead and curled closer to Nuri, her animal guardian, her angel in disguise. The name meant shining light, and she had been exactly that. The wolf huffed a deep breath, her sleeping body still somehow alert and on guard, even while resting. Dilara's head was nuzzled under Nuri's own, and for the first time, she felt safe, comforted. This animal had done something for her that no other human being had ever been able to. Offered her safety, love, and comfort with no strings attached.

The gale of snow had died down outside, but Keitha had assured her it was just a calm before another storm. They were in the height of winter now, blizzards coming fast upon the previous one like a galloping stampede, scarcely a second of peace before another one would charge through. A mournful wind howled against the eaves and whistled down the chimney. Perhaps it was about to start again.

The entire inn, maybe even the entire village, was slumbering peacefully, the tavern's very beams and slats sighing with relief after a long and hard day. She closed her eyes. Peace always seemed to evade her, even in sleep, but this time felt different.

A creak in the stairwell jerked her awake. She held her breath in the blackness, wondering who was up at this hour. It had to be the middle of the night. She jumped and Nuri whined when a blast of wind assaulted the window pains, and she felt a chill run down her spine. Keitha was right. Another storm had come. Turning, she felt the cold air rush beneath the covers, almost as if the wind had made it into this very room. Shivering, she leaned her back against Nuri's warmth, pulling the quilt to her chin as another howl echoed outside.

This storm seemed worse than any that had come before. It was as if the very gates of hell were threatening to burst as another howl sounded after the first, followed by the loud crack of a tree branch as it broke in the gale. She shook. Something felt off.

Another creak outside her door. Perhaps it was Kahru. He had been known to get up once in a while, frightened in his sleep and wandering about the halls as he tried to find Marcus or Fendrel. She didn't want the poor child wandering too far from his parents, so she slipped from the covers, leaving them pulled up to the top of the bed to keep in as much heat as possible. The worn planks of the floor gripped her feet with an icy grasp, and she stifled a gasp at how cold the room had become. The fire had died down to just a few coals, the wind from the chimney doing its best to stifle any last warmth and light.

The door creaked when she opened it, and she didn't bother to make sure it shut. She was the only one in that room now that some of the healthier refugees had moved on to other places in Elira. The Kingsmen had dispersed weeks ago, and some of the invalids had been taken in by other villagers to ease the strain on Keitha and her husband. A stair board groaned again, and she padded softly toward the staircase, taking one step at a time in the darkness, feeling her way along the wall as it curved in the downward, squared-off spiral every few steps. Why hadn't she found Kahru yet? How far had that child wandered? She would need to ask Fendrel if he was sleep walking. Perhaps there was an herb Marcus had that could help. He seemed to have the answer to every ailment. She admired that about him.

"Kahru? Are you all right?" she whispered into the stillness as a barrage of tempest proportions attacked the outer wall, the howl of the wind reminding her of the wolf pack that had haunted her every move during her escape. She shivered again. Perhaps Nuri had been the reason they had never come for her that night.

Hands suddenly grabbed her forearms with a ruthless grip, pulling her down the last few stairs and into the main hall of the tavern. Her breath frozen in her lungs, her body locked up with a fear that rivaled frostbite.

Then the orange glow of the fire fell on the countenance of the man who leered over her, and her knees collapsed like a rag doll's.

"Conri?"

"Thought you could escape me?" His harsh whisper grated against her face like the back of a blade. "I bought you. You're mine. And you'll never be able to outrun my ownership of you."

His breath was hot on her cheek, her fear like frozen ice, trapping her in its biting grasp. His hands gripped her roughly, groping, pulling her against his large, sweaty body and smashing her face against his shoulder.

"No." Her voice was barely audible as everything internal screamed a warning in a deafening volume.

A slap reverberated against her head and rattled her teeth against each other. "This was a waste. You'll regret the day you left me and wish you never had. No one else can have you; you are mine."

"No." Her voice was louder this time, though it shook, trembling in her panic. She had tasted freedom, and she would not return to bondage. Not without a fight. Her frozen mind started sputtering to life, thawing with the adrenaline that coursed through her body, numbing the bruise on her cheek.

His hands squeezed harder, dragging her roughly toward the door.

She kicked, pulling away, pressing hard against him, snagging a chair with a free finger, and wilting inside when the furniture barely moved. "No." Louder, clearer, desperate.

A fist to her side collapsed her legs, and he flung her over his shoulder with a swiftness that paralyzed her for a mere second. The door was getting closer, wind screaming against the window pains.

For a moment, the room taunted her with her last taste of freedom. "God, please." The smell of sweat, smoke, and sundry herbs gagged her as his cloak suffocated her senses. With one last effort, she reached again for a chair, and her fingertips snagged its back. All of her strength was focused on that meager hold as time slowed and one finger, then another, released its grip. With a grunt, she pulled with all her might against his shoulder and watched as the chair started to tip.

Time stood still, and she didn't breathe, didn't move as it slowly fell, finally clattering to the ground with a sound that reverberated through the entire cavern.

Whispered curses sounded behind her, and she cried out in pain before the world crashed down around her head.

A snarl that sent ice through her veins sounded from across the room a brief second before massive jaws, beady eyes, and a flash of fur barreled past and grasped Conri's leg.

His roar rivaled Nuri's growls and barks as she attacked Dilara's captor with the fierceness of a lioness protecting her cub. Sounds from upstairs were muffled in the distance as Dilara kicked against Conri and was dropped to the floor seconds before he fell on top of her as he used both hands to defend himself against Nuri's merciless attack. He scrambled against the floorboards and over Dilara in a useless attempt to escape.

The sound of snapping, growling, snarling, and a man's grunts and cries of pain echoed around the empty room before the darkness burst into light from the flames of a few torches as men dashed down the stairs and into the main hall.

She couldn't move, trying desperately to will her frozen body to do her bidding. She struggled to stay conscious as the adrenaline exploded inside her, heart pounding hard in her chest. She gripped at it with a shaking hand, a yelp sounded, and suddenly, it was over.

Her vision was hazy, snowflake-like crystals crowding out the clarity until she saw Nuri laying still, burgundy blood coating her gray fur. Dilara reached out a hand and was blasted by the wind whipping through the open door that swung crazily on its hinges against the blast. "No."

Conri fled. God had answered her plea for help. But at what cost?

The sounds of snapping and snarling woke him from his sleep, and Marcus shot upright, wide awake in an instant. A medicinal needed the ability to wake immediately upon being called by a patient. But this was no injured human crying out in pain, it sounded like a beast and monster were locked in a battle that was too close for comfort.

He followed the thundering feet of the other men whom he heard dashing through the hall and down the stairs. He wasn't exactly sure it was smart for him to head downstairs if he couldn't quickly get away from whatever danger was occurring. When he passed Dilara's door and saw it cracked open, then noticed that her bed was empty and Nuri was gone, he moved quicker than he ought to as a sick feeling chilled him to the bone.

God, please, no. Protect her. Keep her safe. He didn't know why he prayed what he did, but for whatever reason, he knew that Dilara was in danger. He stumbled on several steps, frantic to reach the main hall, catching himself a few times on the railing. The jolts and worry over pitching headfirst down the stairs did nothing to slow his racing heart and hurried breathing.

By the time he reached the bottom of the stairway, he caught sight of Dilara, crumpled on the floor, the nightdress that Keitha had given her torn at the shoulder and smudged all over by what Marcus realized had been dirty hands.

Someone had come for her.

He took in the scene, his heart simultaneously aching and in his throat at the same time. He felt sweat beading on his brow, and he dabbed it away with an elbow. But then he caught sight of Dilara's face—dazed, unspeakable hurt resting in the depths of her eyes.

With three quick, broad, swings of his crutches he was beside her and fell to his knees. She weakly reached for Nuri, lying on the floor, bloodied. A roar started in his ears, heat winding through him, protective and angry. He wanted to hold Dilara, shield her from danger, but clearly whatever had happened would prohibit him from doing so. He worried that any touch would feel dirty in her mind and set her spiraling, instead of moving her toward the healing light of protection.

Instead, he crawled closer to Nuri. *Please, God, let her be all right. Let me heal her. Let her come back to Dilara. Don't take her away from her, not now.* "Shh, shh, shh." Marcus cooed to Nuri as the creature opened one black eye, staring at him with a world of pain reflected in those depths, and whined, moving her paw a fraction of an inch as he gently rubbed the soft fur by her neck. "It's okay, Nuri," he breathed, running his hands down her side and looking for the slice that had opened her up.

Someone had shut the front door, and Dilara was transfixed. Watching them but seeming not to see them. Her eyes had glazed over, frosted like the panes of glass coated with ice. Her hands were pressed to her face, tears spilling down it, a bruise blossoming on her cheek. Her freckles stood out against her pale skin, brown eyes large beneath dark lashes coated in tears. Her mouth hung open as if a silent scream had frozen on her lips, and she couldn't tear her gaze away from Nuri.

"Dilara, everything is going to be all right." He used the same soothing tone he was using with Nuri, who whined when his fingers found the gaping wound in the side of her chest where the attacker's wicked knife had found its mark. He hissed in a breath. "Sweet one, you gave it your all, didn't you?"

"Can you save her?" Dilara's words came from a raspy throat, and he looked over his shoulder, glad in some small measure to see her returning to a bit of reality.

"I'll do my best, I promise. Keitha—" He turned to look over his other shoulder to the taverner's wife who had a shawl wrapped around her nightdress and her hair sticking out at odd angles, a fireplace poker gripped in both her hands and anger still smoldering in the lines on her face. "Can you get me some hot water, bandages, and my medicine chest?"

With a growl under her breath, she nodded, handed the poker to her husband, and scuttled toward the kitchen, bare feet scuffing against the floorboards.

Heavy footsteps headed toward the door. Marcus looked up, both hands occupied with Nuri's wound, to see Everard wrapping his monstrous cloak over his shoulders and tying it around his neck. He pulled the hood up before reaching for the door handle.

"Everard! Where are you going?" Marcus knew that Everard could take care of himself. At least, logically, he knew this, but that didn't stop his heart from hammering in his chest at the idea of Everard stepping outside into what could be the hidden hands of Dilara's attacker.

Everard turned, gave him a reassuring nod, raised his eyes heavenward in a clear message, and stepped outside the door before Marcus could say another word.

Dilara behind him in tatters, Everard chasing down who knew what in the frozen world outside, and Nuri bleeding out in his hands. *Lord, help.*

"Dilara." That was Fendrel's voice. Marcus drew a breath of relief. Some help at last. He glanced again over his shoulder again as Keitha bustled up behind them, his wooden chest under her arm and a dish of steaming water in her other. Fendrel wrapped Dilara in a blanket he must have fetched for that exact purpose. The group of men who had hurried down at the noise stood a respectful distance away, talking under their breath. Marcus heard Jaromir and his son's voice, amongst a few others.

Though his awareness snagged on what was happening around him, he sought to give his undivided attention to Nuri. Using the hot water to cleanse the fur around the gash and then pulling his needle and waxed thread from his leather pouch, he started stitching immediately. The thinner thread would be used to stitch together the artery that had been nicked before stitching the muscle, then the skin, closing the wound. It would take a few layers, and he poured out prayers as he worked. Sweat dripped off the tip of his nose before Keitha wiped away the remainder with the corner of her shawl.

He could hear Fendrel's soft, soothing voice as he spoke to Dilara, prayers mixed with calming phrases. He glanced at her. She watched his hands, still carefully tending to Nuri's wound, that fearful deer-like gaze transfixed on her furry protector as Fendrel rubbed her cold hands between his own.

Then she looked up at Keitha. "I'm sorry for the mess."

"Tut." Keitha threw her hands in the air and dashed angrily at a tear that leaked past her facade of a tough shell. "Don't you dare apologize. You did nothing wrong, dear one. Sweet lambs like you oughtn't to apologize for the doings of monsters." She reached out her hands and timidly rubbed Dilara's shoulders beneath the blanket, though looking awkward and uncomfortable as she did so. As if offering physical comfort was not a normal occurrence for her.

Stitch, two, three, knot.

"But I… If it weren't for me, he would never have come."

"And glad I am that you were here and that you had the forethought to tip that chair to alert the house. Dear 'un, I'd gladly sacrifice all my chairs if it meant you'd be safe forever."

Stitch, two, three, knot.

Marcus glanced up and saw Dilara move her eyes from his hands for the first time, brows puckered as she caught Keitha's gaze. "Why?"

The low voices in the corner ceased, and Marcus felt a lump growing in his throat. The bewilderment on that doe-like expression snagged his heart. She looked like a child who had just been offered the most underserved gift in the world.

Keitha faltered, and her eyes welled. Blinking rapidly, she pulled her hands to her chin and crouched beside Dilara. "Child." Her voice was breathless, quivering with tears as one escaped her steady gaze and slid down her cheek. "Because you're just as deserving of love as anyone else."

The barriers and frozen shock melted away beneath the heat of a fire of love and acceptance and the walls Dilara had held herself seemed to break. A sob ripped from her chest with a force that made Marcus's hands shake as her face crumpled, and she collapsed into Keitha's arms. The stalwart taverner's wife pulled her into an embrace and rested her chin on the young girl's head.

Stitch, two, three, knot.

Lord in heaven, heal.

There was more than one thing on his heart as Marcus threw that prayer heavenward, his hands coated in the blood of a sacrifice for a girl who didn't know the depths of love that truly awaited her.

Dilara could not remember when she had last experienced such love. Free of exchange or payment, simply there, offered and extended with no thought for what she could give for its return. The pain of her frozen heart breaking free and melting away at the wave of compassion that swallowed her whole cracked like a river releasing to the rushing melts of spring.

Time moved on without her, and she clutched the arms that held her as if she would never let go. A soft hand rubbed circles into her back. The touch asked for nothing, given with no strings attached. The anguish she had held inside, locked tight, was loosed, and it brought a new feeling she almost didn't recognize.

Release.

The arms that gripped her in their embrace were strong, protective, compassionate. Tears swam in her eyes, clouding her vision and filling her with the precious realization that for the first time in forever, she was safe.

Outside of Conri's grasp, away from his manipulation and thievery. He had taken so much from her. Everything, in fact. Everything except her will to live beyond what he had done to her. She realized with another wave of sobs that the time had finally come for that to take place. Her first step outside of his grasp, his control, had begun.

She didn't want to be alone. She wanted to remain right here, in the shadow and shelter of these arms, but she also *did* want to be alone, to shout her defiance to a hard, cold night that had tried to snuff out the life she carried, burning deep within her chest.

"He loves you." The whisper was in her ear, meant for no one but her. Quiet, yet loud enough to shatter mountain rock.

She shook beneath the weight. The God Marcus had talked about. The One whom he said would love her no matter what she had done or what He had to do to prove it. She had prayed. Had asked Him to rescue her.

And He had.

Deliverance had descended, and she was safe. A new life and an offer of something more. Something she didn't quite understand yet.

Fourteen

LOST LOVE AND A HOME

THE FIRST FEATHERY HAND of morning was cracking the sky open, a fiery glow exploding across the crystal snow that tried to cloak the beginning of day in frosted fog. Dilara rhythmically ran her hand over Nuri's fur, her fingers still shaking under the weight of what had occurred last night. Had it truly been a mere few hours? Had her life almost been torn into shreds only dozens of minutes prior?

The house was quiet again, all but a soft stirring in the kitchen as Keitha and her husband prepared for the day ahead. The rest of the house had surrendered back to sleep, hoping to gather a bit more strength for the coming morning. She leaned forward and kissed the side of Nuri's face and was thanked with the softest whisper of a huff from her nose and a twitch of the ear.

All her poor protector could offer.

She rubbed a hand against the soft fur on the she-wolf's face and cupped a hand around the ear, larger than her hand. "Thank you, dear friend," she whispered, her throat hoarse from crying, even while more tears fogged up her sight.

A soft whine met her ears, and she sank down closer to Nuri, her head resting in her hand as she reclined in bed beside the injured wolf.

"Marcus said it's up to you now, Nuri. And you know he always seems to know exactly what a body needs. Just keep breathing. Please." She sniffed, running her hand down the resting body, avoiding the bandages that were twined across the wolf's chest. "Please don't leave me. I've only just found a friend, and I can't bear to lose you, too."

With a shuddering sigh, trying to hold back more sobs, she buried her face into her elbow against the pillow, allowing herself to close her weary eyes.

"God, please, don't let her die. Let her live."

Marcus woke with a start, pulling himself up to a sitting position and reaching for the gauzy, hand-woven curtain that rested over the window pane. A flash of cold greeted his fingers as a hazy daylight flashed into the room. Gray, stormy, and barely there.

He blinked the sleep from his eyes and slid his legs over the side of the cot. Fendrel still slept, his arm folded over his eyes and a soft snore escaping his mouth. Marcus smiled. He'd let the old man sleep. Lord knew he didn't get much of it.

Marcus was tired himself. He could feel the fatigue held off mercifully in the distance, but it was still there. Drawing in a lungful of the chill air, he reached for his crutches. His body didn't take kindly to how poorly he treated it, and it had been weeks of painstaking labor and harsh relapses, only to bounce back quicker than he ought. He was fine for the moment, but he tried not to sense some looming darkness about to descend upon him like a blizzard swooping down from the mountaintops.

He wanted to check on Nuri before heading down those blasted stairs to begin his day. Perhaps he could get the children to help him grind some of his herbal flowers to make a colored paste Dilara could use as paint. Perhaps he could even beg some more paper or sheepskin from Keitha or her husband to give Dilara more space to create another of those beautiful, heart-creations she had a fondness for making.

He smiled as he quietly swung across the floor with his crutches. He loved that he had found something that gave her a bit of freedom as well as helped her to process the things she had gone through.

He sent a prayer heavenward by habit, his thoughts naturally turning to a discourse with his Maker. Prayers for healing, for strength, restoration, and for hearts to be mended in ways that only the Master Healer could bring about. Marcus swallowed. He desperately wanted Dilara to meet the Lord. The One who had saved her over and over again and sacrificed Himself once and for all to save her soul. He knew that would be the ultimate healing that would rescue her soul from frozen torture, but she needed to accept it on her terms. Her heart needed to recognize its need, and her spirit needed to mold with the Holy Spirit in her own time.

He couldn't make that decision for her or force her into that acceptance, no matter how much he wanted to. You can force a child to take the hand of their father, but it won't be anything but a shackle until they do it of their own accord, out of their own desperate need for saving and a heart full of love and acceptance of the sacrifices made for them.

The door to Dilara's room was open as he passed it, and he glanced in, pausing long enough to catch the rise and fall of the furry beast's chest as it lay on her bed, the sleeping girl's arms wrapped around its middle and cradling its head. Locks of her brown hair fell over her face and across the pillow, and he caught his breath at the look of peace on her face. A peace he hadn't seen on her before. A smile pulled at his lips; it made her even more beautiful.

"Finish the healing, Lord. Thank You that You are faithful to complete the good works that You have begun." He whispered his thanks, taking the stairs with another prayer for strength and balance to make it to the bottom.

"Psst."

The sound came from around the bend in the stairs, followed by a set of little eyes peeking around the corner and quickly retreating again, a giggle echoing sweetly off the twisted walls of the stairwell.

Marcus stifled a chuckle and sighed loudly instead.

"I declare, it's going to be such a lonely morning." He spoke with as much flair as he could muster, setting his crutches down a step and swinging again. He winced. The bruises under his arms from the crutches didn't seem to be getting any better; he shifted their position to alleviate a little of the pain.

A blond head poked around the corner again, only to instantly retreat. There were more giggles, another "Shh!" and the sounds of a slight scuffle.

Marcus cleared his throat. "I can't believe my favorite friends decided to abandon me on this lovely morning."

He rounded the corner and was greeted by a chorus of the most un-frightening roars he had ever heard in his life.

Stumbling backward on the landing, he dropped his shoulders against the wall, clutching a hand to his chest. "Mercy me and saints above!" He gasped, throwing his eyes wide and feigning fright from the small group of children who laughed up at him, clearly thrilled with their effect on him. "You nearly scared the life right out of me. In fact, oh, there it goes." He tossed his head back against the wall, positioned his crutches just so, and sank to a seat against the wall, lolling his tongue out of his mouth and gasping for a breath before shutting his eyes.

They laughed and chattered, gathering around him to badger him from every side, little hands patting his shoulders and grabbing his face. "Wake up! Wake up!" they cried, their movement making the wooden floors shake as they tried to hold back giggles.

"Boo!" He startled awake, grasping at them as they squealed and ran down the last section of stairs as fast as their little legs could carry them. "I'm coming for you!" he roared around the bend, pulling himself to his feet with a groan and clumping the rest of the way to the main floor.

"Everard!" Marcus caught sight of the blacksmith as he swung across the dining hall to the table in front of the fire where Everard sat, warming his hands on a steaming mug and drip-drying in front of the flames. "Did you find him?"

Everard shook his head, his eyes meeting Marcus's with a flicker of frustration and a crease between his black brows.

Sighing, Marcus maneuvered his crutches out of the way and, with his bad leg in front of him, settled into the chair opposite. "The skunk." He growled. It had only taken one look at the utter terror in Dilara's eyes to determine the identity of the intruder.

"Worse than. Lost him. Snow covered his tracks."

Marcus nodded then glanced at the large man who shivered and ran a hand along the back of his neck, shaking off the water that had dripped from his hair. "Move closer to the fire. You need to get warm before you catch cold."

Everard sent Marcus an amused glance and rolled his eyes, the slightest of smiles tugging the corners of his mouth. Marcus grinned back. It was nice to have the role of mother hen reversed. For once.

"Come play with us!" The children's little hands tugged at Marcus's tunic, trying to pull him from the chair and in every direction but a useful one apparently.

"I have a better idea—how about you help me make paint?"

"Make what?" Matthias, the inquisitive ringleader, asked, his blond curls flying as he placed his hands on his hips. There was a defiant attitude in nearly everything he said and did.

Marcus tried to keep from rolling his eyes. "It's color. You know how Dilara makes those drawings? This will give her colors to draw with instead."

"Her drawings are scary." Matilda, the small brown head poking from behind the group, was folding her arms over her chest. She barely made it to Marcus's waist in height, and her tiny face showed her nervous nature.

Everard scooped her up and bounced the worried look away as he made the sound of horses hooves with his tongue. Instant giggles and other voices begging for a turn suddenly filled the room, and Marcus laughed. "You didn't realize what you started with that, did you?"

Everard sent him an amused expression that said he clearly *had* known and had done so on purpose.

One of the older girls, Matthias in tow, walked with Marcus to the kitchen to fetch his wooden medicine chest. They crowded around as he lifted the lid, gasping in wonder at the juxtaposition of herbs, mortars and pestle sets, jars, and other medicinal paraphernalia that were strewn about in a chaotic, but also somehow orderly, fashion.

He knew where each herb was stored exactly so, and he could find what he needed without even looking. Bundles of dried herbs were pinned to the lid, jars stacked and held against the sides by netting to keep them from rolling around or breaking in transit. Small trays of even smaller compartments, made of cedar to match the chest and keep the scents separate from each other, were stacked in the middle.

He grabbed a few bundles of different flowers, coneflower, sunflower petals, and hyssop and sage flowers to determine which would make the best blues. "I think we may just have to experiment and see which colors look the brightest." He smiled, handing the young girl, Noam, a handful of the dried blossoms. She threw him a grin, her little nose crinkling beneath her freckles, and dashed out to the dining hall with her prize.

Marcus reached to hand Matthias a mortar and pestle, but the boy's arms were folded. Again. His face wrinkled in disgust.

"Matthias? Is something wrong?"

"Why are you helping the Rusalkan girl?" The spite in his tone surprised Marcus before he could formulate any proper response.

"I'm sorry?" Marcus sputtered.

"Some of the other people in town say that we have no business taking in an enemy. How do we know she isn't dangerous? You heard Matilda; she said she was scared of the drawings she does."

Marcus drew a breath. That was a lot of fear and anger from such a tiny human. "Matthias, who is saying that? So many of the people of Pranvera have been so kind in their care and blessing of the refugees."

Matthias's expression turned into a bit of a pout, and he looked down as he dejectedly scuffed his foot on the hardwood floors. "I dunno."

Marcus laid a hand on the boy's shoulder. "You don't have to be afraid of Dilara. Or of Jaromir and his family. You've gotten to know Kahru, haven't you?"

His eyes cleared a bit. "Yes."

"Well, he's from Rusalka, and you enjoy spending time with him. I've seen you playing with sticks in the corner and laughing and having fun."

Matthias shrugged. "But what about the others? What about the ones who came over the walls? The ones with masks and curved blades? What if they come back? One already did." He brushed a hand beneath his nose and pushed back a lock of his honey hair.

Marcus sighed. He knew Matthias's defiance was more of a mask to hide his fear and memories of the Rusalkans' vicious attack. The last few years since the death of Elgon's father had been trying to them all. But those of the border lands had to contend with ruthless Kingsmen who were more like the brutal Rusalkan warriors than they were the kind and gentle leaders of a free country. He could only imagine the fear children like Matthias must have felt when their towns had been raided before, and now, those from the same country who had treated them ill had come to stay and had furthermore begged help from them.

"Matthias, can I tell you something? Even adults find this one hard to grasp, but I think I can trust you to understand. You're a smart boy, and God has given you a very special gift of leadership. I see it in the way you lead the other children in your games and play, as well as your chores."

Matthias looked up, a conspiratorial gaze mixed with excitement on his face. He was clearly proud to receive such a commendation from the medicinal who had become his friend.

Shifting on his hip so that his standing position was a smidge more comfortable, Marcus took hold of the young boy's shoulder. "Not all of those in Rusalka are like the bad men who come and attack us. They are people, families, just like us. And God loves them just the same. He doesn't care where you come from, what you do, or what country you were born into. He doesn't care what you've done or who you served before. He still loves you just the same. Even if you have done bad things. And it's why He asks us to love our enemies and pray for those who curse us. Because He knows, with His help, that we are capable of the same love Jesus has. He gave it to us, and by His strength we can give that love to others. Do you understand?"

Matthias nodded slowly, thoughtful, his eyes squinting past Marcus in deep thought. "I think so. But does that mean I have to love the bad men with masks?"

Marcus pulled him into a hug under one arm. "You don't have to do anything. But think about Jesus. If Jesus loves them and wants them to meet Him…do you think you could, too? Have you tried praying for them? That always helps me when I'm angry at someone. It helps me to see them the way Jesus does."

Matthias nodded slowly, his thinking so noticeable it made Marcus smile, watching the plotting of his little brain unfold in his expression. "I—I don't know how to do it. I want to see them the way you see them. But…I'm still angry."

Marcus stifled a grin. "Things never feel easy the first time. Or the second. Or even the third. But the doing gets easier over time, and suddenly you find that what you wanted has become a part of your life, whether you realized it or not. But you keep doing and you keep asking. Just because you don't see the answer at first doesn't mean it didn't come. Our eyes do not see like God's eyes. Shall we ask Him for help together?" He gripped the little boy's hand when he received an answering nod. The child clung to him while he prayed for them both to receive mercy to extend to any of those from Rusalka and for their hearts and minds to be molded to see what Christ sees.

Matthias—the independent, willful boy who had enough mind of his own for two people—ducked into Marcus for a lightning-fast hug before scampering out of the room.

Marcus felt a smile brush his lips even as he ignored the ache in his joints and the grind in his hip as he gathered a handful of herbs in each hand and his crutches under his arms.

The heart of Christ could melt even the iciest and hardest of hearts.

Dilara brushed her fingers through the fur of her slumbering protector. She didn't want to move for fear of waking Nuri up, but she was ready to move. She needed to get out of bed or her own thoughts would drive her crazy. But Nuri had given her all for the safety of her adopted master, and Dilara would stay with her until she was out of danger. She drew a deep breath. "Lord, if you're there, please let her live."

"I'm happy to see you might not think I'm telling tall tales afterall."

She started and caught sight of Marcus at the open doorway to her room. She had taken to leaving it ajar when it was in her control and she didn't need the privacy. She was used to sharing common spaces with people, and it helped her feel less alone to know that others walked by nearby. It gave her the security to feel that she had people just a call away, like a warm blanket on a chilly afternoon.

She turned back to Nuri, thoughtful. "He may have answered a prayer last night."

"One of mine, too." The sounds of his crutches made their way toward her, and she kept her gaze focused on her animal friend. She knew if she looked into those deep blue-green eyes, he would somehow guess at the thoughts, fear, and pain tormenting her soul where no one else could see. He had that way about him. As if he could guess her inner wonderings. Even though she thought she had buried them deeper than was humanly possible.

"How is she?" Dilara sat up, pulling her legs under her in a criss-cross pattern to give Marcus room to examine the wolf.

"I do better with human patients, but she seems to be holding her own. I hope and pray she will be fine, but that was a nasty gash, and she lost a lot of blood. I kept it clean, but if infection sets in—well, that's my biggest worry. We'll know in a day or two if she is out of danger."

She watched his hands as they softly probed and rebandaged the wound. Nuri made no sign that she cared except for a soft huff or two when he seemed to get close to a tender spot with his gentle fingers. His hands were pale but calloused. The brown color of all the herbs he used rubbed deep into his palms like a shade that never goes away. She could smell them on him. Always. The constant aroma of leafy and forest things hung around him with the subtle spice and earthy tone of the other medicines he used all of the time.

"I made you some paint if you would like to paint while you are sitting with her." He reached into his satchel and pulled out a few small glass pots with cork lids pressed into their openings. "I thought you might like to try some colors."

Their hands brushed as she took them, and his touch didn't make her startle or feel ill at ease. Instead, she was at peace, calmed. Like the feeling of a hot cup of tea, warming her palms.

Colors? Taking off the cork lid, she dipped a finger into the pungent-smelling paste and pulled it out to examine it. Miraculously, an oily purple coated her fingertip, and she stared, mesmerized, turning it so it caught the light. "How did you...?" She was breathless. Color. Her black paintings of pain would see the blessed benediction of life in the form of color splashed across her pages.

He looked so pleased with himself. Grinning, actually. Those blue eyes were the brightest color in the world, and she hoped she could find a shade to match one day. "My herbs," he said. "Many of them have flowers that the children helped me make into a paste that you can brush across your pages. I mixed the ground flowers with oil from Keitha's pumpkin seeds. She said it helps the pigment stay. The children were thrilled that it worked. I had a few doubts myself."

"It's marvelous," she murmured. "I can't wait to try them out." An image of the cornflowers in the field behind her home that abutted the forest sprang to memory, their blue and purple hues dancing in the golden rays of the setting sun. "I know just what I'm going to paint first." Her fingers smeared colors across the paper, and her heart started to sing. Heavy though it lay in her chest like a stone, it was singing nonetheless.

Marcus cleared his throat, but she couldn't tear her gaze from the paper with dots of purple that would eventually become flowers as she added more colors and shades to the background.

"Dilara, I have something to ask you."

Her hands paused in their work, and she looked up, her elbow dropping to Nuri's side for comfort, just by the touch. There was something in his voice. The she-wolf let out a huff as if sighing over her charge's temerity.

Why did he look so awkward, standing there, rubbing his left elbow with the fingers from his other hand as he let it dangle limp over the crutch?

She brushed a hair away from her face with the back of her hand. "Yes?" Her voice sounded thin and small, and she cringed at her own timidity.

"I had a thought. In light of what happened…Everard went after him, but he lost his tracks in the snow. Despite Nuri wounding him, probably badly, he knows you're here. Fendrel and I have discussed about when it would be time to head back to Padsley, and…well, we thought it best to offer that you could accompany us back."

She stared at him. What was he offering her? Why did her heart melt and skip along all at the same time?

"Only if you want to, of course. We simply are worried that your captors might try to claim you again. It's just Everard, Fendrel, and I on the way back; we have no women accompanying us, but it's merely a day and a night's journey away. There are people there who can house you. I know of a few farmers' wives who would be able to take on another mouth to feed. You wouldn't be hunted there. Wouldn't be…kept."

Dilara knew she should be afraid. Wasn't that what her life had taught her to be? But why was it that this man could offer her a life and a home, and it sounded completely different from the demands and commands of her previous keepers? There was a freeness to his offer, something she had never experienced, yet her heart knew it when it heard it.

"We just want you to be safe. Keitha and her husband would do their best, but after last night, there's no knowing what…" A flash of anger lit Marcus's features and made his lean face sharp in the winter light trickling in from the window. "What that animal might do if given another opportunity."

A chill swept through Dilara at the thought, her gaze flicking to the window and then to the door behind Marucs, almost as if worried that Conri would come flying through it, snarling like the rabid wolf that he was. She could still feel his hands in her hair, his fingers around her neck, and her body being dragged across the floor. Darkness closed in around her vision, and another shudder worked its way up her spine.

"Dilara?"

She snapped back, and a flickering fire filled her heart with warmth she couldn't explain. She had lived with so much tragedy; even the faintest whisper of hope felt foreign to her heart.

"I'll go."

Fifteen

PROFESSIONS OF A NEW LIFE

DILARA ROLLED OVER in bed, her back against that of her protector, and she held her breath as she heard Nuri's hitch. She must be in terrible pain. Having given so much to protect Dilara, she was now paying for it.

A tear worked its way down her cheek. If Nuri died from the infection Marcus was so worried about, she wasn't sure what she would do. The sound of the wind still rattled the panes upon occasion and sent a hollow voice whispering down the chimney, sputtering the flames in the grate. But Dilara snuggled down tighter, the sounds now more familiar and comforting than they were frightening. She had seen what Nuri had done to Conri, and the chances of him coming back for her tonight were slim to none. Tomorrow night, she'd be well on her way to Padsley.

The darkness brushed her eyelids with tender fingers, drawing her deeper into rest, and she let out a sigh, one hand curled beneath her head and the other beneath her chin as she felt each muscle relax and sink into the tick mattress that had been hers for the last few months. While the dead of winter pounded the forest and the cabins outside, she knew it wouldn't be long before spring arrived. It was a special kind of hoping and waiting for the day to come. Hope was assured because, through cloud and storm, the sun still rose, even when one couldn't see it. Its gentle light still shone.

I am like that.

The voice didn't startle her from her restful state. Instead, it felt like it fit. Like it belonged, speaking deep in the caverns of her soul.

She wondered if the voice that had been popping into her thoughts—the one that somehow felt like her own mind, but also spoke things she had not accepted yet—was the voice of the God that Marcus constantly spoke to her of. She would have to ask him to borrow the book he carried in his vest pocket. The one that he treasured so highly and read often, when he had moments to himself. If he would give it up for her to read, that is.

What would it be like to be treasured by someone like that? What if Marcus treasured her that way instead of just his book?

With a shake of her head as the darkness pressed in deeper, she squeezed her eyes against the unbidden thought. Sleep. There was time to worry about where that thought had come from tomorrow.

It was cold. Dilara's eyes popped open. It was cold, and it was morning. The faint gray glow of the winter dawn hovered around the windows, too weak to shine through, but throwing the room into a gloaming. The fire must have gone out. Her heart leapt. *I'm leaving today.*

She rolled carefully to keep from disturbing Nuri, but the bed moved oddly. Turning her head she realized Nuri was nowhere to be seen. She did sometimes slip out, but the cold, the absence her warm body had left behind made Dilara wish for a roaring fire and a hot cup of cider to heat her chilled bones.

She chirped her tongue in the way she and Nuri had been communicating. Keitha had explained to her that it was the sound a she-wolf makes when comforting her cubs, and the realization had made her tear up. Nuri was her saving grace. She needed to make sure she was okay so they could take this journey to a new home together.

Her heart filled with trepidation and an excitement she couldn't remember ever feeling. But more than that, she was just glad that she would feel safe. While she knew at the moment her chances of Conri returning to claim her were small, she still felt like these walls that had once been a haven had been defiled by his presence. His words of accusation and ownership came back to her now with a harshness and a chill that made her shiver as it ran its ugly finger down her back.

She needed to find Nuri.

Letting her feet fall to the floor, she settled the kirtle that Keitha had given her over the top of her head. Its rich brown color reminded her of the fields that had waved with grass in the summer on the mountainside where she had grown up, and its warm, woolen weight settled on her shoulders like a gentle hand of comfort. Not bothering to find her shoes beneath the bed, she wrapped the shawl that doubled as an extra blanket at night around her shoulders and sped from the room. Her thick, hand-knitted socks slid on the well-worn dark wood floors. She chirped again, calling down the hall before heading to the stairs.

No wonder it took Marcus so long to get anywhere; these stairs must be abysmal with his hip. Sliding to a stop at the bottom of the stairwell, she caught her breath. Even though she had spent a couple of months healing in this tavern and eating proper food, her body was still not used to sudden or multitudinous movement. She could hear Keitha bustling in the kitchen, a tavern shanty rollicking through the kitchen in a soft voice often lapsing into hums, but she didn't see Nuri beneath any of the tables or curled in front of the fire.

Where could she be?

She stumbled, catching herself, and reeled toward the kitchen. "Nuri?"

Keitha popped out of the opening to the kitchen before Dilara even reached it, drying her hands on her apron, her hair done up in a cap to keep it out of the way. "What in blazes are you doing up this early, luv? Sakes alive, what is it?" Keitha wrapped her hands around Dilara's shoulders as Dilara tried to look around her into the rest of kitchen.

Why was she panicking? Nuri had stepped outside before...

But not with a stomach full of wounds or with Conri nearby.

"Have you seen Nuri?"

Understanding dawned on Keitha's broad face. "Not this morning. Perhaps Rensen let her outside. Rensen! Have you seen the she-wolf? She's missing this morn."

A deep voice bellowed back from the woodshed that was connected to the back of the kitchen. "Not this morning. She usually comes down and asks for a taste of that bacon o' yourn, but I haven't seen her yet."

"What do ye mean? You've been giving her a taste o' my bacon?" Keitha settled her hands on her hips and darted back through the doorway.

He held his hands up in a pacifying gesture, a hatchet in one and a piece of wood in the other. "Calm yerself, woman. You clearly never missed it."

Keitha bit her lip with a frown, but a twinkle danced in her eyes. "Off with you." Turning to Dilara, she asked, "Have you tried outside, deary?"

Dilara was trembling. Her skin felt drawn tight in a constant chill as if something terrible was about to happen. She shook her head, turned to head toward the door, and ran into a massive chest.

Without a thought but instant flight, she lifted both her hands to guard her face and drew back, her hip bumping against the kitchen table as a gasp drew the breath from her lungs.

"Shh," came soothingly from behind her. "Careful, wee one. Everard won't hurt you." Keitha's voice was soft, as if soothing a crying kitten, and she carefully held out a hand, not touching Dilara until asked.

Dilara gathered her arms around herself, pulling her shawl tight, instantly off kilter and overwhelmed all at once. Everard stood before her, his palms out in a quiet, giving motion that set her instantly at ease. *He's a friend. Not a foe. You ran into him, not the other way around. Take a deep breath.*

"I can't find Nuri. I need to look outside. Have you seen her?"

He shook his head, a worried expression lighting his features. She moved to go past him, but without touching her, he held up a hand, the wrinkles around his eyes pressed into the dark skin and his pinched lips telling her he didn't want her to follow.

"What is it?"

He shook his head and motioned with it toward the door, the worry lines deepening.

She swallowed, the involuntary movement hard around the rock forming in her throat. He must want her to stay because he didn't know what he would find outside.

He disappeared from the room, and a blast of cold air signaled his departure into the frigid morning.

Her feet didn't want to move, but her mind wanted to pace, and as she stepped forward with a lurch, it was like moving a rusty wheel after not being used in many a year. *If You're there and You are watching over us like Marcus says, please keep Nuri safe and bring her back to me.* Her words felt foreign, speaking them to another entity, but there had been something at work in her life. Marcus was right—she had been protected in so many ways. Through Nuri in the woods, then through every single person in this little tavern who had risked everything to rescue her from the field of those dying after she made it over the wall. Then tending her, bringing healing back to her very bones over the last few months, and protecting her in the face of her enemy who had come back to haunt her.

They said a loving God led them to serve her this way. Compelled them to care for her as a child of their own. Gave them a desire to tell her that she was worthy, even though she felt anything but.

Please be there. I can't trust without fear of being betrayed. Not again. She gripped her stomach where her child had grown, and the pain came rushing back. The fear, the loss, her keening cry that met her ears echoed as it had through the moonlit forest, accompanied by wailing wind and a wolf's howl. Her legs gave way, and her knees met the wood floor with a jolt. Nuri was gone. She was sure of it.

"We'll be home in just a few hours." The wagon creaked, and Everard adjusted the set of his shoulders, his arms rubbing up against Marcus's from where they shared the bench seat at the front of the wagon.

Marcus was hollow inside. The intensity of the last few months had gathered like a sickness in the pit of his stomach, and he had been emptied by it. Emptied and broken over the lives he had witnessed that were changed forever. Moments suspended in time had shattered, altered, and corrected course for many people. Soldiers losing limbs, children separated from parents, lives lost in the desperate struggle to survive, slaves freed then taken captive again.

They had hurriedly packed up and headed for home, Jaromir and his family declaring they would follow within the next few weeks when the worst of the snow and ice started to loosen its hold over the world. When Everard had hunted for Nuri on the forest trails around the tavern, he had found blood and footsteps in the snow that could only be those of Conri. Marcus felt an anger toward the man who was more like an animal than he was human—a hunter stalking his prey.

Dilara had come willingly, but Marcus couldn't help feeling that they had all been robbed of a true farewell. Traveling wasn't easy for him, and he would miss Keitha, Rensen, Jaromir, Kahru, and his family dearly. At least Jaromir, his son, daughter-in-law, and little Kahru would be joining them in Padsley, but he might never see Rensen and Keitha again. He prayed that their paths would one day cross.

He smiled, remembering their reaction to hearing of Conri's stalking in the forest outside the tavern. Rensen had juggled a few of his knives before throwing one expertly at the wall and winking at Marcus. "He'll think twice before barging in here."

"Especially when I hit him with one of my kettles, the scum." Keitha brandished a cast-iron pot in the air like a battle ax, her face sternly set as if going to war. "His head might not stay attached to his shoulders after I'm through with him," she had growled.

While there were many things to be grateful for and to rejoice over, now as the darkness descended like a woolen cloak upon the wintery world around them, dusk settling in the corners and crouching around every bend, he couldn't help but feel the weight of sorrow. It always attacked him in the stillness—moments of quiet when pain resurfaced unbidden and hope fled for higher ground. Perhaps their distance would give Dilara not just the safety that she needed to fully heal, but also the peace of mind to know that Conri could not follow her quite so far. It would not be easy for a Rusalkan with so evil a temperament as Conri to make it through the villages and farmland of Padsley without being noticed by at least a few farmers, if not the Kingsmen stationed at the outpost. Especially after they were warned to be on the lookout for such a character.

A feminine cough broke the stillness of the night, the creaking of the harness, and the horses' hooves as they crunched through frozen snow and thudded against the ground. *Dilara.* Why did he feel so drawn to her? He had never felt this way over any of his patients before. He swallowed. Not even Violet. His dearest friend, confidant, and childhood sister... He shook his head. Why was he so attracted to a woman he had only known for a short time?

He had barely been ready to marry a woman he had known his whole life, though he would have loved to give it a go before she met Elgon. But to feel even more strongly drawn to a woman he had known for a few months? One who certainly would rather not have anything to do with a man for the rest of her life. And how could he blame her?

He shoved the feeling of love down like a seed being buried deep into the ground. There was no possibility of the happiness of family life in his future. He was too broken for anyone, let alone a young woman as equally broken and hurt as Dilara. She needed a man who could protect her, keep her safe, hold her tight in his arms, and reassure her that everything would be all right. Not a cripple who couldn't even walk fast enough to keep up with an invalid, let alone a child of his own or a young wife who needed to experience new joy in her life.

His blood boiled within his veins, and he felt the heat waft up his spine, replaced by a chill. The fact that any human being could treat another as Conri had treated Dilara, and perhaps many other young girls… He couldn't fathom it. She had given few words of explanation, but her eyes and body language, the injuries and losses she had sustained—it was all he had needed to hear.

He huffed, pulling his cloak up around his shoulders and settling back into the hood, blowing hot air onto his fingertips, nearly numb with the cold. They would all need some thawing when they arrived. The temperatures dropped under the canopy of the oaks in Raintamount Forest as they neared home. The trees that stubbornly refused to drop their leaves until the new growth threw them off in the spring crowded out the stars in the sky with their dark arms, stretching over the King's Highway like scraggly hands, reaching to cover their prey.

What was with him and all of these dark thoughts of late? His leg throbbed, and he shifted, bumping into Everard, who grunted.

"Sorry."

The hand on his shoulder was more than forgiveness, it was kindness. Friendship. He had no right to feel so despairing, surrounded as he was with people who loved him for who God created him to be, cared for him like a son, and would move heaven and earth to keep him safe.

But with them rallied around him, why did he still feel so empty? So torn and perturbed at the idea of returning to

Padsley? The words he had heard on the day he left rang in his ears like a broken bell, sounding over the hills of his soul with its clashing voice. *"If Richard had left well enough alone, the boy would be out of his misery and wouldn't be a burden to poor Fendrel. I'm sure it would have been much easier for him to die and not experience such a harsh life."*

He gulped, his throat suddenly feeling as though it were coated in burning salve.

The trees whirled overhead, and the swaying of the cart felt exaggerated, the throbbing in his hip sharpening like knives running against his bone. He gasped a ragged breath. *You should have taken me. I could have been with You this whole time. What purpose do I have on this earth? What do I, a cripple from Padsley, have to offer a world dying, a people desperate for a better life?*

"You offer them Me."

Marcus felt his head bounce off Everard's shoulder. Or at least what he thought was his shoulder. Such a bumpy ride. Why didn't Everard stick to the road? It was too rough on this unbeaten path. The knives dug into his bones, the shock ricocheting off of every nerve and tendon, shooting down into his legs and up his spine. Why did he feel like he was falling apart at the seams? Like the very foundations of his body were giving way to the burning fire within?

"Take My hand. And don't let go."

Dilara shivered, pulling her shawl tighter over her head, missing the furry warmth that greeted her each morning with the soft lick to the cheek and deep, throaty chirp that comforted her no matter what she was feeling. Her heart felt empty, hollow, like the last and dearest thing had been stripped from her, and she huddled down, alone, cowering like she had in the forest, welcoming the shelter of the trees and praying they hid her from her captor. Though the Lord hadn't shown Himself all that merciful to her today. Perhaps she was right. She was too dirty for Marcus's Lord to care for her.

The worried voices of the men grumbled in the frozen stillness of the early evening air. They had been traveling for the entire day, having left before dawn, the journey taking longer than anticipated through the snow, and now they were several hours past dark. The chill had set in sharply, like a knife blade coated in ice. Her lungs hurt if she drew in too deep a breath, and she cowered under the blanket when another shiver worked down her spine.

Something was wrong. Everard and Fendrel were talking with Marcus at the front of the wagon, their voices low. Why did his head roll like that?

"Dilara, would you make way, dear? We need to lay Marcus down." Fendrel's gentle but tight voice reached her as the wagon eased to a stop.

Dilara's heart skipped a beat before she gathered a few baskets and trundled them out of the way. What was wrong with him?

Everard had tied off the reins, and he and Fendrel lifted Marcus's limp body and laid him at her feet. His face was pale in the broken moonlight that filtered through the branches of the woods. Surely that was because the light was blue. It always cast such shadows in the winter air.

But the moan that escaped Marcus's lips sent Fendrel to his knees beside the young man. "Everard, drive. We must get home before this cold makes him worse." Fendrel was rubbing Marcus's hands between his own before he flung off his cloak and threw it over his fellow medicinal.

"What happened?" She nervously lifted her extra blanket and lent it to make a pile on top of Marcus, her hands tucking the edges in almost without thinking about it.

Drawn silence met her ears as Fendrel laid his head on Marcus's chest, listening intently.

Marcus moaned, his head rolling to the side, facing Dilara with his closed eyes, and she shuddered. Where was the blue, the vibrant light from within those tender and knowing orbs? There was something wrong about seeing him this way. Something desperately wrong.

"He's having one of his spells." The pace of the horses picked up, and the wagon lurched as it propelled over a pile of snow, eliciting another moan from Marcus. She almost gave an echoing groan, a response to the sudden panic that pressed into her side like a stitch from running too hard and fast.

"His what? What do you mean?" Her voice sounded hoarse, even to her.

"His body wears out sooner than most. I worried this would happen, but he seemed so well. His leg bothered him, but the fevers were gone. I had hoped…" Fendrel's voice broke as his hand rested on his boy's forehead. "I had hoped that he would make it through the season without one."

"One what? What's wrong with him?"

"His spells. He gets attacked by a fever every once in a while. Usually when he's worn himself out or the pain becomes too much. His body can't fight it anymore, and he is too weak to stay strong. Don't worry, Dilara. He is usually fine; it just takes some time. His body forgets how healthy his soul is, and old injuries come back to haunt him. But he is strong of heart, if not of body. He won't be down for long."

The hope in his voice felt forced. Dilara shivered as Marcus moaned again at another lurch of the wagon. Her heart felt heavy. This didn't feel as normal as Fendrel was trying to make it out to be.

The hours stretched on, and Everard had gotten out of the wagon to lead the horses with a lantern in hand, his long strides eating up the earth with a rapidity that astounded Dilara. But with the deep darkness pressing in on every side, it was almost as if they made no progress.

Marcus had started to burn with a fever. A cough came to his lips every few minutes, and she moved the blanket to better cover his ears and head as she shivered without the use of its extra warmth.

Lord, if You care about Marcus as he knows that you do, be with him now. Let him be all right. Please. I know I'm not worthy to ask You for myself, but won't You hear Your servant Marcus and the pain that he is in?

She felt a sob rise in the back of her throat.

Please don't let me lose the only man who has ever cared.

Sixteen

FRESH WHITE SNOW

DILARA DREADED the thought of leaving Marcus's side. It felt wrong. After so many weeks and months spent by her bedside as he cared for her, offering her his strength of spirit in addition to the herbal tinctures that healed her body and the prayers that he was sure did the same, she could do no less. She had stood beside him as Everard had carried him into what she had come to know as Fendrel's home. Waited with ringing hands to be told what she could do to help while Fendrel tended him behind the fluttering curtain to his room. She even sent prayers Heavenward of which she had little to no understanding of their efficacy.

Her heart was heavy like lead in her chest, almost numb, frozen as surely as her fingers and toes were.

"You ought to stand closer to the fire. The ride was much colder than we expected, and you must be freezing." Fendrel's words to her were punctuated by a stifled moan from Marcus, and she fought off the dread pooling in her middle.

Everard was coddling small flames to life, weak but still throwing off enough warmth to be felt, calling her like a beacon from across the room. Rubbing her hands together and feeling her shoulders settle somewhere midway between their normal posture and her ears, she felt the cold of her cloak brush her skin, the material holding onto the night air from outside. It wafted around her like dark fingers trying to remind her of the chill which threatened to bring back memories of the darkest night of her life.

She stood as close as she dared to the fire, feeling a need to keep some distance between her and Everard, though the man had been nothing but kind to her. It still took a trust she wasn't sure she had yet to even stand in a house with only three men inside with her.

She drew a breath and felt a tight constriction of her throat. What was she doing here? She had no one to trust. No one to turn to. Not even her animal protector had followed her here.

A low clearing of a throat in front of her caused her to jump, and she laid one of her freezing hands on top of her chest as her heart thumped, leaping against her fingertips like a bird trying to escape from its cage.

Those dark eyes. Suddenly, she saw Everard in a new way. His chestnut skin tone, that mass of dark hair pulled into a tail at the back of his head, and those thick, black brows. She swallowed against a throat that was closing up and took a stuttering step back, suddenly seeing Conri in this large man's face. Seeing her father.

A light flickered in those deep eyes, and her frightened attempts to back away stilled. There was a fire inside him that matched the one in Marcus, a torch that burned brighter and hotter and harder than anyone else she had ever met. Something strong and steady and sure, trustworthy and lacking that animal greediness she had always seen in Conri. It was more than just humanity. It went deeper, and it beckoned to the broken fissures inside of her, offering something more.

He slowly held up his hands, palms out, and she realized she was trembling. She gritted her teeth to keep them from chattering and drew a breath between them, shuddering in the cold shadows that pressed in from the dark, ice-coated windows. He held out a hand, an invitation, a warm-hearted gesture to draw her into the orb of yellow light that circled the fireplace as the flames grew, the heat tugging at her, begging her to step into it, to warm her freezing fingers and toes...and to thaw her heart.

Why did trust feel like a mountain to climb? She swallowed again, blinking against the tears that threatened. She stared at that offered hand like it was a lifeline. But what if it had strings attached? What if it would require something of her? What if it took instead of giving the safety it seemed to offer?

Her breath came thicker and faster, but that hand didn't waver, and those eyes deepened with a honey glow, their darkness melting beneath the warmth and glow of the flames.

Why? Why couldn't she take that hand? It was like hers were tied to her sides. He didn't move, didn't once hesitate in his offer of something more than she had experienced before. Never had a man offered her anything without also demanding she take it, demanding she live by their rules, demanding she abide by the structure of the exchange they had set out.

"Take it."

But what if something happens?

"I'll be there."

But you left me. The tears spilled out of her eyes and fell down her face in hot swathes that carved through the ice, leaving behind something new and clean.

"I was there all along."

Isn't that what Marcus had said? She wanted to take that hand. Wanted to be protected, held, warmed. The icecap of her soul was creaking and exploding with its need for warmth, desperate to begin its spring thaw.

Something snapped. The resistance was gone, and though it took all her strength, she reached and nearly fell forward in her haste. It was like the dam had broken and her entire soul rushed forward to claim its prize. Her fingers were light in his warm ones, still freezing, but as he slowly, gently closed his fingers over hers, they filled her with warmth that raced up her arm and to her heart, melting something that had already started to show signs of life. Her legs gave out beneath her, and through the hazy tears, she felt herself being gently guided to a seat on the fur rug in front of the flames. The heat licked her face, drying her tears, and she sank into the soft fabric below, her fingers spreading into the fur, her heart aching that it wasn't Nuri.

Words were not necessary with Everard. She looked up into his eyes and saw a knowing there. The same that she had seen in Marcus's many a time. A subtle nod of his head was all he offered her before he turned back to the fire, putting another log upon those that were already crackling.

He started to head across the room, but she surprised herself by reaching out and touching his hand, then pulled back as if burned. She hadn't meant to do that. Who did she think she was?

He turned back to look at her, understanding on his face as he waited for what she wanted to say.

The words came out coated in emotion that was too deep for them to express. "Thank you."

He nodded, the fire in his eyes growing deeper. His hand lifted, and the gentle pressure on her head felt like a benediction. A father's hand, if a father were loving and kind and good. It enveloped the top of her head with its comfort, spilling over and pouring down to her very feet. That was all—a gentle hand on her head. But it cracked the last of the ice and sent healing rushing into a place that had long been broken.

She woke with her head pillowed on her arm, the fur rug gripped beneath her fingers as if it was Nuri, and her heart ached all over again. Where was her precious pup? Had Conri done something to her? Was she gone forever? The one friend in times of trouble had disappeared without even a goodbye, and Dilara felt as though another piece of her heart had been stolen from her. How much did she have left?

She sat up, the embers on the fire needing a good stoking. If she had learned anything from her work over the years, she knew well enough how to stoke a fire. Grasping the metal poker that leaned against the stones beside the open hearth, she stirred the coals, raking them together and blowing on them until they glowed red hot amidst the black. The remaining pieces of wood that had fallen away sputtered into a few flickering flames with another puff, and she settled a few more logs on top from the stack nearby.

Stretching her shoulders, she rolled them, wincing at their tightness. Sleeping on the floor, while warm, had not been the most comfortable. She had grown used to her straw mattress over the last few months. Perhaps she was going soft. Sleeping on the floor hadn't been out of the ordinary in her previous life.

Standing, she stretched the aches in her low back and unhooked her cloak from around her neck. Fendrel suddenly stepped out from behind the curtains and mirrored her as he stretched his own low back. The shadows on his face indicated a late night.

"Can I help? How is he?" The questions came out in a rush, blurred and almost mumbled in her haste.

Fendrel smiled wearily, stretching his arms and crossing one in front of his body, then reversing the movement with the other. "The same. Still feverish, more so than I would like. He can barely keep down a few sips of water, and I don't want him to get dehydrated." He shook his head. "I am going to make him some tea and hope that takes his fever down, but if he cannot drink it, it won't help much." He started for the kettle.

"Please, let me make it. I know how. You should rest."

He nodded his thanks, scrubbing his fingers over his face and through his hair. "All right. Use yarrow, elder flower, and nettle. The first two will fight fever, and hopefully the nettle will bring down some of the inflammation." He shook his head, pouring himself a glass of water and swallowing it greedily. "I've never seen him in this bad of shape. It's been some time since he's succumbed to such a fever."

"Please, get some sleep. He needs you more than me, but I can tend him long enough for you to rest."

Fendrel eyed her knowingly from across the kitchen table as she wrapped her hand around the kettle, divested it of its lid, and started filling it with water from the barrel by the door. "Thank you. You are a godsend. Everard went home last night. Since you were asleep, we figured there was no sense in trying to move you, but he said he would go out and ask around for a place for you to stay with some women folk."

Dilara knew she should take them up on their offer but couldn't deny that her heart sank when it was mentioned. Did she truly want to meet new people and live with someone else whom she knew nothing of and who knew nothing of her? Her stomach sank.

"Can't I stay with you?" The words were out before she could stop them. She blushed and hid it by bringing the kettle to the arm by the fireplace since the stove wasn't lit yet. She would do that next. Fendrel would be hungry when he woke, and the least she could do was offer him food.

He didn't answer her right away, and she finally glanced up at him, wondering what he was thinking. She hadn't expected herself to say it, so she wouldn't be surprised if he didn't take too kindly to her idea. Instead, though, he seemed thoughtful.

"Do you *want* to stay with us?"

"I…I at least know you." Her hand trembled, the water in the kettle sloshing as she set it on the arm and swung it over the fire so it rested directly over the flames.

"There's no shame in that. I completely understand. How about we see how Marcus fares, and then we can decide? I could use the help since you are willing to give it."

She drew a breath of relief. She was far from comfortable around anyone, but these two were the closest she had to friends, and when these were so hard to accept, the idea of finding new ones set her heart racing.

"I'll turn in. Keep him cool as best you can. I've been bathing him with cold compresses on his neck and face. Try to give him swallows of liquid with the spoon. The tea, too, once it's cool and if he'll have it. I won't be long."

"No need to be hasty."

"Call me if he gets worse. I pray he doesn't, but there's no knowing." He paused on his way into a room one over from Marcus's. "Are you sure you are all right taking care of him?"

She nodded.

He smiled in a fatherly way, making her heart light up in response. "Thank you, Dilara. You truly are a godsend."

Alone.

Unwanted.

A burden.

He moaned and shoved the spoon away. The fever pulled every last ounce of strength and coolness from his body with its burning heat, exploding down every limb, inside his very bones. He gasped against the cool rag that touched his face but then thrashed against it as it instantly took on the heat coursing through him, the feeling like a droplet of water sizzling into steam and evaporating when it touches hot bricks.

That haunted face—soft, gentle, but full of strength he had rarely seen—floated somewhere in his sight. The cold touched again before he was plunged once more into the furnace. Is this what Shadrach, Mesach, and Abednego felt like? No, that wasn't right. They weren't burned when they went into the furnace. He drew a deep breath, but the pain in his hip felt like a knife stabbing him, and it wrung a groan from his lips.

"Shh." The voice echoed in the distance. Soft, sweet, a healing balm to his weary soul.

A cold spoon touched his cracked lips, and a morsel of liquid trickled onto his tongue. Barely enough to do anything to quench his thirst, but it stayed down this time.

There were those eyes again. Staring deep into his soul, willing him to get well. He tried to keep them in sight, but the pain seared up his spine, and he had to wrench his eyes shut in an effort to hold back the cry that wanted to tear him limb from limb. Being unconscious would be better than this. Another spoonful touched his lips.

If only he could offer Dilara a life. Why did his heart yearn for her so when there were better men, stronger men, whole men who could love her, adore her, and keep her safe? He could offer her nothing but love and devotion. What must she think, seeing him lie on this bed, wasting away, too sick to move without crying out in pain? What kind of a life would that be? Chained to a cripple like him?

Then why did his heart beat in tandem with hers? Why did he see in her a woman he could not just love, but cherish? A woman whom he so desperately wanted to protect. Wanted to keep safe. Wanted to hold dearly and treat like the treasure that she was? Why, when he was nothing? Could never be anything worthy of more…

She was better than him. Had survived worse than he ever could and carried her wounds with a grace that seemed too far from him. He couldn't protect her; he couldn't even lift his head off his pillow without crying out in pain. And keep safe? If Conri came for her, it would take one fell swoop of his evil hand and Marcus would be flat on the floor with nothing more to give than a feeble cry for help.

He shook his head, the pain from his effort numbing his fiery brain further.

She could be nothing to him. Would never be. She needed better than he had to offer. She needed someone who would be a warrior on her behalf. Who would mend all those broken places within her. He was too broken himself to be able to heal anything.

Dilara held her breath. He had said that he loved her. His face bunched in pain and eyes half-closed as he rolled about in agony… Had he truly understood what he'd said? How could a man so good, so loving, so tender, love her? A woman who was broken, sullied, dirty beyond cleanliness with a heart wounded beyond repair?

No one could love her. Never. She was unworthy of it. Not only had everything been taken from her, but she had not even been able to save her child. Her hands shook, and in her attempt to set down the spoon, she instead sent the cup spinning across the floor, the tea spilling and seeping into the cracks of the planks as the stoneware cup shattered into pieces. They rocked on the floor as she stared. Every touch of hope within her froze.

He didn't know what he wanted. How could he? How could he want her and know all that she was? All that she truly was at her core?

Dirty.

Worthless.

Nothing.

He deserved so much better; he needed a wife that could give her entirety to him. Not a woman who had been shattered. She could not make him bear the shame that should be hers and hers alone.

Shamed.

Broken.

Murderer.

She had never said it to herself before, but now the word stared at her from the depths of her soul as her hands continued to shake and her heart trembled within her.

She was a murderer. She should have been able to save her child. Should have been able to keep him in her womb. Should have been able to fend off whatever poison they had given her. She should have known it was coming, should have given her everything to ensure her baby's safety.

But, instead, it had been too late. She had escaped, but for what? Her child had not escaped with her. If not for her stupidity and worthlessness, he would still be alive.

"Dilara?"

She jumped with a startled cry, her fingers clutching at the collar of her kirtle, desperate for more air, something clean, fresh, light to blow away the heaviness pinning her feet to the ground.

"Are you all right, my dear?" Fendrel stared intently into her eyes, only breaking his gaze away to peruse the room, and then returned his focus to her again.

She shook her head.

"What is the matter? What happened?" He took a step toward her, and she felt as though the whiplash had caught her back. She drew in a breath, cringing and cowering away from him, her hands up to ward him off.

He held his palm out as Everard had done, and the concern on his face was too much. She couldn't take it. How could they treat her like this when they knew what she was?

Maybe they didn't know.

She dashed forward, around him and out the door, snagging her cloak from the hook where she had hung it beside Marcus's as she ran from the house. She didn't know where she went, didn't even know where she was. The cobblestone streets were shrouded in dusk at the day's end, the shadows mocking her from every corner. Every one of them reminding her of who she really was.

Murderer.

Prostitute.

Sullied.

Alone.

So desperately alone.

A few doors closed as she flew past them, and the pain of being rejected, though she knew they weren't shutting for her, shoved the knife lodged in her heart deeper. They did well to bar their doors with a murderer on the loose.

With a suddenness that sent her tumbling onto her backside, she ran headfirst into something hard as she turned a corner, almost welcoming the sting as she crashed to the ground.

The grunt that reached her ears made her want to disappear into the cobblestones, and tears started to her eyes. Was it not enough to wallow in shame privately? But to have it displayed for all the world to see…

"Are you all right?" Whose was that deep voice? And why did it sound so familiar?

Everard towered over her, compassion and worry lacing his deep-toned skin as he held out a hand, offering help to stand.

That might have been the first time she had heard him speak. Surely she had before. Dashing the tears out of her eyes, she still heard that mocking voice growling in her ears, reminding her of who she was, of who she would always be, no matter if Marcus thought he loved her or not. Surely his fever made him think things, deranged things that were not true. He couldn't feel that way about her if he truly knew.

The hand came just a bit closer, as if it were more convenient for her if it were nearer. She daren't take his hand. He should not be seen with her. Her chest heaved with the gasps for breath as her body desperately tried to recoup some of the air that she had expended in her run. Dusk gathered closer, the gray shadows laughing at her, mocking her, pulling her into their darkness.

"You don't have to be alone, Dilara."

The words pierced the night air like a knife, and the shadows shook at the sound, cowering back into their corners like skulking wolves, unsure if their prey was worth the fight.

She looked up at the gentle face bending over the offered hand.

She almost crumpled. "You don't know me." She almost couldn't bring herself to look into those eyes, but when she did, they were glistening with moisture, a warmth there as his look oozed a gentleness she would never have expected from such a large man. From any man.

"I know more than you think."

Confused, she felt her insides quivering. She stood to her feet without the help of the offered hand, wrapping her arms around her middle and trying not to shiver in the cold. With a start, she realized she was wearing Marcus's cloak. She must have snagged the wrong one off the hook in her hurry. Now that she was calmer, she smelled his scent on it, and it was painfully wrong. This cloak did not belong to her, and she worried she would sully it just by wearing it.

"How can you know me?" Her voice was barbed as she shook out the folds of the cloak, brushing off the dirt and straw from the street that clung to the green wool. "You don't. You know nothing of who I am, what I have done."

The words spilled out of her faster than she had intended, and the pain that gripped her at the realization that she was sharing her innermost feelings with a near stranger, who somehow didn't feel like one, sent a shiver down her spine.

"I might have more of an idea than you realize." He held out his arm in a broad gesture, and she realized that the barn they were standing near was glowing from within, the sound of a large fire crackling into the street from the open doorway.

She threw a quizzical glance his way that he answered with a shrug. "My shop," he said.

Dilara remembered that Marcus had told her Everard was a blacksmith, and the soft whinny of a horse from within, along with the idea of warming herself in front of the flames, drew her into the building. He set a wooden box for her in front of the large hearth that was littered with his tools, and she sank down upon it, her shaky legs grateful. She was not used to such exercise and had not gained her strength back just yet. But she would not let him get away with such a statement.

"How could you know me? You've never met me." She gulped as a thought struck her of the bordello she had been taken from to send to the mines when it was found out that she was pregnant. She gulped back the bitter taste of nausea as her stomach turned.

He shook his head, standing far enough away so as not to feel like a threat. "I come from where you do."

Her head snapped up, gazing intently into that face, only now realizing where the familiarity in it came from. "You're...Rusalkan?"

He nodded, pain flashing across his features. That explained his stature. Men from the mountains north of Wood River were said to be tall and stronger than three men put together. She had only met one other that sported his height, and he had simply been passing through. The anger on his face had scared every single one of the girls at the bordello, and his chosen one had been sent to the mines after his visit. Dilara had not even had the opportunity to say goodbye to her.

"But if you have never met me before, how could you know anything about me?" While this man had the same size as the one who had visited the bordello, it was hard to see a resemblance between the two. There was a meanness in the one which Everard did not possess. His strength was tempered with a gentleness she was trying to trust as he proved himself over and over. The softness and tenderness that rested on his face and in the wrinkles around his dark eyes were different enough, but it was the flame from within that he shared with Marcus, Fendrel, and Keitha. The spark of a life not their own, something of another Kingdom shining from a depth she couldn't fathom. It was as if a part of their soul was tied elsewhere, and it shone forth on their countenance.

But the tears that gathered in those eyes now were more of a surprise to her than anything else.

"Because I was once like your master."

Her breath caught, and she clutched her stomach, her womb aching from a place deep within her. The emptiness cried out at the painful prick of memories that assuaged her like an avalanche in early spring.

"How?" she breathed. It was barely a rasp, barely audible.

The pain lacing his countenance like cuts made her heart feel near to bursting. "Conri was not the only slave trader." He choked and cleared his throat. "I was once like him in many ways. But for God's grace."

She stared, unable to move, to breathe, each thought more numb than the last. She didn't know that she believed him. Conri never had the light Everard seemed to carry. How could this be so?

"But…you are not like him."

His face crumpled, his voice following in scattered syllables coated with pain and unshed tears. "Only because our Heavenly King saw fit to redeem a sinner so great as I."

Tears spilled down her cheeks, though she knew not from whence they came.

"Dilara, this is how I know the shame you carry. I was once the cause of it for many like you. And that is why I know to tell you that the shame and guilt you carry, the wounds deep inside you that you feel will never heal, the voices that shout at you, telling you all that you are or ever were... They are not yours to bear. Our Savior can take every single one of those burdens, wash every stain white as snow."

Exposed, vulnerable before this man who hardly knew her, and yet saw deep into her heart. Every word he said was like one of Rensen's knives hitting their mark in the center of the target each time. "Your God—He saved you?"

He nodded. "I couldn't have done it on my own. My sins are too numerous to count. But by His grace, I have been forgiven." The first tears she had seen the man cry spilled down his cheeks. "Washed clean and set free. I only pray you will accept the same from Him."

She felt split in two, even as the weight in the pocket of her cloak—Marcus's cloak—drew her attention. Her hand gripped the small rectangular book of well-worn pages. Without thinking about it, she pulled it from the pocket, turning it over in trembling hands.

"But how can I trust someone I cannot see?"

"Faith is choosing to trust, never knowing for sure before you take the leap."

"But there is blood on my hands!" The words flew from her mouth like flames as her heart broke open, and she sank to her knees. "My child would have lived if not for me." Sobs welled deep from the place of emptiness and longing within her. The part that had failed her child. Failed to carry the little one entrusted to her. "How can He forgive that?"

That fatherly hand was on her head again, and words that sounded unfamiliar but were comforting nonetheless fell from whispering lips as she wept over the book in her hands, holding onto it like a lifeline, hoping against the empty void that it would somehow give her the strength Everard and Marcus held fast to.

"'Though your sins be as scarlet, they shall be as white as snow; though they be red like crimson, they shall be as wool.'" The words met the questions surrounding her heart and settled them with a gentle hand of reassurance, a soothing balm to her soul. "He died for you, Dilara. That guilt you feel… We would live in utter torment if it were not for Christ. He is the sacrifice that took the blame for our sins. Our Heavenly Father loved us too much to see us die an eternal death filled with pain and sorrow."

Every last sin. Every shame, guilt from every sin. Washed off of her all at once. It was almost too good to be true. "If He loves us so much, where was He? Where were You? *Where?* He died in my arms, and where were You?" The words were wrenched from her with a violence that sent her reeling as the bitterness flew from her tongue like flames licking up dry kindling.

"I never left."

"Why didn't you save me?" She held the book fast to her chest as if it would keep her from flying into pieces.

"I have. I am. Trust Me."

The months leading up to this moment flashed into her eyes. Nuri saving her. Marcus rescuing her in the field. Her long road to healing and the friends who cared for her along the way. Her rescue from the hands of Conri in the tavern, and even her escape to Padsley to keep her safer still.

It was as if she was being given new sight. Seeing every single circumstance from her escape to now and how her life had changed, been made new, with new chances, a new life, and new relationships with people she felt as though she could trust. Every gift given from a hand she had been unable to see before.

"I was with you all along. Moving. Caring for you. It may not look like what you would have wished for, but I love you with an everlasting love, and I rescued you from the hell of your life."

Warmth flooded through her heart.

"Repent, Dilara. Ask Him to come into your heart and forgive every shame that you carry. Give it all to Him. They're not yours any longer, child. He carried them for you. Let Him have them."

The ache to reach for the unseen hand that had led her all this way pulled at her from one direction, but her fear drew her another. The pain of the separation flooded her, darkness closing in around the edges of her vision. Her chest constricted beneath the pressure, and her heartbeat was loud in her ears, echoing with every resounding *thud, thud, thud* as she tried to draw a breath. She thought she heard Everard muttering but couldn't be sure as she fought with all that she had to simply breathe as the weight pressed her into the dirt floor she kneeled upon.

"You cannot have her!" The voice was booming, and it sliced through the cloud that threatened to drown her in ice and fire. But the darkness swirled closer, and she saw Conri's face. Laughing at her.

You thought you could leave me? I made you what you are. You are mine. You will always be mine. His laugh made her want to retch, and the weight pressed harder. Her chest. She couldn't breathe. *I bought you. You are mine.* His voice clung to her like chains, and she could almost feel the cold metal cutting her wrists. Air. If only she could get air.

"Be gone, in Jesus' name!" Everard's voice sounded like a roll of thunder that tore through the clouds that held her captive, lightning following with a clap.

"I bought you with My blood. You are Mine, not his. You will never be his. You are My child. He cannot own what I have redeemed."

"Take me. I am Yours." The words barely made it past her lips, and with a desperate plea, she reached forward, shattering the cloud that held her, and the shadow-wolves scattered. She could almost hear their yips of confusion and pain as they turned and ran.

"Daughter, you are Mine. Chosen. Holy. Loved. Made new. Clean. Worthy. Whole. You are who I say You are."

There was no denying the presence, the light. The warmth that she felt in that moment. Tears spilled from her eyes unhindered, the wracking sobs gone and replaced with a peace, deeper and calmer than the mountain lakes. Is this what

Marcus felt? The presence? The peace? The calm? It was like all the world swirled in a wintery tempest around her, while within she sat before the warmest fire. The avalanche came crashing down, and with it the burdens, the weight, the heaviness that had been on her shoulders, the pain that had been her constant cross to bear. The sorrow that had torn her apart on the inside no longer mocked her; she was filled. Whole. The emptiness deep in her womb that ached for more, ached for what she had lost, felt closed up and knit together. Missing but healing, mending beneath the ministering touch of her Healer. "Lord, you are my King. My Father. Have Your way with me."

His healing touch poured through her. Pain washed away beneath the ministering hand of a Savior who could heal the sick and restore hearts back to hope again. Who washed them white as snow.

Seventeen

SEPARATION OF SPACE AND HEARTS

SPRING WAS COMING. She could feel it in her bones—the warmth that was spreading, the snow slowly melting. Instead of ice falling from the sky, the large flakes were mixed with rain, gray mist hovering close to the ground like an animal skulking away from the hunter. Spring was rising to take winter's place, and the snow would not last long.

Marcus had been ill for nearly two weeks. She had pored over his book, the Bible, as he fought through fever and pain. Far too ill to do so himself, she had learned to read it as Fendrel read to them both over her shoulder, her eyes following his finger, tracing the words as he spoke them. Words took on shape, a physical form. Sounds became ink on a page, and her mind, always fast and able, capturing pictures like her paintings, was able to find what the markings meant and the sounds they created. She was far from being able to pick it up for herself without any help, but it was a start.

The more she read, the hungrier she grew, the deeper her longing was to hear more. She hadn't known how much this man Jesus had healed. It seemed as though every page, and sometimes more than once a page, He laid His hands on someone and brought about a miraculous healing. A blind man could see after Jesus pressed mud to his eyes. A lame man walked again. A young girl rose from the dead. A woman with a bleeding womb was made whole. A woman just like her.

Resting a hand on her stomach where her child had dwelt, she felt the longing washed clean. The pain still dwelt within her soul, but there was a comfort to it. As if her wound was shared by another. As if she was being mended, touched, and held through her pain. Shared pain healed instead of making the wound grow deeper with each remembrance. She felt His nearness with her in every moment, felt her heart longing for more of Him. Begging Him, when every thought or memory brought with it a sharp stab. Her heart turned to Him, and He met her there. Even in the darkest and most vile of places.

No longer was she alone in the forest, wandering amidst the dark, threatening trees, crying out in loneliness, afraid for her life from those who sought to devour and enslave her. He walked beside her, held her hand and guided her through, helped her over stones and stumbling blocks, and warmed her against the ice that threatened to bury her.

Dilara worried Marcus fought for his life. The fever wracked his thin frame, divesting it of the fire that burned within him and leaving him limp like a rag wrung dry. His moans throughout the night and cries of pain set her teeth on edge and her heart to beating fast. She wished she could share in his pain as he did for so many others.

Instead, she painted for him. She learned to mix his tea and his herbs, but she also learned how to use them to create colors. Blues from cornflowers and iris, green from nettle leaves. Purple from the elderberries and coneflower. Pink from hyssop. Pages started to fill with the pictures from her mind. Mountain fields strewn with wildflowers. Views of the forest from the plateau. The Kaira mountain ranges. She even started painting faces.

Keitha. Kahru. Jaromir. Even Nuri, though her heart ached with longing as she gave life to that sweet, protective face.

Soon Fendrel's table was full of them. The mantle above the fireplace brimmed with sheets of parchment, paper, and even birch bark, painted with oils and watercolors. Her dreams, too, made it onto the pages—not the nightmares. Though they had decreased, they still occasionally troubled her. But no, the new ones. The ones that filled her mind with a beauty that breathed peace into her slumbering hours.

Dancing in the meadows. Her hand in the larger one of her father. Her mother hugging her as a child. What she imagined her son's face would have looked like as a child.

Pictures became the pathway to memories she wished she'd had. Pieces of her that had been stolen and moments that should have been. Each picture felt like a capture of something she should have been given, and each one painted a picture of hope and healing upon her heart as she created from somewhere deep in her spirit.

Marcus coughed, and she dropped her brush, rushing to his side to lift the tea to his dry and cracking lips. The fever was gone, but in its wake, it left a shadow of the man she had once known.

"I can do it." His voice was raspy, and he choked on the last word, coughing dryly. She ignored his admonition and held the cup to his lips anyway.

Dilara glanced at his eyes; they looked cold now, as if his weariness was sucking the life from him. She could see the pain on his face, though he tried to hide it. Always hiding. Always pretending. He reached for the cup with a wince, his spine stiff against the pillows, the simple act surely slicing through him with pain. She could tell he schooled his features when he grasped the cup, but his shoulders were tense, and he held his breath before letting it out through clenched teeth. He blinked hard, looked up, and his eyes snagged on hers.

"You care for everyone, but why do you not let anyone care for you?" The words, perhaps too honest, hopped out before she could stop them.

His mouth gaped open, the question falling like a spilled glass of water to the floor where it rested like a puddle in the stillness.

"I—" He trailed off, simply staring, and she still held his gaze, determined to understand this man who chose to carry burdens upon a back that was not straight enough to bear them upright.

"I have been cared for by all of you the last few weeks." The tiredness and frustration in his voice was not missed.

"Yes, but you do not *let* them care for you."

The frustration at having no response to her question rose in his chest, freezing cold, as though a bucket of snow had been dropped on his head. Intense, the frustration wasn't directed at Dilara, but at the fact that she was right. So right, and he had no words to argue. He tried to swallow back the reply that came from somewhere cavernously deep within him. But it came nonetheless.

"I do not want to be a burden."

Her brown eyes were persistent, like a doe who had caught the eye of a human in its path, unwilling to relinquish the link between them. He often wondered when he would say or do something that would send her skittering back into the woods of her mind, shutting out any and all connection between them. She had been different since he had awoken from the fever that had wracked his very bones with its grip.

"You are not a burden." Her words were quiet in the little room.

"You are not like I am. You are not unable to move about without the help of a crutch or cane. You do not lie in bed for weeks on end, unable to even lift your head from a pillow. You are not weak beyond reckoning with hands that can do little else but pick and press herbs." He choked in the back of his throat, but this time it was not from the dryness.

She tilted her head, still staring at him, unnerving him with those massive brown eyes. "But if He made you this way, how can you be a burden?"

Silence.

He didn't know what to say, or more aptly, he did but couldn't bring himself to. "I only act like I have all the answers. I can't help but feel that He *didn't* make me this way. I became this way. If I had done anything different, I would be whole and the man who risked his life to save me would still be alive. I am guilty of more than just existing. If I had not been in the way, none of this would have happened. Maybe if I had just died that day—"

"What?" The vehemence in her voice snapped his head up, his gaze to her face, fire behind those eyes that no longer looked like a frightened deer in the woods but more like those of a mother bear.

"What would have happened if you had died that day? Either you were meant to be here, or you are just one mighty accident. And you, Marcus, are no accident. Why do you think I am standing here at this moment?" Tears rose in her eyes, making them swim, and he saw a depth of pain and emotion behind the anger. "If you had died that day, I would have died on a mountaintop, or perhaps a battlefield, or maybe I would have even been dragged back to the bordello or continued on my way to the mines. My life would be a living hell instead of the taste of heaven I've had earthside. All because you were alive to be in a certain place at a certain time and care for a certain person God put in your path. And you have the nerve to think your existence on this earth is nothing but a burden?" Her chest rose and fell rapidly as she struggled to catch her breath.

The anger and strength in her surprised him, like a snap from a log that had been cheerfully crackling on the hearth all this time, the coals suddenly exploding with the built up heat of flame.

"What did I do that anyone else could not?"

The huff that issued from her made his heart nearly stop. He had never seen her this way. How was she so angry, almost hostile, and…stunning?

The tears still brimming in those flickering eyes caught him further off guard, and his stomach clenched. "Is that what you think? All this time you have been someone I thought knew God better than most. I could see it in you. Where did *that* Marcus go? Because this false sense of humility is nothing but a farce. Even I, who was lied to my entire life, can see straight through it. What are you afraid of, Marcus? Of actually mattering? Of meaning something beyond what you thought you could offer?"

The disappointment that filled her voice made him wish to climb out of his pain-wracked shell and flee from the room to escape that look, that voice…that truth.

"I saw Christ's purpose in you. I saw *Him* in you. And yet you are just like all the others—hiding." Pain shot across her face, and she turned sharply, fleeing from the room, the skirt of her kirtle swirling behind her.

How he longed to jump out of this bed, escape the pain and the truth and lies that swirled around him, fighting for supremacy like a snarling pack of wolves. He shuddered. When had the truth become so distorted by the lies he had housed himself in?

Why did things feel so strange? Dilara's feet, clothed in the deerskin shoes Keitha had made for her, pattered against the cobblestones. She needed to get away. Out of this place where people and their inquisitive gazes seemed to track her through the streets. How did a person breathe with so many people all in each other's space all at once? She hadn't realized how much she had missed the trees, the brisk open air, and the sky calling her name.

Just a little bit of space, of freedom, was all she asked.

Outside of the wall that contained the village, she drew her first true sigh of relief. Her feet slowed, the brisk breeze rustling through her hair; she reached behind her head to unwrap the long braid that was tied into a bun with a string of leather. It thumped against her back as she moved forward, the hill behind the copse of trees calling her name. Stepping off the road, she felt a smile reach her lips. The dead grass actually looked like it had some green to it. Bending down, she ran her fingers through it—wet, cold, but starting to show signs of life, much like her own heart.

How did living this new life feel like she was a floundering puppy galloping about a field on its first foray into freedom, unsure of itself, her feet getting tangled up more than making steady steps?

"I am with you in the learning. I will never leave you nor forsake you."

Her eyes filled with tears, and her steps continued on. The wind whistled through the empty branches of the trees, tiny green buds tinged with pink, unnoticeable from a distance, sprouting along the sleeping trees. That verse had been one of the first Fendrel had read to her, and it had instantly been committed to memory.

"I will never leave you nor forsake you. Even when your father and mother forsake you, I the Lord will be with you and take care of you."

He had done that. Cared for her even when those she should have been able to love and trust had forsaken her. Worse, sold her into the hands of another.

Marcus, though wrong about so many things of late, had been right about that. She kicked a stone with her toe, frowning at the offensive member as it stung. What had happened to Marcus?

The healer that had surprised her. Protected her. Brought healing and spoken truth to her, gently leading and guiding her in the direction of the only One who could save her soul. The man who had been right about so many things was now an entirely different person. Was this the man behind the facade? That couldn't be. She had grown to know him. But was it just another instance of betrayed trust in her life? Why did everything she love always become everything she lost?

She hugged her arms tightly around herself against the biting spring wind. It was cold, but it had a taste of the warmth to come as she leaned into the climb. The hill on the eastern side of Padsley was taller than it had first appeared, but she relished the stitch that grew in her side, the puffing that filled her lungs with invigorating, chilly air. It set her nerves to tingling, her mind to dancing, and her eyes set on the prize of reaching the top. It gave her a direction for the frustration she felt.

"Fine. I've given you every other part of my life. You can have him, too. He needs you more than he needs me. Perhaps he never wanted me in the first place."

How Conri would mock her if he saw her talking to thin air. But Marcus had said that God was a God who always hears. Always listens to the cries of his children. Be it about sorrow or simple aches and pains.

Perhaps Marcus's declaration of love for her in his fevered state was only that. A fevered expression of some thought that popped into his head, induced by delirium. How foolish she had been to think a man like him might love a girl like her. She saw her own struggles in his pain, but the same redemptive power that had rescued her was also his. She saw his strength, even in his weakness, and was drawn to him all the more for it.

Perhaps no one ever would love her. Perhaps there would never be a person who would cherish her for who she was, despite what had happened to her. Was being alone all that bad? Perhaps standing on her own two feet would be the making of her. The redemption of her story. Christ in her, strengthening her for a life of solitude. She hadn't known many women who had done so, but if she had her Heavenly Father, then what need did she have of anyone else?

And if that was the truth, then why did her heart yearn and ache at the thought of never having the family she had dreamed of? Why did her arms feel the emptiness and the loss of her child more keenly now that the idea of having another was gone forever?

She crested the hill and caught her breath, staring straight at the start and end of her story. The place where it all had made her who she was—the Kaira mountains rising above the clouds in the distance.

Her story—started, but not complete. What did the rest of the pages hold?

A FEW WEEKS LATER

Marcus dragged himself out of bed again. Yesterday had been an improvement on the day before, and he hoped today would be the same. He hadn't been this sick since the weeks directly following his injury. The expenditure of energy had reached its limit after the entire ordeal in Pranvera. He had even survived a battle. Not literally, but that was the closet he had ever been to one and the closest he ever wanted to be. The months of tending, praying, and caring for those who had been ill had done him in, and Dilara was right. He had slipped into not letting others care for him, speak into his life. He felt heat rise into his face to think of how he had reacted to Fendrel and Everard over some of their coddling.

Just because they acted like mother hens didn't mean that gave him reason to respond in anger and frustration. And if he did, what did that say about the true nature of his heart? Why did being forced to rest, stay still, and perhaps even accept care make him so irritable and angry?

I'm sorry, Lord. Settling his vest over his shoulders, much thinner now than they ever had been, he reached for the familiar lump in his pocket. The book that held all the answers, all the joy, and all the healing he could ever ask for. He ached at the feeling of it. The realization that it was no longer in Dilara's hands. Her absence had been a yearning hole in his day-to-day life, an eclipse where the sun was missing. The winter air had rushed in and perturbed his spirit without the joy of a woman who carried life and spring in her very voice, art from her fingertips, and understanding in those large brown eyes that could flip his heart.

There was a strength in her that he so desperately wanted for himself. Something that he, as a child of God, had not been in possession of. An acceptance of circumstances. A growth through pain that was unimaginable.

And here I've been a complaining fool with nothing to say but grumpily begging for a release from a life You chose to give me. Forgive me, Lord.

"It's good to see you up and about, dear boy." Fendrel was smiling from the doorway, his arms folded as he leaned against the lintel.

"I wish I could say it was good to be so, but it aches more than I care to admit." He winced as his hip grated harshly, bone against bone, as his shaky steps made for the doorway. He missed his herbs, the earthy smell that coated his hands and the healing they gave to those in need.

"It will get better in time."

"I'm terribly sorry for being the worst patient you've ever had."

Fendrel's eyes twinkled as he reached out and offered a helping hand to Marcus in that way he had of making Marcus feel that he did it of his own accord and not because it was needed. "You were that. Though, of course, I will forgive you, as is my Christian duty."

"Thanks a heap," Marcus grumbled, covering a growl from the halting and jerky steps that wrung throbs of pain from the joints, bones, and muscles that had been scarcely used in nearly a month's time.

"Spring is on its way. I'll bet the dandelion and nettle are about ready to harvest. The sunshine and crisp air might do you some good. You missed the ground thaw, but the river is still roaring through Raintamount, and the leaves are starting to bud on the trees."

Spring had a tendency to stay true to its name, springing up like a well of hope, exuberance, and life. The warmer weather treated him kindly and gave him much to look forward to. His joints and bones ceased to ache quite as much, and his crutches were often disposed of for a simple cane. The warmer months were the promise of a life nearly normal, something to look forward to through a winter of cold, aches, and pains.

"I bet that is a sight to behold."

"Especially after the Pranvera mountains. Rusalka is far too cold for my liking. I'll take the mild, rainy weather we get here over the ice and storms that seemed to pelt us like a demon unleashed for weeks at a time."

By now the table had been reached, and Marcus sank with a grateful sigh onto the bench to hide his shaking legs and his trembling strength.

The silence punctuated by his deep breathing passed between them for a moment.

"Dilara is staying with the Milton family. Kenelm said she has been doing well and been helpful to them with the little ones. You know how Mya has much to do with their youngest being just over a year old." Fendrel's words were calm and quiet. Almost hesitant.

Marcus cleared his throat and shoved down the pain of what he wanted. Maybe if he kept thrusting it down further, it would cease to bother him with its presence. "That's good."

"Marcus."

Reaching for his pestle, he avoided eye contact with Fendrel. He knew the man was going to speak his mind, and he wasn't exactly ready to hear it at the moment.

"You know you are worthy of her, and she of you."

His eyes snapped up of their own accord. So much for avoiding eye contact. "What do you mean?"

A small smile tugged at the corner of Fendrel's bearded face. "You said many things in your feverish sleep."

His eyes widened as he sucked in a sharp breath. "What?"

Fendrel couldn't hide his smile as he leaned back against the wooden table and folded his arms across his chest. Was that smugness in his grin? "You might think you have no future together, but don't let that thought sit inside your head. You two would make a beautiful match." Wistfulness joined the soft light in Fendrel's silver-hued eyes.

"But she's been through so much."

"As have you, which makes you even more perfect for each other. You each have some understanding and compassion for what the other has experienced."

Marcus shook his head. "Nothing I have been through could compare."

"It's not a competition, Marcus. But don't deny yourself the emotions you are feeling. They may have been placed there by the Lord, and He knows better than we ever could. I just don't want you to think that what He might have set before you is something that you aren't worthy of. He has made you worthy, and your life is of more import to Him than it could ever be to anyone else."

Swallowing back against the lump in his throat, Marcus pulled dried leaves from the thyme stems one by one, the task taking him longer than it ought. Perhaps there was something to what Fendrel said. Was it not repeating the same refrain he had been sensing in his spirit?

Spring caught up with them like a cart racing downhill. The warm days tripped into each other as the golden glow of the sun stretched deeper and deeper into the evening, pushing back the darkness earlier each morning. Dew gathered on trees like beads on a necklace, catching the glimmering light of early morning and waning evening. With the warm weather, Marcus's aches abated, and his strength slowly returned. He ventured farther and farther from his door every single day, stretching his walks, counting his steps and smiling to himself as the number of them grew with his strength. The greenery exploded over the ground and from beneath the disintegrating leaves on the forest floor, tiny buds and leaves curling out of winter's dead and frozen blanket.

The shadows of the branches grew larger as the leaves sprouted almost overnight, stretching to meet the sunlight so rapidly it was almost like an explosion of spring green and amber, with the occasional shade of pink. Raintamount was returning to its former glory, and the spring rains hugged the spindly branches with fog as the sun played hide and seek behind the clouds.

The world was waking up, and with it, Marcus's soul was coming alive. All except that small part that longed for something more. A certain broken but healing soul who had more strength burning within her bones than he had ever seen.

His knees creaked and were wet with the damp from last night's rain as he dug his fingers into the dirt, removing the dandelion sprout, roots and all. Each part of the plant was precious and could be used for the healing of a body. Nothing the Lord made was wasted.

He started at the thought and blinked rapidly against the moisture in his eyes as he saw himself in the thin and spindly dandelion plants.

"Oh!" The soft exclamation snapped his eyes up to the beautiful face he had been looking for around every corner since he had started venturing from the house. Those large mahogany eyes shone from a face rounder, ruddier, and softer than he had last seen it. The pinched look of pain and malnourishment was replaced with a healthful glow and strength that set off her eyes like those of a gazelle—awake, alive, but still unassured and hesitant.

"Dilara," he whispered. Where had his voice gone?

She glanced behind her, the basket hanging from her arm filled with wild ramps she must have been foraging from the forest. His mouth watered at the idea of a plate full of them steamed. He would need to fill a basket himself.

"I'm sorry, I oughtn't to have disturbed you. I'll go another way."

Why was she so fidgety? "No, don't! You don't have to leave. I was just thinking about you."

The stunned silence that met his words made him want to crawl beneath his basket instead of continuing with the conversation. Why on earth had he said such a thing? How terrible to say to a woman who had been stalked and had struggled to escape from an evil hand.

"I mean…that is to say…" He cleared his throat as his words trailed off.

Her eyes darted everywhere but to meet his as she rearranged her ramps in her basket, as if to create a more useful display of them.

What had happened to the ease of conversation, the comfort they had possessed together? Where was the woman he had grown to care for as a friend?

"Would you like to come to dinner?" He cringed at his callused, hurried tone. If he could have hit himself in the head with his cane, he would have appreciated the gesture.

"I—Mya may need me. I was collecting these…for dinner."

She still had yet to meet his eyes. What to say? What to do? What could he say that would bring her back to her old self and somehow erase all of the uncomfortable feelings that hung in the air between them like a wall that had been erected over night? Where had the comfort and the ease gone? Chased away by the words neither had meant to say? How did one regain a trust that had fled like a bird startled from the heather?

She turned to leave when a crack in the forest stilled her mid-step. The hair on the back of Marcus's neck stood on end, and his eyes scanned the hollow shadows of the forest, the brush still bare and new in its weak attempt at foliage. A darkened figure moved behind the brush in the distance, and he stood, moving to her side in two steps that were sore, tottering, and painful as he took her hand by instinct. She glanced up at him with fear in her eyes, and the terrified darkness that pinched her face made his heart beat hard in his ears.

Another branch cracked, and he gathered his cane in his other hand, positioning it in front of him to ward off whatever came after them. Was it Conri? Come with the thaw to claim what he thought was his? A wild animal on the loose? His hand trembled with the adrenaline that was coursing through his body as her cold, little hand fit snugly into it. Perfect, small, cherished, protected.

The shadow moved closer, and his muscles tensed, readying for whatever it was that lurked in the forest to pounce. Though he wasn't sure how far his limited strength would get them.

Eighteen

BURIED PASTS AND NEW BEGINNINGS

A BELOVED WOLF face bounded out of the woods, and large paws crawled up Dilara's legs, pressing into her stomach and knocking her off her feet. She gathered the large, furry body in her arms as the soft chirping sound she had thought she'd never hear again sounded in her ears, comforting as ever. The wet tongue that met her face filled her with such joy that a laugh escaped her lungs, like a bird set free from a trap.

"Nuri." The name came out as a half-laugh, half-sob as her heart jumped loudly in her chest, the after-effects of the surprise filling her with a jittery, dancing feeling in her belly. She smiled wider. Not only was Nuri alive, but she carried a pup. The wolf's stomach was swollen, probably near to giving birth. The idea of a small version of Nuri bounding around in the spring made her heart ache with happiness.

"You found me. You're all right. I was so worried about you. Don't you dare leave me like that again." Dilara whispered into the she-wolf's ears.

A throat clearing off to her left and a soft moan made her snap her head over to find Marcus, dumped unceremoniously in the soft, new-green foliage, a grimace of pain on his face.

"Marcus! I am so sorry! I didn't mean—"

He shook his head, groaning as he rose to his elbows, feeling around for his cane. "It's all right. It's not your fault."

"All the same—" She rushed to his side, handing him his cane and gripping his elbows to pull him to his feet, her hair falling in front of her face. She blew it out of the way as, together, they hefted Marcus back to his feet, looking up into his face to make sure he was okay.

The wonder on his face, merely a foot from hers, almost made her stop breathing.

"What is it?" Why was he looking at her like that? She pushed her messy curls behind her ear.

"You're so beautiful."

And the wall came crashing down. Agony filled her soul. She was too broken. Too dirty. How could he find her beautiful?

Like a wild animal frightened beyond reason, she ran. Gathered her skirts, left basket and wolf and boy, and ran for the hill. Her heart thudded in her chest, shattering the comfort she had just experienced. Panic. Fear at the bigness of his expression and the words that had flooded from him like water from a tipped over barrel, pouring out before anyone could stop it.

She saw his face in her head. The admiration, wonder—was it love? How could a man like him look at her in such a pure way that made her insides feel worthless? None of the men had ever looked at her that way before. There was always greed. Desire. Pain laced with their own attempts to drown and wallow in something that should never have been theirs to begin with.

But that look? She had never seen a look like that on another's face.

Her feet flew up the hill, the sound of a bounding wolf behind her. She cared not that she had left him behind. Her heart longed to hide, to find solace, to escape the feelings she had seen on his face and the words that had escaped his lips. The declaration of what she believed in her deepest core to be a lie about her. God could save her. He had, but surely He could not make her whole. She had been through too much. He could not make her beautiful. She had been told many a time that such dreams were gone forever, hope lost in the avalanche of shame and degradation and guilt of what she had been made into.

Panic flooded Marcus, but determination won out. She could not run. Not this time. She needed to hear the words that filled his heart like a raging forest fire, licking the trees to ashes in the path of the truth that coursed through his veins. She needed to hear it. She could run and hide forever, but only after she heard him out. He could not let her live and believe herself to be something that she was not. Righteous anger surged through him at what another man had done to her. How others had forgotten that she was human and had treated her as if she was not.

His cane helped him along his way, though it did little once he made it to the foot of the hill. He could see her skirt dancing on the wind up ahead, and his breath almost gave out at the very idea of trying to climb the summit in front of him.

"The Lord is my *strength*." The last word came out as a groan as he stepped onto the mounting ground before him and pulled his weight onto another step upward, small but excruciating. He would climb this hill even if he died in the attempt.

He would do anything for her. Including putting life and limb at risk of never recovering. Words that made no sense to anyone but the Spirit within him flew from his tongue on a whispered breath as his inhales and exhales became more labored, his limbs trembling with the effort, wholly unprepared for this tax on their reserves. She had already disappeared from sight, but onward he climbed. The sun bowed toward the horizon, closer to setting with each tortuous step that he took.

Onward, every step an effort beyond his strength. Every movement added aches to the already screaming muscles. His lungs screamed for air, burning against the sharp sting of the spring coolness.

Upward. Broken, painful. His breath wore thin, and the meager amount of air he was able to suck into his lungs seemed to be of little help in his climb.

His bones begged him to stop. To sit down, just for a spell. Rest long enough to catch his breath or to relieve some of the ache from every single muscle in his body as they cried for a rest from the toil of his climb. But forward he trudged, his steps getting shorter, every joint shaking harder, his hand trembling as he brought his cane forward every other step to use as a pulley to get him farther up the hill. His eyes burned, and tears welled in them at the force with which he pushed forward. His mouth was dry, water sounding like life-giving power from above. His throat tried to close up in an attempt to make him stop, but he continued on. The crest of the hill grew further out of reach as each moment seemed to draw it farther from him instead of closer.

With a sudden thrust that stole what little breath he had from his lungs, he crested the hill, gold and orange flooding the sky as the sun's rays lengthened, and the peak of the Kaira mountains nestled atop the clouds in the distance.

The wind blew his cloak around his shoulders, throwing it about as it danced with more energy than he would ever possess in his lifetime. But her skirt flapped in the breeze mere yards away, Nuri at her feet as he drew himself closer, his mind whirling in prayers that were almost incoherent. He knew the Lord heard as his soul stirred at the peace, purpose, and comfort that flooded him from within.

"Dilara." Her name came out strong, though he knew not where the strength came from. He surely possessed none as his hand shook, lifting his cane forward and dragging himself closer.

She turned. The surprise on her face was swallowed up by pain, sorrow, and anger that crackled like sparks from a log exploding into flame.

"I am not beautiful!" Her words were shouted with every ounce of strength within her, ripping a hole in her gut and her heart as she let them loose. She screamed them. She knew she did. But the beast within her was raging, slamming against her insides, trying its hardest to escape. "I was ripped to shreds from the inside out. Every part of me laid to waste. It can't be healed. *I* can't be healed. Don't you understand? You can't fix me, Marcus! No one can."

The tears that trembled on those brown lashes made his blue-green eyes look like mountain glass. "That's not true."

"How do you know? When was your heart ripped from your chest by the very one who was sworn to protect you? Everything I loved became everything I lost. Everything I held dear was either ripped from my arms or stabbed me in the back. Everything. No one can heal that." Her screaming had settled to a low rumble like thunder as it receded into the distance. She quivered from head to toe, her knees knocking and her heart vibrating in her chest with an uneasy rhythm that felt entirely unnatural. Her hands shook, her lungs floundering like drowning fish within her chest. "Not even you."

"Christ can." His lips barely moved, the snow that had started to fall—the last sputter of winter at this altitude—distancing them, dancing between them and mingling with their pain. Its whiteness mocked the black heart and bloodied wounds of her soul, laid bare for the world to see.

Nuri whined, her large paw batting Dilara's calf, her face sorrowful in the golden light of the lowering sun.

Dilara pushed her away. "You don't know that. You don't know what I've done."

"What's been done *to* you, Dilara." Marcus stood, the pain-filled look on his face an expression of his heart but surely added to by the effort she knew it took him to stay on his feet, weak from the climb. "None of this was your fault."

"Then *why*?" Her voice broke on a sob. "Why did my father sell me? What did I do?" Her words fell to a whisper.

Marcus's face fell, and a tear escaped those beautiful, pure eyes. He was standing right in front of her now. She could get lost in those eyes. Hers were dry, painfully so. But she didn't break his gaze. She couldn't. She was spellbound. Those eyes were the only link to Heaven she knew. Like a portal to a world she only wished she could live in. Her entire soul longed to be counted among those who did, but her spirit knew it was too broken.

He didn't touch her. He didn't have to. His words poured out like ointment on a festering wound, knocking down the flames of pain, shoving them back. "You did nothing. You are nothing wrong. The wrong was in them, Dilara. You are a treasure. Priceless. Like the scarce mountain diamonds that we only hear tales of. You are chosen, not by a man no better than a demon; you were chosen by a King. A pure, holy, spotless, beautiful King who sees nothing but the beauty He created in your soul when He breathed His life into it. His love is unconditional. It's nothing you earn."

Her heart jumped at the pronouncement of his words, as if a chord deep within her had been struck. A string, strummed and reverberating against the tension that held her suspended between pain and salvation. A tightrope between guilt and freedom. Shame and wholeness. Sorrow and healing.

Her words were a whisper now. Aching. "What if I don't want to heal? It would mean I have to let go." She held her arms tight around herself, her hair whipping against her skin in the wind. "I can't move on from my son. I can't. It would be as if he didn't exist at all, but he was real. He existed, and my empty arms are only empty to me, and the world goes on without him. But how can I?"

"He will be with you." The words that spilled from Marcus went deeper than mere speech. Their syllables like cool water, dousing the flames of pain that tore through her. Their truth settling into her spirit and whispering healing just like his herbs had to her body. "'But now thus saith the Lord that created thee, and he that formed thee, "Fear not: for I have redeemed thee, I have called thee by thy name; thou art mine. When thou passest through the waters, I will be with thee; and through the rivers, they shall not overflow thee: when thou walkest through the fire, thou shalt not be burned; neither shall the flame kindle upon thee. For I am the Lord thy God, the Holy One of Israel, thy Savior."'"

She sank to her knees, tears finally spilling from her eyes as the sobs wracked her frame and the wind caressed her wet and flaming face.

"'Since thou wast precious in my sight, thou hast been honorable, and I have loved thee: therefore will I give men for thee, and people for thy life. Fear not: for I am with thee: I will bring thy seed from the east, and gather thee from the west; I will say to the north, Give up; and to the south, Keep not back: bring my sons from far, and my daughters from the ends of the earth; Even every one that is called by my name: for I have created him for my glory, I have formed him; yea,

I have made him.'" Marcus's voice, although breathless, was full of fervor.

"I bought you with my blood. You are Mine. You will always be Mine. I have ransomed you from your enemies. Set you free from captivity. Your pain is Mine. Your child is Mine. Every ache you feel, I carry with you. My heart is for you. My healing touch, yours for the asking. Draw near to Me, My daughter. I am your Father. I will never leave you nor forsake you. I will never abandon you or sell you to another. Betrayal will never come from Me. You are Mine. You are whole. You are enough. You are clean. You are loved. You are free. Forever, you are free."

The arms that wrapped around her were strong in the tenderness of the exploding sunset, its golden rays casting a warmth over them as the last flakes of winter whirled around, dancing in their tossing hair. The new, fresh blades of grass growing from beneath the golden ones of last year comforted her skin with their coolness as her hands gripped the earth as if to hold herself together.

The arms that encircled her were not the strongest, nor the greatest in the world as she rested her aching head against the thin shoulder. But they were strong enough to hold her tight and to protect her from harm. And the tender whisper of love in her ear was as sweet as the One who whispered in her spirit, filling her with healing from the inside out.

ONE MONTH LATER

Today's journey had been forged those weeks before on the top of the hill.

Marcus held her hand and did his best to walk without his limp, though the farther they got from Padsley, the harder it became. She wasn't the strongest due to her own physical struggles, but it didn't take much to be stronger than him. His breath came harsher and faster in short gasps as the pain in his hip increased with each step.

He stumbled over a loose stone and crashed to a knee with a hiss of breath between his clenched teeth. She bent down, her large brown eyes framed with their beautiful lashes and their depths speaking of compassion and—he hoped—something else.

"Here, let me help you." She settled a gentle palm under his elbow, giving her strength to pull him up beside her with the little handful of daffodils clutched in her fist. But if she didn't stop squeezing their stems so hard, there wouldn't be much of them left by the time they reached their destination.

They walked on, slower now as she supported him without taking her hand from where she had placed it to help him up. He was grateful for her added support, though he tried to disperse it as much as possible to his crutch under the other arm.

After this excursion, it might be a two-crutch day, or perhaps simply a day to spend in bed. His heart ached. He wanted so desperately to be more for her. Stronger, to be the one to extend the protection that a woman of her past and heart deserved.

Because no matter what Dilara said, she was worthy of something special. She was worthy of all the love and hope and peace and comfort a man could muster.

And he was less than most men in every department.

The forested hill took it out of him, and he worried that he wouldn't even be able to make it back to Padsley, but his heart was so full of the reason for this outing that he would have given anything to be there. Had, in fact.

She was trembling. He could feel it before the gentle rainstorm of tears that cascaded down her cheeks turned to sobs. They crested the hill and turned their backs to the woods, facing out over the view that he would gladly give of his breath again to witness with Dilara at his side.

She shook like an autumn leaf about to shudder to the forest floor, and he wrapped her hands in his as they stared out over the wooded hill they had climbed to Padsley, the farmland beyond, and the far top of Raintamount Forest as it disappeared in the foggy distance. It took his breath away. Just a few hills higher and one might be able to see the ocean on a clear day.

Then they turned. The sight of the Kaira mountains rising out of the clouds in the distance. Marking where they had come from. The journey they had both experienced to get here. The mountaintop matched the one that shone through in Dilara's painting, her art capturing a picture of a place she had called home but had treated her in a way utterly unworthy of the word. Yet it was a part of her tale. A part of what had made her who she was. It was a part of crafting a story for her life and the little life that had left this side of Heaven far too soon.

"I wish…" Dilara's voice broke, her jaw shuddering with the impact of the sorrow he knew consumed her soul. "I wish he could be here to see this. I want to always think of him with this view. A view of a world he will never see." She swallowed and hiccuped back a sob.

His own heart ached as he gripped her hand tighter. "I can guarantee you that the view he has now is far superior." His breathless voice sank to a whisper of marvel at the thought of Heaven.

A few moments longer and she swung the small wooden board from her back.

There, the words that Everard had carved stood out in a timeless reminder of first love, lost and broken. Snatched away in the wintry depths of the forest, with no audience to the silent passing save the mother who bore him and the wolf who cared for her. No witness save the sighing trees, the moaning wind, and the scattered gray light of winter.

He helped her dig and set the delicately carved wooden monument upright in the ground. There was no body beneath this marker, and Marcus thought it fitting as he swept the dirt back to hold it in its place. The babe did not reside here; he lived with his Father in Heaven, forever comforted, forever at peace. But his memory would not soon be forgotten. Not in the heart of Dilara nor from that of the man who loved her more than life itself.

Dilara swayed and looked at the daffodils clutched in her white-knuckled and dirt-stained grip, gazing beyond them to the name enshrined in the carving.

Asa Chaim.

Loved and not forgotten.

Thou art mine.

Marcus fought back the clenched feeling at the back of his throat as tears started to his own eyes.

Healing life. A name for a child who had gone before but had been the catalyst of the salvation of his mother. A child who would be forever whole, healed with eternal life in the arms of Jesus. A child who had left a legacy that reached far beyond the barren dirt and wooden monument at his feet. Marcus reached an arm for Dilara, and she leaned into his shoulder as she sobbed. Deep, aching sobs of healing and of restoration.

Dilara laid the clutch of daffodils at the feet of the little monument. So beautiful for a life that had not even taken a breath on this side of Heaven. A life she would formerly have done anything to restore to herself, but one which she now did not wish back.

The yellow petals in different shades fluttered and swayed in the breeze that took the long strands of her hair and set them dancing before her already blurred vision. She leaned into Marcus's side and soaked in the peace and comfort that radiated from him in waves, like the green boughs waving in the wind.

Though sorrow still rolled inside of her as it would until it abated over time, peace overtook her heart. Her child, her Asa, the one who had been taken from her, snatched from life so quickly, was at rest. She commended her heart to God. The One who heard and answered every prayer and who could speak life over her wounded soul. The One who breathed hope and passion into a heart that had wished death upon itself. He washed away the shame. The ache that longed to do it all over again. He spoke to the brokenness in her that had felt worthless and beyond saving. The girl who had been trained from so young an age that she was worth nothing but what her body could give.

That girl was now a woman who knew what it meant to be loved by a Savior that had seen her. Chosen her. Stretched out a hand of mercy to her and had waded through the very depths of hell for her.

He had proved that she was more than the sum of this mortal shell. She was more than what could be stolen from her. She was worth more than the pearls and rubies she had been bargained for and priced beneath.

She was worth His life. His sacrifice. His love.

And this life of hers would forever more be a living sacrifice to the One who had given His all to rescue her.

A daffodil caught the wind, and its yellow petal floated toward the flaming evening sun that lit the sky with pink. She smiled through her healing tears.

Daffodils meant new life. New seasons and new birth. She was born anew and bathed in fresh hope, destiny, and healing.

She gripped Marcus's hand and lifted trembling lips to his cheek, damp with his own tears.

"This life of mine, all that I have. It is Yours," she whispered.

"And together we will offer this life to the One who gave it."

"Blessed be the name of the Lord," she whispered before her lips were stolen in a kiss as the wind tickled her face like butterfly wings.

Their walk back to Padsley was one with a tight grip between their hands. Love and longing expressed in that one touch. Dilara's heart was too full for words. How did joy and sorrow mingle in such a way that the melancholy touch of them both intermixed like one of the herbal tinctures Marcus created? Grief wasn't something easily forgotten about or lived without. It was something that flavored life so the joy experienced became so much sweeter for having tasted the depths of sadness.

Dilara felt the weight of that truth all the more after experiencing the loss of her child. His moments on this earth would never be forgotten, but they had spoken and shaped and changed her life, no matter how few those moments alive were.

Marcus wound his fingers tighter around hers gently. She could feel his pulse racing in his wrist, and his attempts to cover for being out of breath made her heart jump with love. She had tried to hide her love for this man. Bury it deep down where even she couldn't find it, but it had been there all the same. Despite having to dust off the feeling of inadequacy and unworthiness that the Lord was slowly healing in her, it was still there. Tender, sweet, gentle, but there.

Words almost didn't have to be said between them. But he was always surprising her. Little tokens and words of love, reminding her of what she had to look forward to. What the continuation of her story would be. This life of theirs…walking forward together, growing around each other like two trees planted side by side. Their roots, ever intertwining over the years, until one day, where one ended would be lost in where the other began.

"I can't wait to call you mine."

Tears flooded her eyes that had already filled more times than she cared to count.

A monster had once called her his. Spoken it over her until she had thought herself too far gone to be reclaimed. But then the Lord spoke it over her. Reminded her that He had ransomed her. Redeemed her. Bought her with a blood covenant no money could afford.

And then the man who would become her husband spoke it over her again. Inspired by the love of the Christ who had set her free, it held new meaning now. Tender, compassionate, putting her first before himself.

They would spend their lives in Padsley for however long God called them to remain there. Their home was even now being built behind Fendrel's. Everard had been hard at work with a smile on his face that threatened to eclipse the sunset which threw golden light at their feet and cast their shadows long before them. His hands had been aided by Jaromir and his son—even little Kahru, attempting to swing a hammer and occasionally use a saw with his little hands.

Community was a new experience for her. People who loved them for who they were instead of for what they could give. But her heart sang at the love that was given. Like a parched plant having survived the darkest and harshest desert, instead of turning away from the love that was showered upon her, she soaked it up, her roots begging for more, growing deeper with every draught of healing water.

The world might be unsure, politics from her homeland creeping closer, but she was loved. By God and by a man who emulated Him in all that he did.

And that was enough.

More than enough. It was everything.

Her life, starting anew, afresh, and unbroken. Whole and redeemed.

"Therefore if any man be in Christ, he is a new creature: old things are passed away; behold, all things are become new."

Epilogue

ONE YEAR LATER

"Push!" he yelled, his blood pumping fast, blurring the edges of his vision.

"What does it look like I'm doing?" She squealed on the last word and grunted, her hands wringing the blankets that she gripped in her fists as she crouched, leaning back against the bed. From his place on the floor, he could just see the head emerging.

"You are doing amazing! I can't believe we are about to meet our child!" He beamed up at her around her skirts from his position kneeling on the floor. Her slight grin turned to a grimace and a moan, erupting from somewhere deep within her. When it gave way to a long exhale, he jumped, repositioning himself to catch the baby.

If she kept up like this, it would only be a matter of seconds, not minutes, before he would be holding her child.

Their child.

"Lord, give me *strength*!" she cried out, her voice loud, guttural, heavy with pain and pressure.

He reached his hands and felt the entirety of the child's head, and within mere moments, he was staring at the pink skin, squeezed-shut eyes, and plenteous hair of a baby boy.

Marcus's cheeks were wet with what he realized were tears. He laughed and cried at the same time, unable to move, transfixed by the wonder of the babe that he held within the shelter of his arms. Nuri shoved her face in with a whine, blessing the top of the babe's head with a sniff and a touch of the pink tongue, gentle as a feather.

Dilara cooed, her breathing heavy as if she had just run over a mountain. She reached out a trembling finger to touch her son's face and leaned back against the bed, slowly sinking to join him in sitting on the floor. Her eyes were full of tears, her riotously beautiful brown hair bouncing in curls and tangles about her face, strands of it stuck to the sweat beading her forehead.

But the rest of her beauty was eclipsed by her smile. Bright. Stunning. His.

"You did it, my love." He smiled through his tears, his heart near to bursting within his chest as he set the baby in her arms.

She rested the child between her raised knees, staring into the tiny face with wonder.

Her smile gave way to tears, though it still remained beneath them. Sorrow and joy married in that moment. One over a heart long lost and mourned, the other over the new life that was theirs to care for. The two emotions were not at war with each other, but they coexisted more commonly and beautifully than many knew. Two strands, when joined with that of redemption, forming a chord not easily broken, but instead strong enough to withstand any winter…and experience spring on the other side.

Her eyes were so full of love and yearning, and she laughed on a sob, looking up at him with those deep, large brown eyes, and their foreheads met. Their breath entangling, sweat, tears, and love mingling together.

He stole a kiss, her lips salty with her tears and perspiration. "I love you so much."

"I love you more," she whispered back.

"Never." His breath set the tendrils of hair around her face to wafting.

She glanced down at the child who had yet to cry, but was looking upon his new world as if taking it all in, ready to encounter it on any given term rather than crying in anger at emerging into it. "He has your eyes."

"Too bad. I was hoping to be able to see your face in more than one place." He grinned, rubbing the knotted muscles in her shoulder with a gentle hand.

She grinned back. "Well then, aren't I the luckiest woman in the kingdom?"

"In the world, I think." He stole another kiss, this time lingering and touching her face tenderly beneath his fingertips.

"I am that." Her smile turned bittersweet. "One here and one in Heaven. What a celebration that will be someday."

He gently brushed the brown locks away from her face, smoothing them with a hand over her head like a benediction. "And we will celebrate every single day until that comes."

Dilara brushed a gentle finger over the child's hair, her face the most beautiful mix of admiration and tender love that he had ever seen. She fairly glowed with a holy, motherly light.

She leaned forward, her eyes speaking more than her tongue as his name slipped from her lips on a whisper. "Tavish. My love."

Marcus touched her hand with one of his own and laid the other over their son's forehead. "May you bring Heaven to earth, my son." His words of consecration rippled through the room with a power which, while tender, held the strength of the Spirit.

Dilara cradled him closer to her chest, her head bending to continue gazing into his eyes as she gripped her fingers over Marcus's with her free hand. "His life for our King. Just as we give Him ours."

Marcus smiled and fought back tears of gratitude. He knew which King she referred to, and his heart soared.

There was no greater purpose than that.

THE END

WANT TO READ THREE BONUS SCENES?

Follow the QR Code to subscribe to my newsletter and receive your bonus material!

ACKNOWLEDGEMENTS

This book was a journey and one that I couldn't have completed if it weren't for so many helping hands.

First of all, thank you so much to my Glory Writer sisters. Tessa, Cherith, Hosanna, Laurel, Livy and Hannah and whoever else was there in that moment during the 2022 Glory Writer's retreat while we sipped tea as the sun set in the sky and I cried over how scared and vulnerable writing this story was. Your support, encouragement, prayer and sweet words of comfort and excitement over what God was doing fuels me still to this day. There is power in Spirit-filled community and your hearts are precious to me!

To my beta's, as always, your encouragement, excitement and emotion of this story helped shape it and give me the breath of fresh air and confidence that I needed. Kylie, Laurel, Naomi, Sydney, Nicole, Flora, Anne, Cherith, Morgan, Emily, Virginia, Marissa, and anyone else who last minute jumped on board. Thank you as always for your kindness and sweet comments!

Alexandria, X, thank you for reading this before anyone else did. For allaying my fears, praying me through the toughest moments, crying with me, flailing at all the appropriate moments, and for believing in these stories as much as I do. Thank you for brainstorming details, processing the depth of plot and arcs, and for catching the vision. Your love and encouragement have been INVALUABLE in my writing and I can honestly say I wouldn't be where I am right now without you.

Livy, sister of mine, thank you for all of the prayers, the encouragement, and the way your heart came alongside mine in the journey. Thank you for being my partner in holy crime and for being the best author in arms a girl could ask for. Can't wait to see all of the adventures God has ahead for us!

To the Glory Writer's staff, new and old, your encouragement and heart has meant the world to me. Livy, Tessa, Kiki, Allison, Alex, Micaiah, and Abigayle, I love you all so much and can't wait to see what God has ahead for us!

Nadine, oh how grateful I am for you. Your tender heart and the way you seem to see mine and speak life over it... I am so touched and honored that the Lord put us in each-other's vicinity. Your heart and life is an encouragement to me more ways than you may possibly know.

Sara, thank you for encouraging me in so many ways and for pouring your tender compassion onto me when we first met. I'll cherish the memory forever and I feel so blessed to have women like you and Nadine to look up to as big sisters in the publishing world.

To the Instagram and TikTok community God has so richly blessed me with. . . You are treasures, each and every one of you. Thank you for all of the ways you have poured out your support of me and this series, for the ways you pop into my dm's and speak encouragement and life just when I seem to need it, and for the absolute party and joy you have made social media.

Micaiah, sweet sis. Thank you for all of your hard work, your fangirl comments and the way that you simply live life. You inspire me, I wished we lived closer, and I'm so grateful to have gotten to adopt you as my sis! Love you, dude!

Abigayle, thank you for your edits, your invaluable ability to be a cheerful critique! I love working with you and am so grateful I got to be on the receiving end of your incredible gift for editing!

Rebecca, thanks dear sister-in-law for cheering me on, for reading my books, and for being the bookish bestie I never thought I would get in a new sister! God is so good to us and I'm forever grateful you joined our family! Thank you for your suggestions, edits, and listening ear as I planned and plotted these stories!

To my family. God is good. And I know His plan is perfect. I love you all so terribly much.

To my King. I serve You and no other. I pray I set captives free, heal the sick, and speak life and hope to the brokenhearted. I serve at the behest of your kingdom.

Till next time,

VICTORIA LYNN

JOIN THE ABOLITION MOVEMENT:

Human trafficking is the most prevalent form of slavery that we know today. While William Wilberforce abolished the slave trade in England, and it was abolished in our nation during the civil war, this new kind of slavery is more pervasive than you could imagine.

What is frightening is that Dilara's story is one being played out over and over and over again on the world's stage every single day. But there is a way you can help…

Some quick stats:

- 25 million people are trapped worldwide in forced labor or sex work according to the International Labor Organization.
- Forced sex and labor generates annual profits of around $150 billion USD yearly.
- Much like Dilara's early entrance into slavery, Nearly 20 percent of trafficking victims worldwide are children.
- This evil happens in our nation and most likely has a foothold in your neighborhood and city.
- The US is one of the top three nations of origin for human trafficking victims (US State Dept.)
- Traffickers often find victims through social media, schools, or in their own neighborhoods.

This evil is heartbreaking. But I believe we can end Modern Day Slavery in our lifetime! Let's set the captives free! Here are ways you can help!

- PRAY: Prayer is still the most powerful weapon we have and one that every single one of us can do, no matter our circumstances. Pray for this evil to come to light, for captives to be set free, for mindsets and trauma to be healed, and for not just the rescue, but also the healing of those who have been slaves.
- EDUCATE: Don't turn a blind eye! The more people who are aware of what goes on, the easier it is to spot, stand up, and speak out! This is happening in your neighborhoods, towns, and schools! Ministries like Women At Risk International, A21 and others offer training and resources on how to spot trafficking and what to do about it!
- DONATE: Rescue missions, after-care, home and job placement all take money that most victims don't have. Donating to a ministry or organization that you trust can be a huge way to make an impact!
- SERVE: If you are feeling called to be what I call a 'boots on the ground' emissary of the gospel, do some research and get plugged in with a local resource center, after-care facility or ministry and offer to be the physical hands and feet of Jesus!

Ministries and Organizations that I personally trust and recommend:

- **Exodus Cry:** Exodus Cry is committed to abolishing sex trafficking and breaking the cycle of commercial sexual exploitation while assisting and empowering its victims. *https://exoduscry.com/*
- **Women At Risk International:** unites and educates to create circles of protection around those at risk through culturally sensitive, value-added intervention projects. *https://warinternational.org/*
- **International Justice Mission:** is a global organization that protects people in poverty from violence. They partner with local authorities in 29 program offices in 17 countries to combat trafficking and slavery, violence against women and children and police abuse of power. *https://www.ijm.org/*
- **A21:** is driven by a radical hope that the cycle of human trafficking can be broken and are committed to Reaching, Rescuing, and Restoring those in danger of trafficking or imprisoned by it. *https://www.a21.org/*
- **Operation Underground Railroad:** has made a significant impact in the fight to end sex trafficking and sexual exploitation by assisting in rescuing and supporting thousands of survivors in almost 40 countries and 50 U.S. states. Our approach is adapted to geographical location, the needs of survivors, and best practices in the field. *https://www.ourrescue.org/*

- **Polaris:** Founded in 2002, Polaris is named for the North Star, which people held in slavery in the United States used as a guide to navigate their way to freedom. Today we are filling in the roadmap for that journey and lighting the path ahead. One of their goals is targeting the systems that make human trafficking possible. *https://polarisproject.org/*

- **Troy Brewer Ministries:** is actively working with orphans and vulnerable children in Mexico, India, Colombia, Belize, Uganda and Southeast Asia. Troy and Leanna have traveled the globe establishing villages in some of the most remote, dark corners of the world. Through SPARK Worldwide, the ministry Leanna founded to Serve Protect And Raise Kids at their SPARK orphanages, Troy and his partners bring hope and the Gospel of Jesus by helping Leanna build schools, churches, medical clinics, water wells and orphanages for the poorest of the poor. *https://troybrewer.com/sex-trafficking-qa/*

FIGHT FOR LIFE:

Dilara's story of infant loss may have been cloaked in some implication, but her story of a forced abortion was one that tore at my heart. I've been in the fight for life since I was a pre-teen, and her story is one that feels all too familiar and heartbreaking because I know it happens on the daily in our country and around the world. While the abolishment of Roe vs. Wade may be a victory, it is but a small one in the massive culture war to bring life and truth and to speak for those who cannot speak for themselves. The latest numbers which are estimated at being low as not every abortion provider is counted was that 602,327 babies were aborted in one year. That's 1,699 babies every single day… just in the USA alone.

1,699 babies that had their lives taken from them every day. Babies like Asa who were denied the opportunity to grow, to experience life. 1,699 babies who could have been the next mothers, fathers, doctors, lawyers, nurses, inventors, ministers, apostles and prophets, and teachers. Their stories do not have to end.

Their stories need to be told, they need to be honored, and their lives should not be lost in vain.

It doesn't matter what your political stance is, what party you vote for, or what religion you ascribe to. There is purpose in Every. Single. Life. And it is our calling and mandate to stand and fight for them. To put an end to the brutal murder of 1,699 babies that occur on our watch every single day.

"Speak up for those who cannot speak for themselves, for the rights of all who are destitute. Speak up and judge fairly; defend the rights of the poor and needy."

PROVERBS 31:8-9

Ways to Get Involved:

- **Pray:** We know that prayer is a powerful weapon and God's heart is that not one should perish. Changing the culture, saving lives, and advocation all start at one place: on our knees. Worlds shift, His kingdom comes, and the Spirit moves when we pray.

- **Get involved:** Use your hands and hearts to minister to those in need. I can't stress the need to get involved on a local level enough. Find a local pregnancy resource center and volunteer. Take a tour. Cover them in prayer. Donate time, resources, or supplies.

- **Donate:** If you don't have a local pregnancy resource center, there are many places that pour into new moms who are in need. Students for Life and Live Action are two amazing places to start!

- **Advocate:** We were not called to be relevant or to blend into culture. Stand up and speak for those who have no voice. Use your platform, your relationships and your community as opportunities to speak truth. Spread the word. Don't be shy about declaring the sanctity of the life that God has given each of us. Change occurs at the most fundamental level… when culture shifts. Don't back down to it. It can get ugly, but God and His truth are on your side.

LEARN MORE AT LIVE ACTION

FIND A
PREGNANCY RESOURCE CENTER
NEAR YOU!

JOIN STUDENT'S FOR LIFE

SECRET VAULT

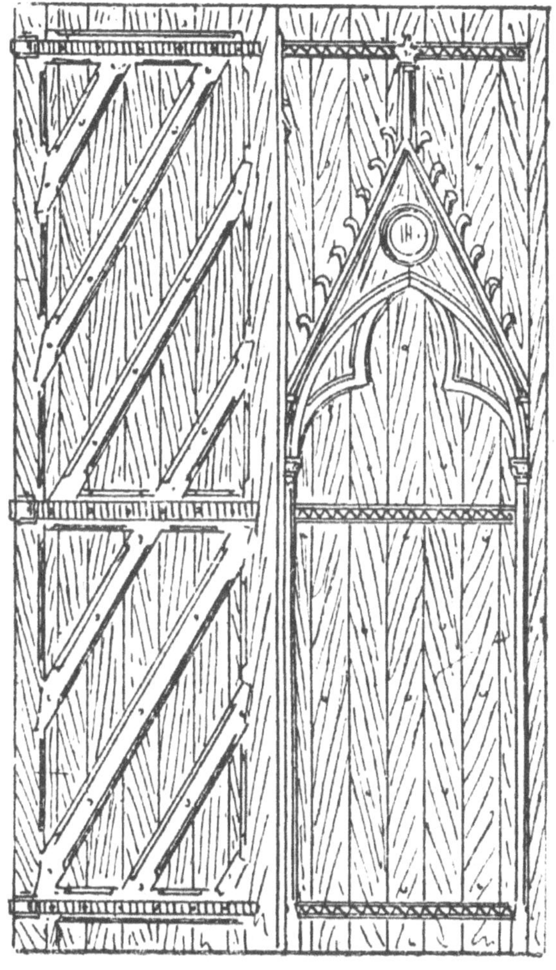

Do not open until you have finished the book.
Spoilers inside.

LOCATION GLOSSARY:

Elira: El-eera – Meaning: *freedom, to be free.*

Niran: Nee-ran – Meaning: *The high place, everlasting and eternal.*

Padsley: Pad-slee – Meaning: *The name is derived from Parsley and the inspiration of medieval times and the significance of the herb. It has been cultivated in Europe and fits with the medieval feelings. Parsley was thought to remove bitterness and although medieval herbalists recommended it for a sour stomach, it was also thought to remove bad or bitter emotions.*

Raintamount Forest: Rain-ta-mount - Meaning: *from the mount of smiling rain or laughing rain*

Pranvera Forest: Pran-ver-a – Meaning: *Forest of Spring*

Pranvera Village: Farthest village on the Southeast border of Elira. (just off the map)

Valhaven: Val-haven – Meaning: valiant or a worth of haven. Valiant haven.

WoodRiver: Wood-River – Meaning: *the river that cuts through the wood.*

Sirene Sea: Sigh-rean – Meaning: *enchanter or enchanting, like in terms of alluring sirens*

Illias Pass: Ill-ee-as – Meaning: *Yahweh is God/the Lord is my God*

Rusalka: Roo-sawl-kaw – Meaning: *Infested with demons and water filled with evil.*

Izevel Mountains: Eye-za-vel – Meaning: *Hebrew origin, to exalt or to dwell. Usually in the context of exalting evil.*

Pavlin: Pav-lynn – Meaning: *Small or humble. Of little consequence.*

Kaira Mountains: Kie-rah – Meaning: *God guides me and Between the rivers.*

CHARACTER GUIDE FOR ELIRA:

Marcus: Medicinal in the village of Padsley, Violet's dearest friend and apprentice to Master Fendrel. Name meaning: *hammer, shining or polite warlike.*

Master Fendrel: The medicinal of the village of Padsley. Name meaning: *Future minded, always looking ahead.*

Everard: The village blacksmith. Name meaning: *brave or hardy: wild boar. Strength of a wild boar.*

Eskel: Stonemason in Padsely. Name meaning: *Divine cauldron.*

Soria: Rusalkan trafficking handler/house mother

Rensen: The *Dove's Tavern and Inn* owner. He has a mysterious past as a juggler. Name meaning: *creativity, curiosity, and charm.*

Keitha: Renesen's wife, Name meaning: *daughter of the forest*

Kahru: Rusalkan refugee child. Name meaning: *little wolf cub*

Jaromir: Kahru's grandfather and Rusalkan refugee. Name meaning: *spring and peace*

Conri: Rusalkan trafficker and slave trader. Name meaning: *'prince of wolves' or fire.*

Nuri: pet wolf and protector. Name meaning: *light or 'light bearer' 'she who brings light'*

Matthias: Pranvera village boy who has a tendency to get underfoot. Name meaning: *gift of God*

Matilda: Rusalkan refugee child.

Noam: Rusalkan refugee child.

Aria: Padsley village girl.

Milton Family: Kenelm and Mya. Farmers mentioned in book one when he came to fetch Fendrel for Mya's delivery of their child.

Asa Chaim: Dilara's lost child, taken at Conri's hands. Name meaning: *Healing and life. 'a life of healing'*

Tavish: Marcus and Dilara's first child. Name meaning: *hillside, Heaven, 'courageous Heaven bringer'*

Drach and Nesryn: Nuri's pups Name meanings: *little dragon and wild rose*

Elgon Indulf: The prince and true heir to the throne. Name meaning: *noble or white, worshiper of the Most High. High minded.*

Violet Frell-Indulf: A farmer in the south country near Padsley. Name meaning: *Purple flower of royal valor. Frell means Free or freedman.*

Richard Frell: Violet's deceased father. Name meaning: *powerful or brave valor*

Miran Frell: Violet's deceased mother. Name meaning: *worthy of admiration and peaceful one.*

Obed: The Kingsman that Violet takes in. Name meaning: *servant of God*

Enguerrand: The Chancellor and usurper of the throne. Name meaning: *Raven. Ravens are intelligent creatures, often solving complex problems with ease. Plotting and calculating.*

Will prey on baby animals of other species. Ravenous for power. Hungry for control.

Galeron: Woven goods merchant. Thin, usually jovial and with a witty joke for everyone. Name meaning: *knight.*

Malcolm: Commanding kingsman of the palace guard. Later, the first knight to the king. Name meaning: *follower of peace, dove*

MARCUS'S HERBAL REMEDIES

**disclaimer* While these herbal remedies have been around for some time and have many benefits to offer, please do not take without the knowledge of a family member or parent or personal physician, or at your own risk. Please do your own research on each of these before attempting to use them.*

Willow Bark Tea: Used for pain relief and as a fever reducer. One of the first uses of Aspirin (see recipe)

Ginger: anti-inflammatory, fights nausea, and boosts the immune system

Turmeric: lowers inflammation. Arthritis patients usually respond well to this treatment.

Stinging Nettles: Known to help with hay fever and allergies, lower inflammation, lower high blood pressure, reduce bleeding and even assist with hormonal disfunction or imbalance.

Wild Yams: Relieves PMS and menopause symptoms, reduces uterine cramps, can lower pain and help prevent nausea. Do not take when pregnant.

Cedar: Can lower chronic inflammation and can be used as a detoxification and to stimulate the lymphatic system.

Coneflower, otherwise known as Echinacea: are a natural antibiotic, and were often used to treat infections. Is known to stimulate the immune system and can assist the body in fighting viruses and bacteria alike.

Activated Charcoal: a purifying agent and for purging of impurities. Can assist with vomiting, abdominal discomfort or viruses.

Sunflowers: Topical applications of a paste or the oil can assist with migraines, and ear aches. Oral decoction can fight the common fever and mitigate the effects of poison.

Sage: Can support brain or memory health, can ease menopause symptoms, support oral health, alleviate diarrhea, and support bone health.

Hyssop: eases respiratory issues and coughing. Supportive during colds and fevers, aids digestion, and can help ease pain and bruises.

Forget me nots: Can be used to tighten open wounds. May also be a remedy for many eye diseases when applied in a lotion.

Motherwort: is a uterine stimulant and has a calming effect. It can also be used as a hormonal/menstrual cycle regulator.

Yarrow: reduces fever and opens the pores to allow the patient to sweat. It also is a natural antiseptic and has been used for centuries to stop bleeding and dull pain.

Elder Flower: are often used as an immune stimulant, nervous system support, and can also be used to soothe itchy eyes, reduce joint inflammation and pain, and are a natural antihistamine, and when taken prior to the appearance of pollen can ease seasonal allergies.

Wild Ramps: are a wildly growing form of onion and garlic and can be used in household cooking.

RECIPES:

WILLOW BARK TEA

INGREDIENTS:

4 tsp white willow bark

2 cups water filtered

1 cinnamon stick optional

2 tsp honey optional

INSTRUCTIONS:

In a saucepan, take water and white willow bark. Boil it for 5-10 minutes. Turn the heat off.

Let the willow bark steep for an additional 20-30 minutes. You can add a cinnamon stick in it for additional flavor.

Strain the tea in teacups. The tea is bitter-tasting and you can use honey to sweeten it.

TURMERIC (GOLDEN) MILK

INGREDIENTS:

2 cups milk (dairy or dairy-free)

1 teaspoon ground turmeric

¼ teaspoon ground cinnamon

pinch black pepper

1 tablespoon maple syrup or honey

INSTRUCTIONS:

Add all ingredients to a saucepan over medium heat and bring to a simmer. Simmer for 10 minutes to let the flavors meld. Pour the golden milk into a cup and enjoy.

SAGE ECHINACEA TEA

INGREDIENTS:

1 cup water

1 teaspoon dried echinacea root

1 teaspoon dried sage

INSTRUCTIONS:

• Place 1 cup water in saucepan and add 1 teaspoon dried echinacea root

• Bring water to a boil, then reduce heat and simmer, covered for 5 minutes.

• Remove from heat and add 1 teaspoon dried sage.

• Allow to sit, covered, 5 minutes, then strain and pour into small jar. Tea will keep for 24 hours at room temperature. Make fresh daily.

GINGER CANDY

INGREDIENTS:

• fresh ginger root

• water

• granulated sugar

• salt

• (OPTIONAL) vanilla or orange extract

INSTRUCTIONS:

First, prepare the raw ginger root by peeling it completely and slicing it into thin rounds. The pieces should look like small potato chips.

Place the ginger slices in a large 6 quart saucepot. Add the exact amount of water called for in the full recipe, and bring to a simmer. Cover and let the ginger simmer for about 30 minutes, until just softened but not mushy.

Remove the lid and check the liquid levels. There should be approximately 1/4 – 1/3 cup of water in the bottom of the pot. If needed, scoop out some water with a ladle, or add water, to make sure you have about ¼ cup.

Next, stir in the sugar and salt. Bring the sugar syrup to a simmer. Simmer, stirring regularly, for 15- 20 minutes, until the syrup starts to crystalize and become sticky. The color will range from pale cream to golden.

Remove the pot from the heat and stir in the vanilla or orange extract, if you are using it.

Then set out a baking rack, and spray with nonstick cooking spray. Use tongs to move the ginger pieces to the rack, and spread them out evenly in a single layer.

Allow the ginger to rest on the rack for 2-4 hours, or until all the pieces are completely dry.

Place in an airtight container. The ginger candy will last for at least 1 month if kept in a cool, dry place. There's no need to refrigerate!

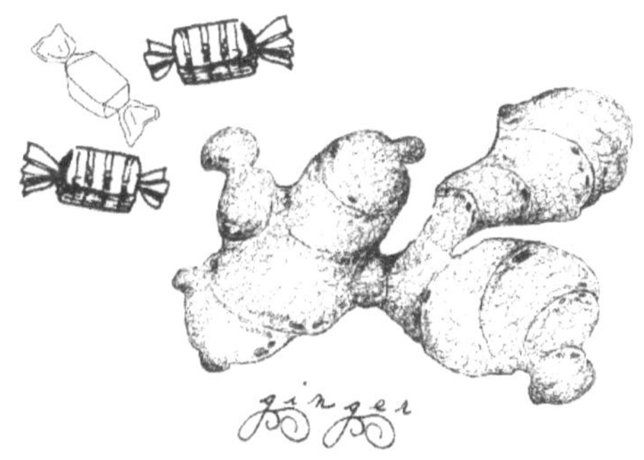

VICTORIA LYNN has an insatiable desire for truth, light and beauty.

Traveling to destinations of beauty created by our Heavenly Father, reveling in creative pursuits that fill her with joy, or pouring her heart into words of life are some of her favorite things to do.

She seeks to bring the life giving words of the Savior to a dark and broken world that desperately needs to know of His sacrifice.

A writing and publishing coach, author, journalist, seamstress and creator, she loves spending time with any of her 8 siblings or nieces or nephews, exploring her native state of Michigan, and sewing gowns fit for a princess.

VIOLET lives her quiet life in her sleepy village, trying to remain as dead to the politics that are threatening their world as possible. She follows the rules, stays out of trouble and does her best to remain out of sight from the dreaded and overbearing Kingsmen.

With the new regent on the throne till the prince comes of age, the country has been thrown into a turmoil. Unlike the kindly king before him, the new ruler is overbearing, frightening and tyrannical in his rule. Taxes are bleeding the people dry and without the money or goods to pay, they have been forced into penal servitude and imprisonment by the Kingsmen, who show no mercy. The despair and fear that has taken over their lives has ruled out any level of hope.

When Violet stumbles upon an unconscious and injured Kingsman in the woods, despite the consequences, she is compelled to take care of the injured man. When he wakes and has no memory of his identity or past, she takes the only precaution that will keep her and her grandmother safe; she destroys the evidence of his past life.

If Violet's lowly Kingsman regains his memory, will she survive the consequences? And will the Kingsman be able to live with his past life? Who will fight to free Elira?

Enjoy these other works by Victoria Lynn!

London in the Dark

With a sudden death in the family throwing a brother and sister together, there is bound to be some conflict when one is the leading detective in London. When a string of thefts suddenly seems tied to their family legacy, can Cyril and Olivia find the answers to their questions? And their struggling relationship?

Bound

When two children escaping abusive families encounter each other at the same lonely train station in the middle of the night, throwing their lot in together seems to be the best option for them both. But when injury lands them in the hands of their worst nightmare - foster care - will they be encountered with the love of God or dragged back into their broken lives?

When Beauty Blooms

Marjorie Kirk is a woman with no fortune, no prospects, no family, and no skills. She is awkward, shy, and the farthest thing from any semblance of a society lady. The new minister keeps turning up in the most awkward of places and she can't help but feel that her life is doomed to one of embarrassment.

A story of a young woman with social anxiety and how she learned to bloom.

What is Glory Writers Press?

What started with a dream for a community that stood for light in a world of darkness, turned into a vision for a Hybrid publishing house. One that supports authors, gives them a platform, and provides the knowledge, advice, and expert service needed to get them selling books that honor Christ and His sacrifice.

Because we are tired of compromise. It has crept into every nook and cranny of the publishing industry, and we believe as followers of the one true God that:

- We hold the answer to all of life's problems - Christ Himself.
- We should be sharing the Gospel message to this hungry world.
- Standing strong in our faith and convictions is a powerful way to draw others into His Kingdom, while also encouraging the Church higher.
- We do not need to pander to society to sell books, nor should we.
- As Kingdom creators, we have the mandate (and the ability) to shape culture according to His Kingdom; speaking truth over a generation that has fallen prey to confusion and deceit.

And one of the most powerful ways to do that is through a story.

What does Glory Writers Press publish?

Glory Writers Press is dedicated to providing Christian Fiction that:

- has a unique voice, intriguing storyline, and out-of-the-box storytelling skills with biblically sound faith.
- Clean fiction with no smut, sexual content, or glorification of lust. No cussing, or gratuitous violence. Think PG-13 max rating.
- Books that seek to glorify God, all while encouraging and edifying its readers.
- Christian Middle Grade, YA, and New Adult for a market that is saturated with bad fiction
- Books with mission driven storytelling and execution

Where Can I Find Out More?

Follow the journey and stay in the know on our Instagram account below!

https://www.instagram.com/theglorywriterspress/